CW01604634

East

A History Interrupted Novel

Lizzy Ford

Copyright © 2015 Lizzy Ford
http://www.LizzyFord.com

Cover art and design copyright © 2014 by Eden Crane Design

Photography copyright © 2013 Cathleen Tarawhiti

Cover model: Georgia Stanwix

Fleuron © spline_x - Fotolia.com

Excritura Pro font © 2014 by Linotype

Published by Kettlecorn Press

All rights reserved.

No part of this book may be reproduced in any form or by any electronic or mechanical means including information storage and retrieval systems, without permission in writing from the author. The only exception is by a reviewer, who may quote short excerpts in a review.

This is a work of fiction. Names, characters, places and incidents either are products of the author's imagination or are used fictitiously. Any resemblance to actual events or locales or persons, living or dead, is entirely coincidental.

ISBN-13: 978-1-62378-186-6

FIRST EDITION

Acknowledgments

This book was inspired by a *Hardcore History* podcast by Dan Carlin. I had never thought twice about the Mongol Empire and knew next to nothing about it prior to the fourteen hour podcast! After listening to it, I was so intrigued by the world Dan painted with his narrative, I knew my time traveling heroine had to visit!

Special thanks to Dan Carlin for the inspiration and the incredible amount of research that went into such a presentation.

Other reference material included:

Secret History of the Mongols: The Origin of Chingis Khan, Paul Kahn translation

The Secret History o the Mongol Queens: How the Daughters of Genghis Khan Rescued His Empire by Jack Weatherford

Genghis Khan and the Making of the Modern World by Jack Weatherford

A few other random history books I flipped through at BN but balked at purchasing because of the price

Ancient Mongol naming and linguistic websites

And … yes, Wikipedia. I don't care what anyone says. Wikipedia is for curious people who have no attention span. People like me.

Prologue – from "West"

ONLY I WOULD KNOW THERE ONCE WAS A GOOD MAN NAMED Taylor Hansen, whose sole wish in life was to retire and live in peace with me.

He deserved so much more, and I had taken everything from him.

The tears began again. I made no effort to stem them this time.

The shadowy figure pressed a large thumb to the back of my neck. I waited for the brilliant light or maybe, for him to chop off my head the way he had halved Nell.

Something smashed into my head instead, and I slid into darkness.

Gradually, I became aware once more. I was engulfed in brilliant light and heat, caught between the sensations of moving rapidly and floating in place, distantly aware of sonic booms and cracks, as if traveling between times required ripping the fabric of the universe.

This trip was smoother than the first and felt shorter. Seconds after the sonic boom, the light cleared, and I was left on the ground in the dark.

It wasn't rainy – but it was *freezing.* Bone-deep coldness gobbled up the heat generated by time travel, and I began shivering before I opened my eyes. Sunspots blinded me for a moment. I tested out my body as I waited for my vision to clear. I was uninjured from the travel, simply disoriented.

How many times did Taylor travel like this? I almost sighed. I'd hoped Carter would wipe my memory, if that were even possible. I was hurting once more, unable to stop thinking about my first trip through time and how I was the sole person left standing when it ended.

The empathic memory chip was strangely silent, and I realized how much chatter had been going on in the back of my mind. Now there were just my sad thoughts and the dread of guessing what Carter had in store for me next.

I sat up. Moldavite chunks steamed around me in the crater. I wore the same clothes I'd changed into before leaving the eighteen forties and gazed at the sky. The stars were brilliant and bright, the moon a sliver and sky completely clear. I'd never seen a night like this with all the light pollution in my home of southern California. It was too stormy for me to notice the sky in Indian Territory. But this … this was absolutely breathtaking.

And cold. Jesus – had I ever been this cold? It hurt my nose and lungs to breathe. I wrapped the riding habit around me more tightly and tucked my face into the tall collar. Making my way to the edge of the crater, I climbed out onto what looked like the steppe: a wide, open land of short cropped, verdant grass that glowed silver in the moonlight. In the distance were mountains, and between them and me …

Nothing.

"It's freakin' cold here!" I muttered. The air was still but had begun to penetrate my wool coat.

There was no Taylor to rescue me this time. The reminder left me feeling more desolate than the steppe stretching out before me.

The sound of movement and shuffling reached me, and I turned, letting out a startled gasp.

An army of forms on horseback extended behind my crater towards another set of mountains, as far as I could see. The men were watching me in complete silence that defied the size of the force. No one stirred. I doubted anyone was even breathing. They were as still as statues, until one of them dismounted.

He dropped all sizes of swords and knives on the ground at his feet before approaching me. Removing his helmet, he stopped a good six feet away, his gaze on the distance between us. He seemed to be thinking about whether or not he wanted to get any closer.

I took in his appearance and dress, trying to place where – and when – I was. His face was round, his eyes almond shaped and skin tone pale olive with ruddy cheeks. He wore layers of clothing: thick, bulky wools and fur-lined leathers over loose trousers and a wide belt cinched at his waist.

I'd never seen anyone like him. Of everything about him that intrigued me, his hair was what I fixated on. Beneath the bowl-shaped helmet, he wore two long braids of grey that marked his seasoned age, one on each side of his head. The rest of his head was shaved.

"Father Sky sent you to bless our battle," he spoke.

Father Sky. At no point in college had I studied ancient religions, so placing the reference was beyond me. I had no idea where I was. Somewhere in Asia, maybe. Not China, not India, certainly not Europe or the Middle East. Like many Americans, I could probably find India and China on a map, but I had no clue what countries lay in the vast space between them. It would be just my luck to end up in one of those places.

"The moon guides us with its white path," he continued with a low bow. "It is an honor to be blessed by Father Sky in such a way."

I understood half of that. "Nice to meet you, too," I managed awkwardly.

A ripple of whispers went through the first several lines of horsemen able to hear me. The man before me broke into a wide smile. "We have milk and meat for you, Goddess of the White Path. You will eat with us this night, and tomorrow, you will accompany the silks and slaves to the Great Khan, so that he may witness this honor."

Great Khan. Now *that* I recognized. Alarm ricocheted within me, and something Carter said when we first met blared through my memories.

Tell that to Genghis Khan when you meet him!

"Oh, Carter. You did *not* send me back to the era of Mongol conquest," I whispered.

"Bring my finest horse!" the man ordered over his shoulder.

If I thought peeing in a bordalou was bad, I didn't want to know what awaited me here.

Chapter One

THE NEXT SEVERAL HOURS OCCURRED IN A FLURRY OF ACTIVITY that rendered me a speechless observer. Where there had been an army on horseback, suddenly tents began springing up in every direction, as if growing out of the steppe like fat mushrooms. I was too cold to do more than huddle and shiver next to the horse brought to me. I was dizzy from traveling and in no shape to ride, so I stood by the animal and struggled not to freeze to death while the camp took shape.

The Mongol warriors moved with quick discipline and barely spoke above a whisper. Their communication among one another was nothing short of baffling: hand signals, grunts, and orders given in the forms of poems or chants. The thump of drums filled the air, coordinating their movements. Their commander remained near me, and I was ringed by warriors that towered over the rest of the men who were closer to my size.

"What was it like to be cast from the sky, Goddess?" the

commander asked me.

"I am not a goddess," I said through chattering teeth.

"The Eternal Blue Sky sends a great gift, goddess or woman. Father Sky does indeed bless us," he said, unconcerned. "You fell from the moon to light our path." He pointed to the thumbnail moon above. "If *Goddess* does not please you, then do you object to *Moonbeam*?"

I shook my head. It sounded like a total flower child name from the seventies. Moonbeam was pretty, and I was too cold to correct him and provide my real name.

And … giving him my real name seemed too personal. I wanted no connection to this place and people after how my first trip ended – with everyone around me dead.

Huddling next to the horse, I sneaked a look at my cell phone.

There are pills in your pocket. Try as I might, I didn't get the time right. After you meet HIM, take all the pills at once, Carter, my handler and the man who sent me back in time, had texted on the magical phone that worked when it shouldn't.

Reaching into the other pocket of my gown, I pulled out a pouch filled to the brim with pills. My fingers were too frozen to open the bag, but there must have been more than twenty of the horse pills within. I clumsily typed him a response, not trusting his intentions now that I had witnessed how much he lied to me.

Why?

Carter was waiting for me, apparently, because he was fast to answer. *I can't move you forward in time. What I can do is put you into a stasis where you'll need no food or water and you won't age. Basically, it's like a poor man's cryogenics. The pills will put you under, and you'll wake up in a hundred years or so.*

I really wished I hadn't asked.

"That's insane." First the empathic memory chip that allowed me to read dead people and had to be turned off with a blow to the head, and now poor man cryogenics. Just when I thought he couldn't say something else to surprise me …

"Moonbeam?" the commander asked. "Are you comfortable?"

"Cold," I responded. "It was a very long … uh … fall from the moon."

He belted out orders to those around him, and two of the guards dashed off into the midst of the camp. "You have traveled far to be here. You will not wait much longer," he told me.

I didn't know what to say to him or Carter and so I tucked my phone away. Moments later, a woman dressed nearly identical to the male warriors approached. The main differences I could see: she had no belt, and her hair was piled on top of her head under an elaborate headdress. She wore the same mix of robes and pants split for riding. There was a bow and quiver of arrows at her back and a white feather tucked into her dark hair.

She gave a low bow to the commander, and then snapped in a tone quiet enough for only the two of us to hear, "Why do you keep her waiting, husband?"

I blinked, not expecting the saucy remark to the man in charge of an army.

"I will not send Father Sky's gift into any *ger* but ours, wife," came the surly response.

"So you will let her freeze."

"The affairs of the army do not concern you."

"The affairs of the *ger* and guests do." She strode to me and bowed her head then leaned forward and sniffed me. "You will forgive my husband for your suffering. Please, come with me."

Distracted by her sniffing, I automatically sniffed my shirt, too, before glancing from her to the commander, not wanting to piss off anyone who ran an army.

"Go on, Moonbeam," he called gruffly. "Ghoajin will make you comfortable."

I followed the woman through the organized chaos of the encampment springing out of the steppe. Two of the massive warriors accompanied us, and she led us towards the middle of the camp and to a small tent with a rounded top.

"We will rest here while my *ger* is erected," she said and entered.

A fire burned at the center of the round tent, its smoke curling up through a hole in the roof. Carpets were scattered over the short grass of the steppe, while a table for preparing food and drink was at the north side of the tent. Three beds were pushed against the walls, covered in thick wool blankets of dark colors.

It was warm and toasty already in the tent, a relief from the cold.

"Please, sit."

I settled onto a pillow beside the fire while she went to the table and poured milk into a goblet.

"Drink." Ghoajin brought it to me and then sat on the pillow nearest me.

I sipped the milk. It was a little bitter, chilled from the cold, and thick. Definitely not the skim milk I was accustomed to. Not wanting to offend my hostess, I drank it down. It settled my stomach, which was still churning from the trip through time. The faint headache that accompanied both my trips through time faded as I drank and rested.

"What manner of dress is this?" Ghoajin asked, puzzled, as she touched the wool riding habit. In the firelight, I could see how pretty she was with large, dark eyes, delicate features and gleaming, blue-black hair. She appeared much younger than her husband.

"It's, ah, how we dress far away." I replied awkwardly. When exhausted, I wasn't the best conversationalist.

She stood. "You will not be warm enough. Wait here."

Ghoajin left the tent.

I sneaked out the cell to check for any more bizarre messages from Carter. The adrenaline from the travel was starting to wear off, leaving me with the memories I came here to escape.

There was nothing from Carter, so I texted him quickly. *What am I here to do????* I knew better than to assume he had sent me back without a purpose and understood this time around the purpose he gave me might not be the truth, either.

The worst part of all if this: I was at the mercy of a man I couldn't trust whose motivations were too far beyond my understanding to predict. I knew he was using me, but I didn't know why. My appearance in front of an army wasn't the most inconspicuous entry into this time period, but maybe there was a reason for it. He had done his best the first time around to place me somewhere safe, and from my reception here, had done the same. They viewed me as divine or near divine after witnessing me survive a fall from the sky. As long as no one needed a demonstration of magical proportions, I was safe enough for now.

I despised Carter for that, too. My life was in his hands. Unable to understand him or what he did, I at least was able to take some interest in witnessing worlds and times and people no one in my era ever had. My favorite television show was Doctor Who, and pretending to be one of the Doctor's human companions helped me view the world around me as a little less scary.

Despite the sorrow and fear twisting my insides from my first trip back in time, I found myself curious about the place and time I knew nothing about. I was extroverted by nature and interested in people and their lives. When feeling returned to my hands and feet, I stood and went to the wall of the tent, wanting to know what kind of material could completely block the cold and wind of the open plains outside.

"Felt," I murmured and traced my fingertips down the thick, plush wool wall. It was too sturdy to be soft and so dense, not the faintest whisper of a breeze penetrated it.

The walls managed to block most of the ambient sound from outside as well. I opened the entrance without leaving, watching as a tent seven times the size of the one I was in was being erected nearby under the stern gaze of Ghoajin. More women were in this part of the camp, some with headdresses and others who appeared to be waiting on them.

The two guards that followed me from the front of the army were at the door. Neither spoke or moved when I took another step out, and I gazed at them. They wore layers of wool and leather without the fur that lined the clothing of the commander. The blades of their swords were curved, the sheaths plain and they carried bows at their backs. Knives of varying sizes were at their waists, along with thick leather belts inlaid with iron filigree in the shapes of animals.

Ghoajin motioned for two women bearing burlap wrapped bundles on their backs to follow and led them back to me. I entered the warm tent once more, a little nervous about how they would receive someone who seemed to fall from the sky. I was in desperate need of a nap and had no idea what social protocol I should know about this time period. I didn't sweat the eighteen forties and shrugged my shoulders.

Carter wanted something from me. I was safe here, at least until I did what he wanted.

I watched the woman in charge sort through the contents of the bundles.

"I have brought my best clothing. My ceremonial clothes," Ghoajin told me and carefully unrolled long gowns of wool like hers.

"You don't have to do this," I said, surprised.

"It is my duty, Moonbeam." She gave me an odd look. "You

cannot meet our Khan dressed as you are."

I glanced down and tried not to smile. I was dressed in my twenty first century pajamas and a long, wool habit from the mid-eighteen hundreds. If nothing else, I was going to freeze to death if I didn't change into something more suitable.

She motioned the two women towards me. They were more plainly dressed and their gazes on the ground. They approached and briskly began undressing me.

Not normally self-conscious, I would've lost any sense of being so during my first trip to the Old West, where I had a governess who dressed me daily.

And then died after she tried to kill me. The memory made my breath catch, and for a moment, I was lost in recalling how my first trip ended.

"Did they displease you, Moonbeam?" Ghoajin asked, breaking into my thoughts.

I blinked to clear my mind and realized the two servants had stepped back and were waiting.

"No," I murmured. "I am ... tired from my journey."

"From the sky." A note of wonder filled Ghoajin's voice. "What is it like to be so close to Father Sky?" She snapped her fingers at the servants, who sprang forward to continue stripping me.

"Very hot," I replied, uncertain how to respond. "The journey was like floating in water and moving so quickly, your mind cannot keep up. It was like someone tore a hole in the sky and dropped me here."

She appeared satisfied, if not mystified, by the simple response.

I shivered as the last of my clothing came off. With the pills in one hand and the phone in the other, I waited while the servants seemed to be going over my skin.

"What are they doing?" I asked.

"It was a long fall from the moon. We wish to be certain you are not hurt," Ghoajin replied and joined them. "Your hair is almost white, pure moonlight." She unwrapped the bun from my head and ran her fingers through my light blonde hair. "Your eyes are the color of Father Sky."

Sweeping my hair over one shoulder, she ran her fingers over the tattoo at the base of my neck. I got it when I was seventeen, against my aunt's wishes.

"You bear the pink lotus," she said, hushed. "A sign of divinity."

"I'm not a goddess," I replied. "You can see I am a woman like you."

"Not like me but yes. You are a woman with a divine mark." She stepped away and motioned for her servants to continue. "You were sent to further our Khan's quest?"

"I believe so."

"You bring special knowledge or talent? A gift from the Eternal Blue Sky?"

Dammit. Without knowing for sure why Carter sent me here, it was hard for me to answer the direct question honestly. "I … speak languages," I said somewhat awkwardly. "When I am better recovered, maybe I can remember why else I was sent."

"Languages." She appeared interested. "What languages?"

"All of them."

"Every language under the sky?"

"Yes."

"This is a great gift. No one man speaks all the languages of the Silk Route, the dialects of China and our own Empire and in the tongues of the West. Without the barrier of language, the Great Khan's words will reach the four corners of the world before his armies."

"Ghoajin, my favorite wife. What have you to tell me?" came a gruff voice from outside the tent.

"We have been blessed, husband," she responded. "If my *ger* is not prepared immediately to receive our guest, you will not sleep inside it this night. We cannot dishonor the Eternal Blue Sky with our sloth!"

I choked back a laugh, not at all certain it was appropriate but unable to prevent my reaction to her bluntness with her husband.

"Bring her water!" Ghoajin barked at one of the servants.

I downed another goblet of water and did my best not to get in the way of them dressing me. Two layers of linen later, they added a third, this one of much thicker wool and pristine white. It reached the tips of my fingers and tops of my feet and was followed by a white cloak and stole made of soft, grey fur. The layers were loose enough to prevent me from overheating and I guessed thick enough to stop the cold night from chilling me again.

It was bulky but far more comfortable than the girdles I was forced into during my journey to the eighteen forties.

"It is ready, wife," the commander called.

Ghoajin opened the entrance to the tent and stepped aside. "Come and meet our blessing."

I was itching to text Carter and ask a few pointed questions and instead, faced the opening of the tent. The commander entered and walked around me twice, trailed by men I assumed were sub-commanders or advisors by their seasoned age and the fact they wore fur.

"Like silk," he said and picked up a strand of my hair. "I have dispatched a rider to the Great Khan, who seeks peace in the mountains. It will arrive a day or two ahead of you to warn him of the honor that comes."

"How far is he from here?" I asked.

"But ten days. You are fortunate you fell here where we are close."

Ten days was nowhere near close in my mind. But at least it would give me the space to figure out what I was doing there and formulate some sort of plan.

"I overheard you say you speak all languages. Would you show us?" he asked.

"Of course," I replied readily. Carter installed three microchips in my brain: a language chip that allowed me to understand and speak every language under the sun, a history chip currently not working and the controversial, experimental empathic memory chip that caused my brain to start hemorrhaging during my first trip. It was a shame to lose it. The empathic memory chip let me read the memories of whoever was closest to me. It was an incredibly effective tool for self-preservation.

However, I'd rather have my brain not explode in my skull than use the chip. From what I could tell, the only technology in my brain working was the ability to speak languages. I didn't need to read a history book to know Mongolians of this time period didn't speak American English.

"Come to our *ger* where you will take the seat of honor," Ghoajin said.

They led me out of the small tent and into the much larger one. The fire in its center reached my waist, and there were pillows lining either side of the blaze. Some were occupied by men while servants lingered in the shadows.

Ghoajin took her spot near the door while the commander ushered me to his right hand side as he sat on the pillow at the head of the men. I sat easily under the weight of the bulky clothing and then just as quickly struggled back to my feet when approached by two men.

The commander nodded for them to address me.

"Moonbeam, it is an honor," one said and bowed. He was dressed very unlike the Mongols in clothing that reminded me of the paintings I had seen in a museum from pre-Renaissance Europe. "I am Lorenzo, an emissary of His Eminence the Pope."

"The honor is mine, Lorenzo," I replied. "I have been to Rome."

"Did it please you?"

"It was one of the most beautiful places I've ever visited."

"I am honored, Moonbeam." He smiled somewhat hesitantly.

The man beside him wore ruby and gold, his style of dress marking him as Persian or Arab. "I am Mohamed, a merchant from the city of Baghdad."

"Baghdad," I repeated, curious about the city. "Is it large?"

"Yes, the largest city in the world, and very beautiful," he answered. He kept his eyes at my waist. "With golden domes on mosques larger than the steppes. We are the center for religion and trade."

"I would like to visit one day." Small talk wasn't easy with these men. Mohamed appeared shy or maybe, reserved, while Lorenzo glanced frequently at the Mongol commander, as if to ensure he wasn't overstepping his bounds.

"Impressive. But how are you with tribal dialect?" the commander asked me.

It all sounds like English to me. I didn't understand the technology Carter put in my brain or used to talk to me via a cell phone nearly a thousand years from my own time.

The other men were murmuring. Several of them spoke. I assumed they were testing me, though none of them sounded any different.

Finally, the commander appeared satisfied that I spoke every language he could think of, and the men of his war council were equally pleased that it was a sign from their god.

Exhausted from my first experience in the past and from the time travel, I eventually sat down and tried to focus on listening to them talk about the route they were sending me to meet their leader as well as their destination.

The servants kept refilling my mug with milk. It didn't take long for fatigue, warm milk, and a blazing fire to knock me out. Whether or not I should have tried harder to stay awake, I didn't know, but I dropped into a deep, dreamless slumber not too long after passing my language test.

***

The vibrating of my cell phone against my hip woke me sometime later. I rolled onto my back and gazed up at the ceiling of the tent, recalling where I was. I was warm and snuggled under about four layers of blankets.

Shifting to reach my phone, I ducked beneath the covers to check it.

Your mission isn't actually there, Carter had written. *It's later but still within the Empire about a hundred years past this point. The Mongols had a history of slaughtering anyone not deemed useful, so … make yourself useful. Is your history chip working?*

Carter was the worst history tour guide ever. I suppressed a sigh and shot him a quick response. I already figured out they respected someone who spoke multiple languages, which I hoped made me useful enough to survive an encounter with the legendary Genghis Khan.

Lowering the phone, I started to doze off again when Carter messaged once more.

Okay. From what I can tell, you're in the middle stage of his campaign to take over the world. He hasn't reached the Arab countries or Turkey. He's been focused on China and the east after consolidating the Mongol tribes. He just returned from a defeat with the Chinese and is regrouping in the mountains of his home. He's in his fifties now, and has four sons, an unknown number of daughters but assumed to be at least five. The Empire eventually becomes more diverse. You'll see the influence of Islam on the western tribes and Buddhism on the eastern. Shamanism is central to their religious beliefs and they are very superstitious. Nine is a lucky number and they are huge on loyalty and honor. The women are expected to shoot a bow and ride a horse as well as the men, and …

I read the brief history, curious about when I was. Carter gave me a general rundown of the era and also cautioned me about what was known of social protocol and norms. I was too tired yesterday to offend anyone, and I took note of what he told me as far as dealing with those around me.

When I finished reading, I sent him a fast response. *Neat. Got it. Um – about the 'poor man's cryogenics' … are you serious???? What happens to me while I'm under? Is this experimental technology like the empathic memory chip that almost killed me??What if someone drops me like a statue and I shatter?*

The sound of movement and shuffling came from outside my safe little cocoon. I waited impatiently for Carter's response.

I've got it covered. Don't worry!! When you see Genghis, take his pic. No one in nine hundred years has seen what he looks like!

"Worst response ever, Carter."

I debated sending a heated response and reminding him about how well he had my first adventure covered.

But in truth … I felt too angry about what happened. About the fact Carter purposely eliminated the best man I'd ever met from the face of the planet and used me to do it. I didn't want to give Carter an ounce of any part of my emotions or thoughts. He didn't deserve them and worse, I had a feeling he'd find a way to use them against me.

I hated Carter for hurting Taylor, my husband of two days in the eighteen forties, and yet was doomed to do what Carter wanted. He was my only link to my world, my only hope of maybe one day getting back home.

I considered his messages for several minutes before tucking the phone away. Nowhere near as eager as I was on my first adventure, I was also excited about being somewhere so completely new, a witness to events still spoken about during my time a thousand years later. It was here where I needed to focus, not on the memories trying to pull free from my mind of watching the man I cared about disappear from all of creation.

Pushing my covers down, I prepared myself for a day of learning and exploration.

A large form in layers of wool and leather rendering him even larger was near the entrance of the tent, back to me. I swung my legs down from the waist-high bed and tucked the blankets back into place before looking around. The servants, commander and Ghoajin were all gone.

"Excuse me," I started quietly. "Do you know where …"

He faced me, and I stopped. He wore a leather mask over his features, and a familiar sword was sheathed at his side.

It's not possible. I shook away the sense of familiarity, knowing the man who saved my life in the eighteen forties, who chopped my governess in two when she went to shoot me, couldn't be here in the Mongol Empire with me now. The two men were dressed similarly, yes, but that may have been coincidence and perhaps, a little paranoia.

"Sorry," I murmured. "Do you know where Ghoajin is?"

He held out a pouch in response. I checked my cloak pocket and found the bag full of pills gone.

"Um, thanks." I drew near enough to grab them then stepped back quickly, not liking the fact he was wearing a mask and dressed like the man who helped Carter send me back here.

He tossed me a water bladder. It landed at my feet.

My stomach began to sink. "Thanks. Again," I said and picked it up.

"Swallow them."

I shook my head and moved away from him, the sense of danger making my heart race.

The stranger with a voice barely above a whisper drew his long, curved sword slowly. The sharpened metal gleamed, and I stared at it.

"You don't know what these are," I said. "It's not the time to-"

"Now." He smacked the flat of the sword against the leather armor over his arm. The sound made me jump.

Reaching for my cell phone, I froze when he started towards me.

"Swallow them. Now," he repeated. "Or I kill you here."

My mouth went dry, and my mind wildly sought some sort of reasoning behind this. "You saved me at the well," I managed.

He gave a nod.

"Carter sent you?"

"I can force them down your throat, Moonbeam," he replied.

Shit. I had no idea what was going on, who this guy was or what happened to me during the poor man's cryogenics. I didn't even know if I was ever going to wake up and if I did, what happened if someone dropped me over the next hundred years, and I woke up with my limbs missing?

The man started towards me again.

"Okay," I whispered. "I'm taking them." Fumbling with the bag, I manage to tug it open and pull out one large, black capsule. "All of them?"

"All of them."

I hope this doesn't hurt. Praying silently to wake up in one piece, I began to swallow the inch long pills. I felt nothing as they went down my throat and settled into my gullet, except for a mild bloating caused by the amount of water pills that size took to choke down.

When I finished with the last one, I held the pouch upside down to show him. "Okay. Now what?" I asked.

"Now you sleep." He sheathed his sword.

"Will you at least tell me if Carter sent you to do this?" I asked once more.

"He did not."

My mouth dropped open, and for a moment, I couldn't summon words. The shock wore off quickly. "Then who did?" Taylor, my late husband from the eighteen forties, had once mentioned his people, an organization of time travelers who went throughout history to protect the natural course of events from people like Carter and those Carter sent back in time to alter history.

Maybe they found me. I fished out the cell from my pocket, starting to panic. It was one thing to know I couldn't trust Carter. It was another completely to fall under the influence of an organization I knew nothing about, one with the ability to do anything to me.

With agility that caught me completely off guard, the man was suddenly by my side. He snatched the wrist holding the phone and pried the cell away from me. Even his hands were gloved; I saw no part of him that might tell me who he is.

"Who sent you?" I repeated.

The world was growing fuzzy. Colors and objects blurred and ran together, much like I was underwater.

With some difficulty, I focused on the man and watched helplessly as he took my connection to Carter and stuck it in his pocket. He pressed something else into my hand, but my eyes had ceased to distinguish shape and only knew light and dark. I wasn't cold, though my limbs were no longer responding to my mental commands.

The world around me faded sense by sense until finally, even light was gone.

I slid into darkness.

Chapter Two

COLD. SO COLD. I BREATHED IN WATER AND CHOKED, TOPPLED INTO darkness and awoke again only for the world to appear as if I were gazing at the blue sky from the bottom of a pond.

More darkness.

More light.

And always so cold.

The cycle went on like some sort of horrific nightmare I wasn't quite able to pull out of. The first sense that appeared to work correctly was that of sound, and I heard the strangest noise, one so unusual and gone so fast, I wasn't able to capture whether or not I really heard it let alone determine what it was.

Tingling of my skin came next, followed quickly by smell. My stomach was roiling, my limbs wooden and mind either too far ahead or too far behind. Either way, I was scared.

Light burst upon me as if the sun had dawned in my face and nowhere else. At once, my senses caught up, and I reeled at the whorl of color, scents, voices, and sensation.

Rolling onto my stomach, I threw up. I blinked away tears and grimaced at the mess beneath me. It was black, oily, as if I'd vomited motor oil.

The world began to right itself, and I wiped tears from my eyes and rolled onto my side. I was on a table, covered by a blanket. It wasn't exactly comfortable.

"Your name is Moonbeam?" someone asked with a combination of cautious curiosity and disbelief.

My surroundings cleared. A warm, evening breeze cascaded through white walls, past curtains so sheer, they appeared to be silk. The sky beyond was gorgeous. Splashes of pink and orange were being gobbled up by the dark blue of night. The scent of jasmine accompanied the breeze.

"Moonbeam?" the voice asked again.

I shifted onto my back and twisted my head to gaze at him. An older man with a head wrap, long white robe and warm brown eyes sat beside me. His beard reached mid-chest.

I smelled food. Holy hell was I hungry.

"We did not think you would awaken." There was a light in his gaze, one I'd characterize as hope if anything. He looked briefly across the room at someone else before returning his attention to me. "Can you understand me?"

"Yes." My voice was hoarse and raspy.

"Are you in pain?"

I stretched my body and pushed myself up. A little dizzy, a whole lot hungry, I was again in a strange place. Fortunately, it was warm here and my surroundings appeared pleasant. Green tile lined the white walls around a hearth. The shapes of the windows and geometric décor were distinctly Islamic in style. "No," I responded, looking around.

He handed me a bronze goblet of wine. I sipped it, wanting water instead. No sooner had I swallowed than the urge to vomit hit me once more. Leaning precariously over the table, I had no time to thank the middle-aged man who caught me before I fell and instead, threw up again.

More black oily stuff. I stared at it, my thoughts moving slowly. It looked a lot like the inky blackness of …

Carter's pills.

Did I really survive his poor man's stasis? I had all my limbs, too. As far as I could tell, I wasn't missing any part of my body.

Carter was brilliant, though a bit on the psychotic side to kidnap people and send them back in time. I was more relieved about his genius than his actions at the moment and hoped there were no lingering side effects.

The middle-aged man lowered me to the table once more. "When you feel well enough to eat, I will feed you," he said and then stood. Motioning whoever lingered in the shadows closer, he spoke in an excited voice. "Tell our master she has awoken."

The servant or messenger or whoever left fast enough that the door slammed closed behind him.

"Can I ask … where I am?" I managed. My body didn't quite feel right yet, so I remained where I was on the table. I was wearing different clothes. These felt like well-woven cotton – soft and light. A nightgown maybe.

"Kharan, north of Baghdad by a fortnight and a week east of Baku and the Sea."

I really didn't know where that left me. One of the Stans, maybe?

"You are in the home of the only royal blood remaining after the barbarians destroyed the city of Baghdad," he added in a sadder voice. "We fled here and have been hiding for seventy years."

I was at least seventy years in the future, then. For a moment, I was frozen between horror at being completely vulnerable in a coma for seventy years and realizing if Carter got me this far, he was able to get me farther. I could wake up every seventy years until I hit my year and resume my life.

The realization made all the difference. My spirits lifted at the idea of seeing my home again.

"Moonbeam, do you wish food?" my caretaker asked.

This time, I almost laughed at the name. It was adorable, though I didn't think the Mongol who gave it to me meant it to be.

"Yes, I think so," I replied and pushed myself into a sit. The edges of the room were a little wobbly still, but the world was starting to feel more solid. I was in a simple dress with no sign of anything else around me, like my phone. "Was there anything with me when you … wait. Did you find me? Hide me in the basement for seventy years? How did I get here?"

He glanced up, giving me a curious look. "You were brought to us," he explained. "We heard the myth of the Mongol goddess who fell from the sky and blessed the barbarian's destruction of my world. We searched for many years to locate you and then, we hired someone to obtain you from the depths of the Empire." He lifted cloth off a round breadbasket and withdrew a warm piece of unleavened bread the size of a small tortilla.

I accepted it. "Oh. If I did that, why did you want me?" I asked. "Revenge?"

"No, Moonbeam. So you can convince them to spare us."

The sobering response unsettled me. "You didn't put me into the sleep or hide me. You just found me and want me to help you?"

He nodded. "We paid someone to bring you here."

That's terrifying. What if someone else had found me? What if I'd been tossed around from place to place like a sack of potatoes for multiple decades? There were days when I swore up and down I'd kick Carter's ass when I met him again.

And moments like this when I realized I wasn't just out of place and time, I was out of the place and time I was *supposed* to be, too. Anxious to figure out what was going on, I rested one foot on the stone floor then the other. They held, though I was wobbly and headachy.

"Was there anything with me?" I asked.

"Instructions on how to wake you and that your name was Moonbeam, the Goddess of the White Path."

"I'm not a goddess," I said with a grunt.

"Of course you are not. There is but one God," he agreed. "But you are not … normal. Perhaps the djinn cursed you."

"Maybe," I replied without understanding what a *djinn* was. Some words didn't translate well. My legs held me, and I walked around the table. Pausing to lean against it, I sighed and nibbled on the bread. The light, fluffy food was a little salty and delicious. "This is amazing."

He shifted from his position on a pile of pillows near the fire and motioned for me to join him. At a low table before him was a small feast consisting of what looked like meatballs, honey drizzled dates, rice, more bread and …

Hummus. "Oh, I love Middle Eastern food!" I exclaimed.

"It is a meager meal, but it is all we can offer," he said with some hesitation. "Does it please you?" He pushed the food to my side of the table.

Nodding, I dug in without hesitation, my appetite roaring to life. I had seventy years worth of eating to catch up to. "This is the best food ever."

He smiled. "You will consider helping us?"

What else was I supposed to do? I had no cell phone, no clue why I was there or what I was supposed to do. Not only that, but someone left *just-add-water* instructions on my body. What was Carter … or whomever … thinking?

I didn't think refusing this man's request was going to win me any favors, either.

What would The Doctor do? He'd help, of course, and hope for the best.

"If I can. What do you need me to do?"

He twisted in his seat and motioned to someone in the shadows. "It is simple. When they come to destroy us, convince them to spare you and her."

The girl in the corner emerged somewhat shyly, dark eyes on me. She wasn't more than seven with long, dark hair braided down her back. She wore a long robe that reached the top of her slippered feet.

Startled by the request, it took me a moment to process it. "They're coming to destroy you?"

"It is what they do. We defied them years ago, and they have not forgotten. They rule the lands as far as you can see," he said softly. "She is the heiress to the royal bloodline. Her father died in a skirmish with the Mongols and her mother at birth. There is no one else."

I gazed at the girl. No consideration in a million years would keep me from doing as he asked. I didn't understand anything about their bloodline, but I did know I wasn't going to let a child get hurt. "Why do you not ask me to help all of your people?" I asked, puzzled. "If they will spare her, why not all of you?"

"It is not their way. We must submit and pay them tribute or die. We did worse. Fifty years ago, her forefather ruled Baghdad and killed their emissary. They destroyed the city. Burnt it to the ground and slaughtered all who dwelt within. They will not rest until his seed is wiped from this earth."

The amount of damage he was discussing was beyond me to

imagine. "You think they'll listen to me."

"We know they will."

I swallowed hard. I didn't exactly look forward to trying to reason with a Mongol army.

"We did find this with you," he added with some hesitation. "My master did not think it wise to return it, but … you are willing to help. It is not right for me to keep it from you." He handed me a pouch.

Opening it, I dumped the cell phone onto my palm. *Oh, thank god!* Except …

It wasn't mine. My cell was white. This one was black. Tapping it awake, I spotted a single message on the screen.

Do as Mahmood asks. Protect the girl for two months.

A chill drifted through me. "You're Mahmood?" I asked him.

"I am."

Not caring what he thought of my actions, I took a break from eating to send a message back. *Who are you????*

Setting it down, I began eating again, my mind racing and heart pounding. Thank god, I had a means of contacting someone. I just didn't know who it was, what they wanted and how to find Carter again.

But as long as I had a phone, there was a chance, however slim, of making it home. Profound relief bolstered me, and I scarfed down the meal before me.

The princess sat beside the older man, watching me.

Full and content, I sat back finally. "Do you have a plan?" I asked Mahmood.

He appeared to debate for a moment before responding. "Not yet. I had hoped you would know how to deal with them."

I was with them less than a day. I had no idea how to respond.

"We captured one of them," he added hopefully. "He has refused to speak a tongue we understand during questioning and what he does say in our tongue, we can't fully understand, but maybe ..."

I waited.

"Maybe you can speak to him and he will tell his people to spare you, since they believe you to be a goddess."

"I like that idea." I shifted uneasily. "It was so long ago that I saw them. I don't know if they'll remember me."

"They do not forget."

I wasn't feeling so confident. I didn't even make it a day there before someone kidnapped me. I looked at the phone. Whoever my new puppet master was, he or she wasn't talking.

"How do you feel?" Mahmood asked.

"Good," I said. "That doesn't seem right, though. I was asleep for so long."

"It is not natural," he agreed. "But God has made this possible and blessed your journey to us, and I am grateful. The barbarians are at our walls now. Do you feel well enough to begin?"

My heartbeat quickened. I didn't exactly understand what that meant, but I had a feeling he was short on time. With a nod, I climbed to my feet, staggered at a wave of dizziness, and steadied myself.

"Good as new," I said with a forced laugh.

Mahmood appeared concerned. "Go, your highness," he said to the girl. "Moonbeam, there are clothes and a servant to help you." He indicated a dressing screen sectioning off one corner.

With some effort, I walked to the screen and behind it. A female servant stood waiting, her eyes on the floor. I recognized a copper pot similar to those I had seen during my time in the eighteen hundreds and quickly relieved myself, disgusted when I peed black oil. My body was purging the pills that put me under, and it was really gross.

She washed me down with a sponge, an act that would've had me in stitches had I had full confidence in my body. As it was, I felt a little wooden, in need of a good hour or so of yoga or hot bath to bring my muscles back to life.

Drizzling scented oils over me, the servant then helped me into a long, black flowing gown and draped a lace scarf in black over my hair. She braided my hair next and tied the scarf at the base of my neck.

Walking was getting easier. Mahmood waited for me, his gaze out the window at the dark night sky. I joined him. For a moment, I forgot to breathe. We were in a white tower. Beyond low buildings of the small city was a wall and past the enclosure, campfires dotted the horizon as far as I could see.

"There must be thousands," I said, surprised.

"Tens of thousands. They will burn the city to the ground and kill every inhabitant."

The city itself didn't seem very large, maybe a few thousand people, but the savagery he described seemed almost … impossible. Or surreal.

The sense of not quite being a part of my world sneaked over me, and I was on my knees before I realized the spell was coming. Taylor once told me it was a side effect of time traveling, a sense of displacement or perhaps, the trauma of travel.

"Moonbeam, are you well?" Mahmood asked urgently.

"Yeah. Sorry." I shook my head and took several deep breaths to clear the sense. "So … are we going out there to talk to them?"

His dark eyes studied my features with worry. "The scout we captured remains in our custody. I had thought, if you were to meet him, and he knew your legend …"

"… then he might be able to get us out of here."

Mahmood nodded.

"One way to find out," I said cheerfully and pushed myself to my feet. "We don't have much time, do we?"

"We do not know why they have waited this long. The armies have been at our walls for three days. It is likely they will not wait much longer, or possible they are waiting for the command to attack."

My eyes went out the window once more. It seemed miraculous that men on horseback could travel from so far away as Mongolia let alone conquer. In my era, we had planes and ships to transport people and machines. The amount of time and effort and sheer willpower it would take in this time to defeat entire nations …

It was incredible, horrifying and mind blowing.

"Come, Moonbeam," Mahmood said and hurried to the wooden door.

I went. My gaze was a bit blurry from the spell, my step not as certain or quick as it usually was. As if sensing this, Mahmood kept his pace slow and led me through narrow halls to a winding stairwell that twisted several floors down until we reached a basement.

Or maybe a … dungeon. It was dark and smelly. I couldn't imagine people voluntarily being down here.

"All we know of him is his name, Batu. He has said nothing else that we can understand," Mahmood said.

We continued down a hallway with an uneven stone floor that smelled of rot, must and men. My nose wrinkled.

"But he's speaking to you?" I asked, a little nervous about confronting one of the men Mahmood feared.

"I wouldn't call it speaking."

The odd sound, the one that woke me originally, filled the air. It didn't sound human: a low, bass hum combined with higher pitched staccato notes that fluctuated in a quick-paced rhythm. The near-growl penetrated the walls and emanated from behind a closed door.

"What kind of instrument is that?" I asked.

"It is no instrument," Mahmood said, amused. "It is the singing Mongol."

"Singing?"

"The song of the steppe. They call it throat singing. He does it all day."

That can't be singing. I frowned, not understanding how anyone could sing two notes at once let alone growl that deep.

Mahmood paused in front of the door from which the sound came. "Do not speak," he cautioned. "Let us observe first."

I nodded.

He opened the door, and we stepped into a large room. Heavily armed guards in chainmail were stationed every ten feet around the perimeter for a total of twelve. Torchlight illuminated the plain, stone room void of furniture or any other comfort items. In the center was a man, hooded and bound, seated on a low stool.

The sound came from him and reverberated in the enclosed space.

I'd never heard anything so peculiar in my life, and I definitely didn't consider it singing.

Mahmood motioned for me to follow him. We circled the captured warrior at a safe distance.

He was much larger than those I'd seen in the army of Ghoajin's husband. He resembled the bodyguards they assigned me the night I arrived: over six feet tall and thickly muscled with biceps larger than my thighs. I immediately understood why there were so many guards. This warrior was simply dressed in a tunic with ties open at the throat and baggy pants. He was barefoot, and I saw no braids or hair from under the hood.

The odd song stopped suddenly. I blinked, not realizing its hypnotic effect, like listening to the low, soothing yoga CD featuring the chanting of monks, until it was gone.

"I smell you," said the man on the stool. "You bring a woman this time." His head twisted towards us, though I doubted he could see us through the thick hood.

I inched closer to Mahmood, who appeared likewise uneasy.

"Where is my hair, imam?" the Mongol asked.

"Can you understand him?" Mahmood turned to me.

"Yes," I replied, recalling the two were speaking different languages. "He said he can smell us and knows a woman is here. He asked what happened to his hair."

"He reeked like a dog," Mahmood said with some disdain. "We shaved his head, bathed him and burned his clothing. He slaughtered twenty of our men yet howled like a bath was torture."

I started to smile, noticing for the first time how clean and neat Mahmood's clothing was. There were no stains on the white robe, and everything down to his fingernails was pristine.

Doubting I wanted to give a word for word translation of this one, I debated what to say to the warrior and finally decided not to mention anything about his hair at all.

"Ask him when they will attack," Mahmood directed me.

"Batu," I said and stepped towards the prisoner. "We came to speak to you about the warriors outside the walls."

"You speak my tribe's dialect," was the curious response. "What magic is this?"

"It's not magic. I am gifted with languages."

"Are you as beautiful as you sound?"

Startled, I barely caught the laugh that bubbled forth. He was relaxed in his spot in the middle of the room, clearly unconcerned about being a prisoner if he was flirting with me.

"I am uglier than a horse. My nose is huge, my eyes small and I have no teeth." I replied, unable to help the saucy response.

"Bah. What do you want, ugly one?"

"I want to know when your people will attack the city."

"How long have they been at your walls?"

"Three days."

"Tell me what you see outside your walls."

I hesitated and turned to Mahmood, catching him up. He frowned and nodded for me to continue.

"To the east there are tens of thousands of campfires," I said slowly.

"And the other directions?"

I asked Mahmood, who shook his head. "The river lies to the north, and there is nothing to the south. The west is protected by a moat."

Relaying the message to the prisoner, I waited for him to speak.

He nodded. "They have already begun. They will not come from the east but from two directions, likely the west and south. There will be nothing standing by dawn."

My heart jolted. "You're telling the truth?"

"Yes."

"But why reveal their plan?"

He shrugged. "It does not matter anyway. The sword of the horde will cut the city at its roots. Whether or not you know we come, you will be dead before you can stop us." The factual, confident response surprised me.

It took me a moment to recover. In an era where warfare occurred between men with swords, I wasn't able to fathom the idea of an army that couldn't be stopped. Didn't it just take another army of the same size to stand in the way? It wasn't like they had missiles or air support or heck, even guns.

"Why have you not told him?" the warrior asked.

"Because I don't understand," I replied honestly.

"You understand the words. You speak too well not to. Does

battle strategy confuse you?"

"You made it simple enough," I said. "This is not … my way. I guess."

He shifted forward and twisted in my direction in sudden interest I took to be a bad sign. His frame was tense, the muscles of his forearms roped and bulging as he tested his bonds. "You are not from here, ugly one," he observed. His ease and amusement was gone, replaced by a note of threat. "It is simple: they submit or they die. They chose to die."

Mahmood and I stepped back, closer to the nearest guard. I rapidly explained to Mahmood what had been said. His alarm rendered him speechless for a split second before he crossed to the door and spoke too quietly for me to hear. The guard darted out. Approaching me, Mahmood's grim concern was clear in his tight features.

"I must address the master myself," he said to me. "You are certain this is what he said? South and west?"

"Yes," I replied.

"Have you told him who you are?"

I shook my head.

"Do so if you feel it wise. I will return as soon as I warn my master and prepare the princess."

Without waiting for my response, Mahmood started away.

I faced the warrior without moving, not at all agreeing with the idea to remain. He suspected something already, and I didn't know enough about this time or his people to know why he was tense.

It scared me. The stories of Mongol tenacity and savagery on the battlefield were known in my time. I sensed if he wanted to be free and decided to kill everyone in the room, he probably could. Maybe it was fear or Hollywood hype or not knowing for certain, but no part of me wanted to be here if he succeeded in freeing himself from his bonds.

"Will you sing again?" I asked quietly.

"Why do you fear me, ugly one?" he asked, amused. "Am I not tied and surrounded by … eleven guards?"

Ugh. How he knew how many remained, I didn't know or like it. Hesitating to tell him who I was, in case he wasn't at all moved or interested as Mahmood thought he would be, I hugged myself.

"I will sing if you remain here," the warrior offered, relaxing in place once more.

"I suppose," I murmured.

"A song of the water? Sky? Grass?"

"Um, sky."

One of the guards brought me a stool and set it a little too close to the warrior for comfort. But I sat. Sensing me with instincts sharp enough to scare me, the warrior began his strange throat song once more.

Puzzling over how a person could make such animalist sounds, I listened. The low drone like that which knocked me out on an airplane, combined with the higher pitched notes and rhythm, was hypnotic. I found myself relaxing despite the strangeness of his song, enough so that my eyes drifted closed.

I was more tired than I had thought. Adrenaline spurts were shorter than usual, and the sense of displacement, of detaching from the world, drifted over me once more. For a moment, I was back at the well in the eighteen forties, standing beside the place where Taylor had been …

… Right before he ceased to exist. Not dead, not gone. *Uncreated.* I still wasn't able to comprehend such a thing or believe Carter and I were the only people in all of space and time who remembered him, because we didn't exist fully as part of the time where we were.

You made a difference.

They were Taylor's final words to me. He knew what was happening to him. I didn't, until he was gone, and nothing but death lay around me. The memory was so sharp, it hurt, and I clutched my chest and bent over with a soft groan.

The song stopped, and I blinked back into my new reality, shaken and not fully present. Tears were on my cheeks, and my chest was so tense, I was breathing shallowly.

"Where did the song take you?" the warrior asked.

I glanced up. He was completely relaxed again, his hooded head facing my direction, as if we were having tea and he wasn't a prisoner in someone else's dungeon.

"I don't know. Too far," I whispered.

"The Eternal Blue Sky has no bounds. Its song might take you farther away than you wish." He was matter-of-fact. "Are you fully returned?"

"No." I was struggling. How he knew that, I had no idea.

"It is easy. When your spirit tries to flee, you force it back."

"How?"

"See. Hear. Smell. Touch."

I blinked, confused. "What?"

"On the steppe, our senses keep us alive. You must learn to ground them, so they can be used as weapons or to protect you."

"You want me to focus my senses back in this moment."

"It is how you survive on the steppe. See. Hear. Smell. Touch."

The simple wisdom of his words settled into me. I studied him and did as he suggested, listening to his baritone voice.

I repeated his words silently. The spell faded faster this time as I took in the details of my surroundings. I sighed.

"You are back," he stated.

"Thank you, I think." I righted myself. "Where did the song take you?"

"To the steppe where I grew up. I will return one day soon."

"You'll probably have to escape here first."

"Escape?" he echoed. "I am where I want to be, ugly one."

The light-hearted response sent a chill through me. "You … meant to be caught?"

"Yes."

"You killed twenty of their men!"

"I had to convince them they captured me. I could not let their victory be easy. We do not surrender."

I wasn't feeling like me yet, but the memories were at the back of my mind and my chest slowly unfreezing.

"Who are you, ugly one, that you speak my tongue and that of the West as well?" Though far more controlled than his initial attempt to identify me, there was still an unmistakable edge in his voice.

"Why does it matter?"

"Maybe I came here to find you."

"Not likely," I replied, mind going to the princess the Mongols were after.

"Unless you fell from the sky."

I froze. It wasn't possible he knew anything about me just by my knack with languages. He was messing with me; he had to be. Deception was obviously a tactic of theirs. He was looking for something, and I had no idea what. In the meantime, he was toying with me.

Sensing my reaction, the warrior gave a grunt or growl of satisfaction. He shifted forward once more, far enough I was able to see him fiddling with the hands tied by rope behind his back. I had a feeling I was better off facing the attacking hordes than remaining with him.

I stood and moved towards the door.

"Do not go, ugly one. I am not yet free," he called. "It will be easier for me to take your head if you are close."

"Don't rush on my account," I replied and then faced the guard nearest me. "He's about to escape."

It seemed to jolt all of them into moving. I pushed the door to the hallway open while the guards closed in around him.

"Moonbeam?" Mahmood hurried down the hallway from the direction of the stairs. "What is it?"

"I think he's about to get free," I said with some concern. "Was he right about the attack?"

Mahmood nodded and waved for me to follow. "Quickly. We must hide you and the princess."

"I thought you wanted me to talk to the Mongols," I replied without one small shred of interest in such a task.

"There is a … division within the house of my master. Those who want to negotiate, and those who feel surrendering, and thereby, turning over the last of our royal line to the barbarians, is a fate far worse than her death," he explained. Reaching the stairs, he took them two at a time. I struggled to stay behind him at the pace, not completely recovered from either of my travels back or forward in time. "Those who prefer the bloodline's demise are organizing a coup may try to hurt the princess. We will hide you from them. The barbarians will dispose of them and find you, and you can negotiate with them."

This is sounding like one of Carter's ill-planned ideas. I heard Mahmood's desperation and understood he and his mysterious master were operating out of fear and partially, out of knowledge their own fates were likely already sealed.

No matter what, though, I wasn't able to stomach the idea of some poor little girl being chopped down, royal or not. I owed it to them to help. What choice did I have? I had to assume whoever sent me here was less likely to help me if I failed.

My only option was to go with the flow, however bizarre the path. Patting the phone in my pocket, I took some comfort in knowing I had an outlet to someone from my time who might one day help me.

He led me up the stairs and to a wide hallway. Armed soldiers lined the hallways, along with several servant women stationed outside a door. Mahmood moved past them all into the bedchamber of the little princess, who sat beside the fire, dressed in servant's clothing and appearing scared already.

The sounds of fighting came from the streets. I crossed to the window. The princess's room overlooked the inner city. Fires had sprung up around the edges of the city moving in our direction. People jammed the streets and fled towards the east. I wasn't able to see the attackers from this angle, but I assessed the prisoner hadn't been lying about the siege coming from two directions. The surreal scene struck me once more as almost too unfamiliar for me to process.

It's like when the Cybermen invade earth on Doctor Who, I told myself finally.

"Moonbeam!" Mahmood called. "Come with me." He took the girl's hand and led us both into the hallway. The soldiers had grouped around the two stairwells leading from the floors below, one on either end of the long hallway.

Mahmood took us down another hallway and into a parlor style room. Five other women accompanied us in nervous silence.

"You must stay here, no matter what," he warned me. He held out the hand of the girl he held. "Hide there." He pointed to a tapestry stretching from floor to ceiling.

I took her hand and nodded. This was starting to feel real – and I was scared.

The princess and I went to the heavy tapestry. I pushed it around until we were able to move behind and was pleased to find a cutout in the wall where we could hide without the weight of the tapestry. It was heavy and stuffy, but we made it to the cutout and huddled together. The girl's arms went around my waist.

This is crazier than the Old West. Though in fairness, I at least knew who the enemy was here.

We waited and listened. The sounds from the room were muffled by the heavy tapestry. Women were talking and soon fell quiet. I didn't imagine the raiders had reached the home of the princess so soon, but it wasn't long until the sounds of banging on the door reached us.

The girl hugged me more tightly, and I rested a hand on her back, pulling us both deeper into the crevice in the wall. Screams burst from the women in the room followed by the clash of metal on metal. I couldn't imagine what was going on and wondered if these were Mahmood's people fighting over the princess or Mongols fighting Mahmood's people.

I closed my eyes, willing this to be some sort of nightmare or at least for us to evade discovery forever. If we survived the raid, I could ask my new puppet master what to do next.

Silence fell, and I held my breath.

"Ugly one."

Oh, shit. This voice I recognized. I didn't think the prisoner was here for me, but how did he know the princess was with me? Better yet, how did he know I was even here?

The warrior prisoner smashed something on the other side of the room, a wardrobe or wooden screen being knocked to the stone floor.

Something else crashed to the ground. He was moving closer, tossing the room in an attempt to find us.

He thwacked the tapestry, and the princess gave a startled cry.

"Hello, ugly one," the prisoner said, satisfied.

"Stop!" Someone shouted from the direction of the door.

"Stay here," I whispered to the girl. Prying free from her, I waited a moment until I heard the sounds of two swords clashing before inching to the nearest edge of the tapestry to peer out.

My eyes went instantly to the bodies on the floor and pools of blood. My trip to the Old West was an eye opener, the first time I'd ever seen anyone die or be killed. This was something else, though. The bodies of at least six women lay where they'd fallen, along with the forms of several more knights dressed like those guarding the prisoner.

My stomach churned. Death and killing … they weren't anything I'd ever thought I'd witness let alone be a part of like this.

I didn't feel able to process it with my twenty first century morals and understanding of post- Geneva Conventions warfare. My heart hurt for these people. I had seen all I wanted to of death in the eighteen forties; I didn't think I could live in a world where this was common.

The princess was crying behind me. I blinked away my fear and stepped back behind the safety of the tapestry.

Movies. Halloween blood. If I didn't find a way to … accept, at least temporarily, what I saw, I'd break down and bawl until someone chopped off my head. *It's just like watching a movie or video game. Fake blood from the haunted house you went to when you were seventeen, Josie.*

I repeated the words until the sense of panic subsided enough for me to remember why I had to get a hold of myself: the little girl crying in the cutout two feet away.

Swallowing hard, I peered out at the surreal scene once more. The bald prisoner's back was to me as he fought off four of the knights with a familiar curved blade. He appeared comfortable without shoes and fought with ferocity and brutality I didn't ever,

ever want to face head on.

He threatened to chop off my head. The thought held me in terrified suspension for another long second or two.

"Moonbeam!" The hiss came from across the room.

Mahmood was peering out of what looked like another hiding spot. He waved to me. Anxious to be anywhere else, I ducked behind the tapestry and took the girl's hand. She stayed on my heels as we crept between tapestry and wall and peeked around it again.

There were more soldiers in the room to occupy the prisoner. Not that it seemed to matter; he was chopping them down quickly.

Easing out from the tapestry, we started towards Mahmood.

"Do not leave, ugly one!"

If anything, the warning spurred me on. A flash of steel soared in front of my face and planted itself into the wardrobe on the wall nearest me. I froze, horrified by how close it came to nipping my nose.

"Stay, ugly one," the prisoner ordered once more.

I faced him, uncertain how he was able to keep an eye on me and the men he fought simultaneously. He managed to angle himself to do so and glanced at me with large, almond-shaped eyes of dark brown set in a heart-shaped face. There was a savage beauty to him, a combination of flawless features and ferocity that was absolutely terrifying to behold.

The princess was crying. She hugged me once more. Mahmood crept from his hiding place towards us, but I signaled him to stay out of sight. The prisoner had wicked aim; I didn't want my nose or Mahmood's head gone.

I watched the fight for a distraction to give us space to run. The prisoner turned his back on us, and I darted forward, all but dragging the girl with me.

Mahmood ran out to help us.

Suddenly, he snapped to the side, a sword piercing his chest and pinning him to the pole of the large bed at the center of the chamber.

Unable to register what happened, I stared dumbly at his form as it sagged. The light in his eyes vanished, and he went completely limp.

The sounds of fighting behind us stopped. I wasn't able to look away from Mahmood's lifeless body or really understand how he was here one moment, pinned to the bed the next. It happened so fast, I hadn't even seen the blade that claimed his life. I was splattered with warm droplets of his blood.

Halloween haunted house. The best ever special effects on a horror movie …

A sword swiped the air in front of my face, breaking the spell. I backpedaled automatically, the girl clinging to me.

"You must learn to listen," the warrior from the basement chided me. The cool tip of his sword lifted my chin.

I stared at him, my senses slowly catching up. He was even bigger than he appeared seated on the stool with bulging biceps and hands that looked strong enough to crush someone's skull. He watched me closely, breathing hard from the battle yet fully in control.

I stepped back until I hit the tapestry and pushed the princess between the wall and me. He moved with me, the tip of the sword pricking the skin of my neck. I was trembling out of fear and horror and had the urge to breakdown and fling off my blood speckled clothing.

"You can't have her," I said and swallowed hard.

His eyes moved to the girl behind me. With no ceremony, he lowered the sword and shifted forward, grabbing one of my arms. He spun me to face the tapestry and planted a hand at the center of my back, pinning me against the wall with ease. Sheathing the sword, he yanked off the scarf covering my hair and pulled down the back of the robe I wore to display the base of my neck.

"I did not come for her, Goddess," he said and traced a thumb over the lotus tattoo I was now beginning to regret ever getting. A new feeling trickled through me, one of dread. Maybe my aunt was right about tattoos attracting the wrong crowd.

He sniffed me. I resisted the urge to ask what it was with his people and sniffing, too afraid to ask.

"I'm not a goddess." It was a stupid time to protest and even stupider to ignore his claim, but the words slipped out before I could stop them.

He spun me once more, this time resting a heavy hand on my collarbone to keep me in place. "You are not ugly, either, Moonbeam," he said, amused. He reached past me to grab the girl.

He knows who I am. I started to block him, but he pushed me back against the wall. He hauled her up by the robe and suspended her in the air, not hurting her but scaring the hell out of her by the expression on her features.

"Who is this?" he asked. "A slave?"

I hesitated, uncertain how to respond.

He met my gaze, waiting. He appeared sincere, as if he neither knew nor cared whom the girl was. His size and strength left me thinking I'd never really understood the meaning of *intimidating* until this very moment. It was humbling to know without a doubt if he meant to act, I had neither the strength nor the speed to escape or survive.

My death would at least be quick.

Unable to form a response under his intense look, I nodded.

Shouts came from the hallway, drawing his attention. "Do not run, Moonbeam," he warned me once more. Releasing us both, he drew the sword and picked up another from one of the men he'd recently brutalized. He lingered, and I swore I saw him slice off the man's ear and put it into a pouch at his waist before he then disappeared into the hall.

I'm going crazy. No one chopped off dead men's ears, even this guy.

I released the breath I'd been holding, about to have a nervous breakdown yet knowing it was the wrong reaction if I wanted to live. Instead, I knelt and took the arms of the princess. We were both shaking, and there were tears on her face. "Do you … know a way out?"

She nodded and pointed up.

I followed her finger and stood back, gazing at the buttresses and exposed beams of the ceiling. Those nearest to the floor were about ten feet up. They extended along the walls and connected to beams twenty feet up that ran between rooms.

"Brilliant," I murmured. It had been a while since I was on a balance beam, but at the moment, I really didn't care. "You know where they go?"

She nodded. "Out … outside."

"Come on." I stood and picked her up, hurrying to the wall nearest us. The Mongol's rampage of the room did us some good. We stood on the wardrobe he toppled to reach the windowsill. I was able to stretch and reach the beam. With some graceless experimentation, I finally managed to walk my way up the wall to the beam and straddled it. I leaned over to grip her hand and hauled her up with me.

It was hard to see what was in the next room over from here.

The princess was quick on her feet on the beam. I trailed, my focus split between the sounds of fighting and my balance. Squeezing through the space between ceiling and wall, we walked above the corridor outside her room.

Chaos was below us. The prisoner, the soldiers from the house, and on one side, two more men in distinctive Mongol warrior dress were fighting over piles of bodies. Blood drenched the walls, and I looked away quickly, disgusted by the sight. My stomach roiled. I forced myself to breathe steadily, aware we'd both be dead if I threw up over the corridor.

The princess led us down a second beam running parallel to the hallway before shifting to take us over an unoccupied room. She didn't stop here, though, but went to the outside wall facing the city and moved through the opening in the wall and out onto a roof.

"Moonbeam!" The Mongol warrior's bellow almost cost me my footing.

I caught myself against the wall and hurriedly squeezed through the opening onto the roof. The night air was warm and the breeze light. The A-frame roofs were steep, the space between them barely wide enough for my foot. One misstep, and we'd both tumble into the city below.

Near my wit's end, I sagged against the eave nearest me.

The girl gasped from her spot at the edge of the crawlspace we were on. I pushed away from the roof and went to her.

The city was almost completely on fire. People poured out of one of the city's gates into the dark night while smoke clogged the sky above us and blocked the stars.

I had thought Mahmood prone to exaggeration, but this was exactly what he said would happen.

"Where do we go from here?" I asked the princess in a choked voice.

"I don't know." She sounded ready to cry. "I … I used to come here to … hide." She sank down into a sit and hugged her knees to her chest.

Double shit. We were trapped. If someone started this place on fire, there wasn't anywhere for us to go.

I paced the length of the short crawlspace before determining we had a better chance of facing the Mongols than navigating the steep rooftops of the small palace we were on.

I sat beside her and sighed. I had no idea what to do next, unless it was possible to wait out the fighting like Mahmood had suggested to face the Mongols on our terms. If such a possibility existed with an army whose motto was *submit or die.*

The thought of watching Mahmood die made me sick to my stomach. He had known his fate and seemed okay with it, but it didn't help me deal with it any better. It took all my willpower not to vomit and instead, I concentrated on surviving the night with a kid I knew nothing about.

"What's your name?" I asked her.

"Rabiyah."

"I'm … Moonbeam." My gaze slid to her, and I realized I was probably already doomed to have a personal connection here.

"I know. Do you not have a real name?"

No connections. No attachments. No heartbreak, especially not from the direction of a sweet little girl whose face was wet with tears and eyes looked at me like I was supposed to save her. "It's a long story," I murmured. "I fell from the sky one night and landed in front of an army of Mongols. They adopted me and named me Moonbeam. I like it better than my real name."

A smile tugged up the corners of her mouth. "If I were to choose a new name, it would be Flowers."

I grinned. "Love it. Want me to call you that? And you can call me Moonbeam?"

She nodded.

"Then no one will know who you really are."

"No one must know." She grew serious. "Mahmood said all these people are dying to save me."

Talk about burdening a kid … I sought some sort of explanation I could give her. "It's not your fault your forefathers did something to upset the Mongols. You bear none of that responsibility."

"I am a princess. I must bear it all."

"No, sweetie, you must not." I smoothed back her hair. "The past can sometimes return to haunt us. There's not always an explanation for what happens or why …" I drifted off, thoughts on Taylor. "But I guess in the end, everyone has a choice to move on. We'll make one, too, to live through this and start anew elsewhere." *Somehow.*

"You will come with me?"

"Yes. Mahmood thought that was wise, and I agree. Don't you?"

She nodded.

Something stirred from the direction of the room outside which we were perched. I pressed a finger to my lips to quiet her, and we both crept forward to see what was going on below us.

The room was being searched and tossed while fighting raged on in the corridor outside it.

The men left, and the door stayed open.

Easing back, the princess and I huddled together and watched her city burn. The fighting stopped in the corridor not too long after. We didn't leave our safe place, though, for fear of being caught. She hugged me, and I pulled her into my lap, leaning against the sloped eave behind me.

This is a nightmare.

I couldn't begin to figure out how to get out of this mess. Mahmood could have been right or approaching the Mongols could get us both killed. I really had no idea, and I was terrified of being cut to pieces by a sword.

Chapter Three

SMOKE SWIRLED OVERHEAD FOR THE REST OF THE NIGHT AND EVEN managed to delay the sunrise, or so it seemed. Billowing black clouds stretched out from the city towards the horizon. The rising sun was soon visible in the east, the murky ball appearing before the dawn had managed to pierce the smoke.

I waited for Flowers to fall asleep before checking my phone. My mystery handler had responded to my question.

My identity is none of your concern. Do as I direct you.

"Jackass," I muttered, taken aback. I stared at the message, torn between anger and hurt and god knew what else. I had never pulled punches with Carter, but I felt comfortable with him, even when he was planning to pull the rug out from under me and leave me stranded in the past. There was something … familiar about Carter. Even now, it was hard for me to be angry with him.

But this stranger, who kidnapped me from Carter and sent me on a mission without even bothering to give me his name …

Who the hell do you think you are? I typed. *Who do you think *I* am? I'm stranded in the past in the Mongol Empire on a roof waiting for them to chop down me and some little girl, and you're going to refuse to give me your name because … what? You're waiting for me to die here and now? Because my life doesn't matter? Well IT DOES MATTER. Either you get your shit straight and get me out of here or I tell the Mongols who this girl is and take my chances they won't kill me because I'm a goddess!!*

It was probably the least diplomatic thing I'd ever said. I wasn't prone to outbursts or anger or even grudges. But at this moment, I felt like unleashing all three at the stranger. I had no intention of turning over Flowers to anyone, but I was banking on my handler not knowing that.

The corridors nearest us had long since grown quiet. Fighting continued in other parts of the city. Achy from the awkward position dozing off and on, I straightened when the princess awoke. She pulled away to observe the damaged city through tear-puffed eyes. I automatically smoothed out her hair.

"It's quiet here. I think we can find some food or something," I murmured. "Are you hungry?"

She nodded.

My new handler hadn't responded. I wasn't surprised.

With a deep breath, I stood, stretched briefly and squeezed back into the room. Already I was able to see the bodies in the hallway and the blood covering the floors and walls. Steeling myself, I began walking across the beam, back towards the girl's room. She trailed me and waited while I climbed down first then caught her when she leapt off the beam.

Her room was eerily quiet. I looked around, unable to pinpoint what was setting off my red flag, if not for the death and destruction around me. A sense of being watched, one I'd experienced several times in the Old West, tickled the back of my neck. If my empathic memory chip were active, it'd probably be trying to warn me of something. I saw no one, though, and brushed it off.

The bodies lay where they had fallen, and the scent of metallic blood was thick in the air. Queasy, I covered my mouth and made my way towards a pitcher of water. We both drank our fill.

My phone buzzed. Not expecting a response from the asshole who sent me here, I pulled it out to read it.

Is your empathic memory chip working?

I muttered a few curses under my breath, hating the mention of the chip. It'd definitely come in handy right now, but I kind of liked my brain enough that I didn't want to ruin it. I sent a quick response.

"Where would we find food?" I asked Flowers quietly.

"Kitchens."

"Where are they?"

"First floor."

Ugh. I hesitated. A tiny voice wanted me to leave her here and fetch us some grub, but my instincts told me the biggest mistake I could make was separating from her. I took her hand, and we found a path through the gummy blood and heaped bodies to the stairwell she indicated.

Reaching it, I was dismayed to see even it clogged with bodies. I had the urge to break down and sob again, followed by vomiting for half a day. Instead, I swallowed the acrid taste in my mouth and picked my way through the dead.

We paused to listen at each floor and ensure there was no one waiting to ambush us or fighting too close to the stairs on the level we approached. The closer we got to the ground floor, the more activity we heard. Fighting raged in parts of the castle, and we slinked cautiously from floor to floor. Twice we had to stop and wait half an hour or more for those near the stairwell to move farther into the hallways.

"I don't think we're going to make it," I said finally, alarm growing at the noise coming from the two bottom floors.

"Me neither," she agreed.

Frustrated but valuing my life more than breakfast, I turned and led her back up the stairs to the quieter floors. Rather than return to her freaky room, we went to another void of the bloodshed that would make the best horror movie's effects team envious.

Closing the door, we sat down near the far wall.

I checked my phone to see another message.

Your psych profile says you won't turn her over. Who I am is irrelevant to your mission. When she's safe, contact me, and we'll discuss the possibility of returning you home.

"Now that's more like it," I said, pleased by the response. I was letting the comment about my psych profile go for now, more interested in the idea of returning home. Carter had said he didn't have the technology to send me back to my time, but Taylor claimed his people did. If his agency was the one calling the shots now, I had a much better chance of seeing my home again than before.

If I survive this adventure.

"What is this?" Princess Flowers asked and tilted the phone down to see the screen.

"It's … uh … a tool," I answered.

"What does it do?" She took it from my hands and examined it.

Wow. I had no idea how to answer the question.

Voices stirred from the hallway, and we both froze.

"Rabiyah?" came the soft call.

"It's one of my guards," she whispered to me.

"One who wants to help you or kill you?" I asked.

She gazed at me, large eyes sad.

"Let's wait here." The shadow of someone passing appeared

beneath the door and floor. He was followed by several more. I didn't know the politics or people well enough to understand who to trust, and judging from Flowers' face, she didn't either.

Mahmood would.

Thinking of what happened to him made me hold my mouth. When this was over, I was going to be sick for days.

"Search the rooms," someone directed.

We couldn't reach the lowest of the ceiling beams without knocking over or moving a piece of furniture. My eyes went around the room. I stood and hurried to the tapestry running along one wall and ran my hands across it, seeking another hiding spot. The center of the heavy woven tapestry gave. I waved for Flowers to join me, and we pushed aside the covering to crawl behind it.

The cutout was the same size as the one in her room, barely large enough for both of us.

The door creaked open, and we clung to one another as someone entered.

"Princess, are you here?" a male voice asked.

She looked up at me. I shook my head, and her grip around me tightened.

More men joined the speaker, until it sounded like a party in the hallway. Where had they all been hiding when this floor was cleaned out by the raiders? Mahmood would know … I didn't think the princess did, or we would've ended up somewhere other than the roof.

Fighting broke out a short time later, and the door to our room emptied and slammed closed. I worked free of her and peeked out.

"I think the roof is safer," I said, watching the flurry of shadows beneath the door. "C'mon."

With the men fighting, there was no chance of moving furniture drawing their attention. I braced my back against a heavy table and slowly shoved it towards the wall where we could reach one of the beams. Reaching the wall, I plucked up the girl and set her on the table before climbing up beside her. She was shaking and scared again.

"Okay. Back to our safe little spot," I said cheerfully. "Ready?"

She nodded.

I hefted her over my head to reach the beam. She clambered onto it.

Someone rammed into the door, and I jumped. It cracked open but no one came through.

"Go on!" I whispered to her, my pulse racing.

She stood and walked the sloping path to the beam above.

The door slammed open. "Ah, Moonbeam." Batu, the Mongol from the dungeon, gazed at me and then up, attention settling on the little girl. "Clever little monkey. This is where you hid." He sheathed his sword and started across the room towards me. He wore boots this time.

Rather than hop down from the table, I climbed on top of the eight-foot wardrobe nearby.

"What do you do, Moonbeam?" he asked, gazing up at me with a small smile. "You intend to climb to the moon?"

How someone like him, at a time like this, could crack a joke was almost as horrifying as realizing the pouch at his waist where he'd put one ear in now bulged, probably with more ears. I wasn't able to reconcile humor and mass murder. It just … didn't … click. Frozen in disbelief, I didn't move until he leapt atop the table.

"No!" I yelled a little too loudly. "Leave me alone!" I pushed myself to the opposite side of the wardrobe.

Batu swiped at me. "Come down, Moonbeam!"

"So you can kill me?"

"I will not kill you."

A shout from the door drew his attention. He leapt off the table and drew his sword to face the four knights spilling into the room.

"I don't believe you," I said and shifted, eyeing the beam.

"It is … true." He grunted and began fighting the knights. "There has been a guardian assigned since you appeared long ago. When one dies … a new one is … chosen … in case you return. I am your guardian."

"What if I never returned?"

"You did."

Rolling my eyes, I watched him for a moment, until he stabbed a man in the stomach and ripped him open from navel to chin.

Squeezing my eyes closed, I fought the sense of detachment and urge to vomit.

"See, smell, feel, hear, Moonbeam!" he shouted from across the room. "If you pass out, you die."

He was right. I didn't want to consider what these people would do to me if I got caught. I repeated the chant he taught me in the dungeon and then opened my eyes, forcing myself into this reality and time.

He had killed three knights in the time it took me to rope in my senses. Shaking, I slid off the wardrobe to the table once more and started towards the beam.

A knife thunked into the beam ahead of my face, barely missing me once more. I sprang back.

"How can you claim to be my guardian and throw knives and swords at me?" I yelled somewhat hysterically.

He didn't answer.

I heard the last of the men drop to the floor but didn't move, afraid of Batu knifing my hand or worse.

"You belong to the Empire as determined by the Eternal Blue Sky. I do what I must to protect you," he replied.

"Even if that means hurting me?"

"Yes. You were gifted to us. You will remain with us."

I faced him. "I don't belong to your people," I whispered, overwhelmed by the too accurate image his words painted. "I think, as a goddess, I can choose to leave when I please."

"No, you cannot." He was serious for once. "You are a lamb, Moonbeam. I am a wolf. The more you struggle, the deeper my teeth sink. Do you understand?" He studied me. "If you choose not to go, I will take you in as many pieces as I must."

My eyes slid to the pile of bodies behind him. No part of me doubted his terrifying claim.

"I can start by breaking your fingers." His tone was almost one of conciliatory offering, as if breaking my fingers was better than his original plan of cutting them off.

This willingness to spare me was what Mahmood counted on. It struck me how wise the Imam had been.

"I would like the opportunity to accompany you without any broken bones," I said as politely as possible. "But she must come with me." I pointed overhead to the princess watching us both.

"You can bring your monkey." He turned away and bent over the nearest body.

"What are you doing?"

He held up the ear he'd just sliced off and tucked it in his pouch. "Taking his ear."

"I see that but, I mean … *what* are you doing?"

"Accountability."

Did the language chip stop working? Because I had no idea what that meant.

The princess worked her way down the beam towards me.

"*Why* are you doing that?" I tried again.

"There are no bones." He held up the ear. "It is easy to cut."

"Why just one ear? Why not both?" The hysterical note was back in my voice.

Hearing it, Batu straightened from his task. "One ear per one man killed. Thus, our commander will know how many died and also that his orders were carried out. Each warrior must return with ten ears."

This was … beyond definition. "I really don't want to go with you."

He sheathed his sword and approached.

I backed against the wall.

With no ceremony, Batu snatched my arm and dragged me off the table and into his hard, muscular body, my back to his chest. The sense of being rendered completely vulnerable by his pure size and power left me shaking and scared once more. He wrapped his arms around me and pried one hand free.

"I can start with this one." He took my left pinky in his large hand and began squeezing.

"No!" I gasped and tried to pull free. It wasn't possible, not with his strength. If anything, his grip around me tightened.

"You have a low tolerance for pain." He sounded satisfied. "Let us both remember this." He released my finger without releasing me. "Let us both remember, Moonbeam, you are also protecting my enemy, and I am allowing it." These words were quieter, spoken against my ear.

My eyes found the princess again. She was waiting for me to help her down from the lowest beam.

"Lamb and wolf. Do not forget," he added.

Overwhelmed, the sense of detachment crept over me again, a combination of fatigue, time travel and adrenaline brought on by terror. I felt myself go limp in his arms. The world began to slide away, and this time, I didn't care if it did.

"See me. Hear me. Touch me. Smell me," he repeated in a low voice.

I ignored him and willed the spell to claim me. Maybe this time, when I woke up, I'd be elsewhere once more.

He jostled me to face him. One arm locked me against him while he rested his palm over my mouth. I blinked, not at all accustomed to being treated like a sack of potatoes or feeling like a delicate piece of china in the hands of a brute.

"See me," his order was low. He held my gaze with his dark eyes, his look penetrating. His heart-shaped face was out of place for a man who slaughtered everyone who came within a foot of him. His head was shaded from the growth of new hair, his rounder face and high cheekbones giving him a purely exotic look I found intriguing. "Hear me. Smell me."

I found myself obeying even though I didn't want to. He smelled of man, steel, horses and his own dark musk.

"Feel me."

Not that I hadn't noticed the rock hard body against me, but in that moment, I truly *experienced* it, the way my softer frame molded to him, the power of his thick thighs, the arm holding me against him, the width and hardness of his chest, even of the calloused hand across my mouth. For a moment, there was nothing in any time period but us. We managed to transcend the thirteenth and twenty-first centuries, to connect on a primal level that defied time.

My senses filled with him, and he pulled me back from the brink where I sort of wanted to be. I doubted it was his intent in any regard, but if not for the blood, fear and time distortion, I'd almost call this strange experience … erotic.

"And you are back," he said, reading my expression. His own softened, the amusement I couldn't remotely understand returning to his eyes. "Fetch your monkey. We must go."

He released me suddenly enough, I groped for the table to catch my balance. I was breathless, and this time, it wasn't from fear. It was from whatever experience just happened.

I didn't want a connection with anyone. Not the princess and certainly not him. The last person I noticed everything about, from the roughness of his hands to his musk, was …

Taylor.

Pain shot through me at the memory I didn't want.

"Her name is Flowers," I corrected Batu. He was already at the door, the delay between him speaking and me long enough to make my cheeks warm.

"Her name is Monkey, ugly one."

Whatever. Shaking my head to clear my jittery senses of *him*, I climbed unsteadily atop the table once more and held out my arms for the princess.

She climbed down.

A little uncertainly, I helped us both off the table and took her hand, gazing at Batu, who waited at the door, sharpened gaze on whatever activity occurred in the hallway. His sword was tucked away and the pouch of ears dripping blood. He hadn't bothered to change clothing, and the shirt hanging off him did nothing to diminish the size of his frame.

"Why did he not kill us?" Flowers asked me.

Realizing she hadn't understood the exchange, I sought the simplest explanation possible. "Mahmood was right. Batu's people won't hurt us and he is going to help us leave here."

She wrapped one of her arms around me despite my attempt to reassure her, her gaze on the bodies between us and the door.

Batu waved at us to follow him and stepped into the hallway.

I didn't want to walk through the carnage or risk being killed. I wanted to return to the rooftop and … what? Starve to death up there? Risk he'd follow through with hurting me until I broke down and did what he wanted?

I really did like my fingers and ears where they were. Mahmood seemed to think this was the best way, and my handler had only said to ensure the princess was safe.

On the surface, I had a lot of room to make my own decisions and do what was best. In reality, there was a Mongol warrior standing between me and any other path but the one he chose for me.

"Time for us to leave, Flowers," I told the girl.

She said nothing and clung to me as we went to the door.

Batu waited at the end of the hallway. His people had taken care of the newest challengers and were bent over, slicing off ears. I focused on the man alleging to be my guardian and went to him.

Unaffected by the death and carnage around him, he shoved bodies out of his way with his feet and led us down the stairs.

There's no way I'm staying here longer than I have to.

Chapter Four

THE JOURNEY OUT OF THE CITY WAS ANOTHER LEVEL OF SURREAL. My senses were overloaded by the fire and smoke, the screams of slaughter and the sense I'd been dropped into a video game without a controller.

Batu strode through his fellow warriors to cheers and teasing about being captured. They supplied him with two horses – in exchange for ears, which weirded me out to no end. As if suspecting I was one heartbeat from fleeing, he rode with Flowers in front of him while I had my own horse. I followed him closely through the maze of fire and death out of the city, unable to take in the world around me – but sickened by my own cowardice. All I could think of was that I was glad I wasn't one of Flowers' people being beheaded or killed, that I was happy to be alive when the rest of the world was on fire.

The thoughts and relief didn't seem … natural. Or healthy or *right.* I didn't wish any of the people around me dead, but I was glad not to be among them, either.

It was a strange mindset to be in.

The rocky land beyond the city was cool and dark. We cantered through the fires I'd seen from my window, and I was able to see they were indeed decoys. There was no encampment here, only campfires evenly spaced to give the appearance of an army.

Beyond the hill, to the south, straddling a narrow river, were the familiar mushroom tents of the Mongol army. There were thousands in the quiet valley and herds of animals that stretched as far as I could see into the darkness.

Batu wove through the tents before stopping before one and dismounting. I followed his lead. This part of camp was quieter than the edges, though there was still a great deal of activity.

"I will take her to the children," he said, motioning to Flowers, who remained on the horse.

"What?" I asked. "She can't stay with me?"

"We travel elsewhere," he answered.

I gazed up at him, wanting to ask or say so many things but pretty much failing to voice one word.

"She will be well, goddess," he added at my stare. "And you will have a reason to stay."

Blackmail. Or something like it. My stomach was already in knots, but it managed to twist into one more.

"I will return to the battle. I am short two ears, then take her to safety."

"How can you be short? You killed over thirty people!"

"A few of my kin were late to the battle. I gave them some of mine."

If we were talking about anything other than human body parts, I might regard him as considerate if not kind hearted to take care of his family. But we weren't, and his sacrifice of ears was morbidly horrifying.

"You are to remain here," he instructed me. "I will be gone following the battle to take Monkey to the other children. My uncle will watch over you." He strode to the tent beside us and peeked his head into it. "Uncle! I am leaving my goddess with you!" Without waiting for an answer, he returned to his horse. He wound the reins of the spare horse to his wooden saddle.

I was stuck on the vision of him collecting more ears. Blinking my way out of it, I faced him. "Gone? Aren't you my guardian?"

"No harm will befall you," he assured me. "You are an honored guest, a goddess."

"Or thereabouts," I murmured.

"Or thereabouts," he agreed. He took the reins of my horse.

"Batu, I ..." There was no right way to tell him I didn't want to be here or worse – I didn't want him taking the princess and leaving me alone.

He waited.

"I'm going to cry and vomit for the next two days," I managed.

"If it please you, ugly one. Do not try to leave." He mounted his horse once more. "Lamb and wolf. I can hunt you wherever you go."

Unless I time travel before you return. I rolled my eyes. It was an effective and somewhat freaky analogy, one that left me no doubt what happened to a lamb that challenged the wolf one time too many.

"Moonbeam." The princess leaned away from him. Moonlight glinted off my phone.

I stretched to take it. "Thanks. Don't be scared, okay? He said he's going to protect us."

She didn't appear convinced.

Tugging my horse behind him, Batu trotted off with the princess. She leaned around him to gaze at me, a little scared and unfortunately, also trusting. I had no idea if Batu planned to do with her what he said he did.

I watched them then gazed at the tent. It was hard to feel my normal spirit of adventure after being dropped into a bloodbath. I focused on keeping my wild emotions at bay. Survival was my priority. I had to suppress anything that didn't serve me making it out of here, including the horrific images in my head of what was left of the city.

My stomach growled, and I took a deep breath. No matter what, I needed food.

Stepping into the tent, my gaze was drawn first to the remains of a small feast on a table on one side and then to a loudly snoring man who appeared to be passed out on a few pillows near the fire. He was dressed for battle but hadn't left the tent. A goblet of spilled wine was by his hand, and I assumed he'd been too deep in his cups to join the charge into the city.

I didn't think twice about waking him and instead, went to the food to pick through it. There was meat of some kind, most of which appeared to have been gnawed on. I found a few chunks without teeth marks and gobbled them down, drank warm milk and then rounded it off with flat bread.

The wine was much smoother than I expected, and I drank a full goblet before the horror of my trip began to fade and warmth filled me. Only when I was calm once more did I approach the snoring man.

He was out cold. After my run in with Batu, I wasn't really excited about meeting another of the ears-first-questions-later approach of the warriors. Instead, I stood once more and shook out my nerves then decided to do what I always did when I was stressed: yoga.

I wasn't remotely good at it. The deceptively simple movements took all of my concentration and helped me shift my thoughts from the nightmare of the city to my awkward attempts to balance and move. Soon, I was in the zone, centering my emotions and suppressing the images of the massacre in the part of my mind that also stored Taylor's death. My body moved less fluidly than usual, a side effect of being frozen or immobilized for almost a century. Even so, I was amazed to be in the shape I was.

"What spell is this?"

I didn't notice the snoring had stopped. Dropping my arms from the warrior two pose, I straightened and turned to face the man. He was on his feet, propped against a pole, his bloodshot eyes on me yet glazed from too much alcohol. His face was jaundiced, an unhealthy shade of yellow, which I took to mean he'd pickled his liver with alcohol over the years.

"It's not a spell," I said, puzzled. "I'm … uh, Moonbeam. Batu dropped me off here."

"I know who you are." He was staring at me hard. "I do not know what magic you were performing."

"It wasn't magic. I was stretching."

"You will refrain from such stretching in my *ger*."

"Okay." What did I say to that?

"Tomeid!" He belted.

I jumped.

Seconds later, a man poked his head into the tent. "Yes, my lord?"

"Bow before the Goddess of the White Path, fool."

The man named Tomeid's eyes widened. He obeyed and dropped to the ground.

"Fetch her robes and milk!"

He crawled out of the tent and disappeared. I started to say something but stopped, not liking the way Batu's uncle was looking at me. As if making some internal decision, he strode towards me and snatched my wrist. He drew a knife.

"Whoa, wait!" I said, startled. "What are we doing to the goddess?"

"The illness in my body. Your divine blood will purify me. The shaman has said only the divine can cure me."

"First, my blood isn't divine. I am a woman who is blessed by the Big Blue Sky or whatever you call it," I said and yanked at my hand. "Second, Batu said I'd be safe here."

"You misunderstand. I will not hurt you," he said.

"Then how will you draw my blood?"

"The divine do not feel pain."

"Not true. At all." I shook my head vehemently.

"We shall see."

Before I could register what happened, he sliced my palm open. Fiery pain shot through me. He flipped it to face the ceiling so the blood pooled in the center.

"That definitely hurt," I whispered, another wave of nausea and dizziness washing over me.

"My family has waited for you for many years." He didn't appear concerned about the wound. He moved away, towards the wine on the table.

Oh, shit. My world was growing fuzzy around the edges. Of all the places to pass out, now seemed more dangerous than in the castle.

I sank to my knees. "Why?" I managed, struggling to stay focused on my surroundings. I stared at the throbbing wound on my hand. Black streaks were in my blood, too, the lingering effects of Carter's magic pills. *That can't be healthy.* I made a mental note to ask him what he'd done to me, assuming I ever spoke to him again.

"You brought victory and great wealth to the empire. Your appearance saved the lives of every man in the *tumen* headed for battle. There was an ambush waiting for my grandfather, but he stopped when you fell from the sky, and the ambush was discovered a day later."

"That's … good." I was having trouble making out his words.

"I would not be here, if not for you." He knelt beside me with some effort, given his weight. Tilting my hand, he squeezed blood into a goblet filled with wine. "You will save my life from the poison."

Ugh. Why do I end up with the crazies? I shook my head. Even the pain of him squeezing more blood out of my wound couldn't pull me back.

"You will be given a place of honor in my council, and you will serve me, a living goddess at my command," he said more quietly. "This is what is meant to be."

I didn't think gods and goddesses *served* men, but I also suspected he was drunk.

Maybe when the alcohol wore off, I'd be better able to convince him I wasn't a goddess. He wasn't buying it now. My eyes closed. I heard movement around me without understanding exactly what happened. Unable to pull out of the in-between place, I drifted into restless sleep.

And snapped awake sometime later, groggy and disoriented.

I was surrounded by men, whose talk silenced when I pushed myself up in alarm. It took me a moment to recall where I was and another to register what was going on. I was dressed all in white, in layers of silk, if I had to guess, with my hair in a long braid and my feet in slippers so light, they almost tickled. Something dangled on my forehead, and I touched the delicate metal, filigree tiara encircling my head and held in place by pins. I wasn't able to see what was on my forehead, but it felt like a pearl.

A little self-conscious with everyone staring at me, I shifted into a sit, afraid to test my temperamental body by standing immediately.

A tug at my neck made me frown, and I felt the choker style necklace with my fingertips before realizing I was connected to a silver leash. At the other end, seated in a wide chair, was Batu's uncle. He pulled at me again, and I slid closer to him, uncertain what exactly was going on.

I almost laughed at the random image that flashed in my mind: that of Princess Leia chained to Jabba the Hut in his court.

Laughing didn't seem like the correct response, though I had a feeling The Doctor – or maybe Carter – would find it amusing if no one else did. My gaze returned to the men before me, and they all dropped into deep bows.

"Hair like moonlight and eyes like the Eternal Blue Sky," Batu's uncle said triumphantly. "Did I not tell you? I am blessed, as was my grandfather."

He wasn't slurring today, and his eyes were clear. I studied him. He appeared much healthier than he did last night when we met. I never recovered from a hangover so quickly; I was tempted to ask his secret. A closer look at him revealed the jaundiced appearance from last night was also gone.

Doubting a night of sleep fixed him, I couldn't guess what helped him, unless I was too traumatized last night to see him right.

"Cease your bowing and join me in a toast to our guest," Batu's uncle said to the others.

They rose. Tomeid, the servant from last night, circulated among the men handing out goblets of wine.

"To new levels of wealth and victory," one of the men said and raised his goblet. "Welcome, Goddess. You have brought new life to Chaghan already."

Several murmurs of agreement went around, and they toasted and drank.

Tomeid gave me milk. I frowned at it and then at my hands. Both were bandaged instead of just the one that had been cut. Not only that, but the bandages extended up my arms. My body was dimly aware of distant aching and pounding, of pain kept at bay by some sort of sedative, the way it was when I had my appendix out. If I was drugged, it definitely explained my grogginess.

I set down the goblet and pushed up the sleeves of one arm. The bandages ran to my elbows. Blood spotted several places, mostly red but with flecks of black, too. Not one to willingly go to a doctor, I had the urge to have the weird stuff in my blood checked out. Was it normal after being put into cryo-sleep for seven decades?

Was cryo-sleep normal in any era?

Dammit, Carter. Couldn't tell me straight up what you were doing, could you?

"Shall we tell them?" Chaghan asked me with a small smirk.

I glanced up from examining my arms. "Tell them … ?"

"My sudden turn of health, the healing of my liver, was a gift," he told the others. "It was brought by the goddess. I have conveyed the magic to all of you as a sign of my gratitude for your service to the Empire."

The men appeared pleased, while I bit back a snarky response. Batu's uncle knifed me up to drug his men. There were nine of them, dressed in furs with signs they had come from battle in the city recently. Only one wasn't drinking his wine. He was frowning as he listened to the uncle of Batu.

Seeing him, Chaghan lowered his wine goblet. "What troubles you, nephew?"

The man didn't look similar enough to be Batu's brother. Aside from his size towering over the others, he had a narrow face and larger eyes.

"With respect, uncle, I am aware of how this magic was granted," he said with a nod of his head. "I feel it does not honor the Eternal

Blue Sky and the gift he sent us."

"This" Chaghan yanked on the chain connected to my neck "is a gift for us to use as we need. Her language skill, her knowledge. Her blood, if it grants us life."

"Blood, Chaghan?" Another asked and peered into his cup. "Blood is sacred."

"Did you have her permission?" the frowning nephew asked, leveling his dark gaze on me.

No way in hell. A glance towards Chaghan, however, made me swallow the response. He was giving me a look that made me want to protect my ears. It didn't help that he began pulling me closer by the neck.

"Did you have her permission?" the nephew asked again.

"I did not need it, nephew," came the icy response. "When you all awake tomorrow, you, too, will benefit from the magic of her blood. It is the gift from a commander to his loyal warriors."

No one spoke. I was almost relieved to see the warriors were as uncomfortable with the idea of drinking my blood as I was. It wasn't normal, then. I had managed to attract yet another crazy man.

"Uncle," the nephew tried again.

"Enough!" Chaghan's shout made me jump. "Leave! All of you!" His face was flushed and his eyes glittering.

I had no idea what was going on except that I was chained to a madman. The men left quickly. Not one of them took the goblets with him. I remained where I was.

Chaghan paced, fuming at the rejection of his disgusting gift. He jingled the leash as he walked.

I straightened and climbed to my feet. For the first time since waking, I felt the pain of what he'd done to my hands and arms.

"You really believe my blood cured you?" I asked cautiously, unable to understand what might be going through his mind.

"I know it did. I was a dead man."

I shook my head. "It doesn't seem possible." *Unless there was something weird in the sleeping agent Carter created.*

"It was not only me." He appeared to be calming, tolerant of a goddess where he wasn't of his men. "Tomeid! Bring him!"

No one else was in the tent, but I sensed his servant was never too far, either. Less than a moment later, Tomeid entered, all but dragging a young warrior who didn't look much over fifteen.

They both dropped to their knees.

"Last night, the boy was brought in, close to death from his wounds," Chaghan explained. "He drank your blood as well, and we both awoke healed."

I was balanced on my feet, a little lightheaded. "Those are … miracles. They aren't because of me," I said.

"You are a miracle," he reminded me.

I wanted to roll my eyes but didn't. "Listen, Chaghan, I believe these healings happened. I don't think they're tied to me."

His face was growing red once more. "You do not bleed like any other!" he snapped. "There is magic in your blood. It is visible!"

To demonstrate, he yanked me closer. I stumbled and landed on my knees in front of the two men waiting silently to be dismissed or acknowledged. Chaghan pulled up one arm and slid the blade of his knife across one finger. I flinched.

My red blood was dotted with black.

Damn you, Carter. What the hell did you do to me this time? I knew nothing of science or medicine, but I was almost able to rationalize some sort of preservative in my body that kept me from aging or deteriorating while I was under for so long. I woke up perfect – not one scratch.

"So maybe there is something unusual about my blood," I murmured.

"I only took a few drops."

"It's potent." I glanced up, and my whole body went rigid. He was looking at me the way I imagined a starving vampire considered his victim. "I have many other talents."

"Languages. This I know. But you can heal an army. Surely this gift weighs far more than speaking to our enemies!"

This was not going the way I planned. I sought some sort of reasoning without really understanding the culture I'd been dropped into, aside from the fact they seemed to be always at war.

"What other gifts do you have?"

I sat back on my heels, wracking my brain for an answer that would matter to him. My brain wasn't working quickly this morning. My gaze fell to the two men listening from their positions groveling.

He yanked on the chain.

"The uh … sky god doesn't always tell me," I managed. "I am here for a purpose, one he hid from me."

Chaghan appeared to be considering this.

"And this? Does it contain more of your magic?" He pulled my cell phone from a pocket and held it up.

I sucked in a breath. If I'd been a little less numb from painkillers, I'd feel the panic I was certain was racing through my blood at the thought of my only connection to my time and home in the hands of a madman. "It's a … a tool," I stammered. "It can only be used by me."

"What does it do?" He was watching me with the same penetrating look Batu had given me, one I took to mean they were trying to determine whether I was truthful.

"I can't really explain it," I replied.

"Does it affect your blood? Your languages?"

"No."

"Will it help me win the war?"

"No."

"Then it is of no use."

Before I could react, he had dropped it on the ground, drawn a curved sword and stabbed it through. As if that wasn't enough, he then ground his heel into it until the circuits and glass screen formed a puddle of chards around it.

And I stared, unable to react, not sure *how* to react to the sight of my way home being destroyed.

"Uncle." The same nephew from earlier, who had refused to drink his wine, peered into the tent. "May we speak?"

Chaghan didn't appear pleased. "Go," he barked at the two men near me.

They scrambled out of the tent. Chaghan tied my leash to a pole before approaching his nephew at the entrance of the tent.

Barely aware of them, my attention was on the remains of my cell phone. Of all the things to think about now, my mind was on Taylor again.

If there'd ever been a place where I wouldn't have minded being stuck, it was probably with him in the large farmhouse on the plains. I had been struggling not to think of him at all, because of my ambivalent emotions, but it was impossible not to see my way home destroyed and recall what he'd told me the night after we were married.

I was the only woman in ten thousand years he had chosen to stay with. While true I hadn't loved him, it was also possible for me to believe that one day, I might've been able to. With quiet strength and a sense of honor I'd never seen before, he was a good man to the core. I cared for and respected him, even if the emotion of love hadn't yet formed.

I didn't understand how I became the person to erase his existence from the universe and all of space and time when I couldn't kill a spider in my bathtub. I didn't pull the trigger, but I was nonetheless the tool that killed him.

I deserve to be trapped here. Was that what this was? Penance for hurting someone like him? Was my fate to be cut daily by a madman to keep his army on the warpath?

What was I thinking the night I met Carter and agreed to go back in time? In a matter of weeks to me, I'd gone from carefree with no regrets to wishing with all my heart I could go back to that day and walk away.

"It is settled!" Chaghan's near-shout pulled me from the trance I was in. I opened my eyes to see him angrily striding towards me from the direction of the entrance. "There will be no consulting the council."

"Uncle – " his nephew objected once more.

Chaghan yanked me up and hauled me towards the entrance. "You will drain all her blood by evening." He thrust me at the warrior.

His nephew caught and steadied me. "You risk displeasing the Eternal Blue Sky, not to mention the Khan."

"The Khan will see what I do: a means to increase our ability to fight. Heed my order, nephew, or you will follow her!"

The warrior holding my arms glanced at me. I sensed his unease, though his face was stoic.

I cursed myself for not paying more attention to their discussion, for letting my thoughts get pulled into emotions I couldn't afford to humor.

"As you command," the nephew said finally.

"Wait!" I cried. "I would ask you to … spare me. For a day, so that I can … prepare myself for what comes." It was the stupidest excuse I probably ever made. My heart raced, and adrenaline began eating away at the numbing effects of whatever drug they gave me.

My arms were hurting.

"To pray," the nephew said.

"Yes, to pray. You asked, Chaghan, if there were some other purpose for me being here." I faced his uncle. "If the Eternal Blue Sky reveals one during my meditations, then I will tell you. If not, then in the morning, you can … do as you wish," I rushed on. *In the meantime, I'm getting out of here.*

He looked from me to his nephew.

"I believe this to be wise," his nephew added. "The battle for the city is over. One day will not prolong our plans."

Chaghan drew a breath. "Very well, goddess. You will meditate here, in my tent." He indicated a cubbyhole between a bed and a table. "You will have all the milk you need, and candles."

"Thank you," I breathed.

He didn't appear happy and brushed by us, out of the tent.

"My uncle is not evil, goddess," his nephew whispered. "Forgive him, and plead for Father Sky to forgive him as well."

"Bleeding me to death isn't going to win him any favors," I replied.

"I know." He released my arms. "I sent for Batu already. He is your sworn protector, and my uncle is obligated to heed his advice when he will not take mine. But …" He glanced over his shoulder and moved closer. "… do not wait until morning. My uncle's mind is less well when he drinks, and he will celebrate his victory this evening. When he has drunk himself to sleep, leave."

"To where?"

"The river is east of here. Follow it to wherever the Eternal Blue Sky wishes you to go."

I had no time to thank him let alone tell him how frustrating his answer was before he backed away into the sunlight visible outside the tent. Needing time to think, I went to the cubbyhole to sit and at least pretend to be praying while my mind raced.

The quietness of the tent had the opposite effect of what I hoped. Rather than hammering out an escape plan, my thoughts returned to Taylor too often. I forced them away multiple times to focus on my predicament.

Batu's cousin was right; I had to leave. I had nowhere to go and no idea where I was, but if I stayed, I'd die.

My eyes went to the pile of pieces leftover from my phone. I crossed to the mess and picked up several of the larger fragments.

There was no fixing this. There was no going home or escaping to some other time period. I replaced the pieces and sat back to stare at them, the ache in my chest growing stronger as I realized I really was trapped here.

Did it matter if I escaped Chaghan tonight? He'd unleash hell to find me again, and I was out of tricks. I'd make it half a mile on foot before they chased me down on horseback. Was there something at the river that might help me? A boat? A crossing?

I was completely blind to my surroundings. It was an adventure, for sure, but a very dangerous one.

I can do this. I drew a deep breath. I was the sole survivor of the doomed eighteen forties trip. I was going to live through this, too.

If Taylor's people found me in the past once, surely they would again.

Assuming my purpose wasn't already served by saving the girl.

My stomach churned. With fear joining the regret in my belly, I stood and returned to the cubbyhole, hoping to remain unnoticed while I spent the day waiting for my chance to escape.

When I was free of Chaghan, I'd figure out what to do next.

Chapter Five

THE DAY PASSED MORE SLOWLY THAN I WANTED. IT DIDN'T HELP that whatever drug they gave me wore off around mid-afternoon. Pain kept me from the amount of thinking I needed to do and instead, I floated in a rather miserable place. Chaghan kept his word and had Tomeid bring me candles and milk. Without him present most of the day, I was able to sit and meditate or nap away the pain and worry.

I was alone until sometime around sunset, when Chaghan returned with his commanders and several others for another feast around the fire in the middle of the mushroom tent.

Tomeid brought me more … milk. No food, just lukewarm, thick milk. It wasn't bad, but it wasn't a pizza either. After a day in a pain-filled haze, I straightened to listen to the men talking for clues about where I could go or anything else that might help me.

"Goddess, if I may disturb you." Batu's cousin spoke as he approached.

I opened my eyes and gazed up at him.

Taking the acknowledgement as permission, he sat down in front of me, accompanied by a man dressed much as Mahmood had been.

"This is The Persian," he said and indicated the dark-skinned stranger with one hand. "He is related by marriage to the royalty of the Golden Horde."

"It is a pleasure," the Persian said and bowed his head, one hand going to his heart. He was around my age with solemn features – but a gleam in his eyes that warned me he was more than he let on. "Khulutei has told me you are divine among his people." He appeared curious, willing to meet my gaze where Mahmood and the Arab merchant I first met weren't. "You came from the moon?"

I glanced at Khulutei, sensing I wasn't able to tell anyone the truth about me. "He is a scholar and a storyteller," Batu's cousin explained. "He travels the Empire to record events."

In a world without internet, Khulutei sounded like the closest thing they had to a blogger.

"Not from the moon exactly," I said. "But I am from a different place."

"What is it like?" The Persian asked. "Plains? Desert?"

"From near the ocean," I replied, mind on my home in southern California.

"A sea," Khulutei repeated. "Better than the moon."

I raised an eyebrow in puzzlement.

"The sea and moon are feminine," The Persian explained. "When you fell from the sky, they thought the moon sent you to guide them the way it lights their path at night. They call this guidance the White Path, for the moon will show them the way with her white light when the night is too dark to navigate. The sea and water are equally sacred, the blood and essence of the living earth. They will associate you with both now, I believe."

He definitely had a way with words. I didn't notice my pain when he spoke. I was fascinated by his flowery explanation.

"Your eyes are of the sea, not the sky," Khulutei said as if proud of himself for figuring out the mystery of me. "I must tell my uncle." He rose and hurried away.

"Is it that important?" I asked The Persian, watching Khulutei's retreat.

"To them it is." There was mild humor in the response.

I returned my attention to the storyteller.

"I cannot explain your appearance or likeness or how you are the same now as reported many years before except that the one true God made it possible," he added. "It is their way, not ours."

"Will that get you in trouble?" I asked.

"No. I do not agree with many of the Empire's ways, but they do allow their people to worship what god or gods they please. In their capitols, the mosques of my god sit beside the churches of the Crusaders and the altars of the lotus worshippers. There is no common tongue or god to unite them. The Empire is held together by power, obedience and the wealth that trade along the Silk Route brings."

Even Carter's historical summaries paled when compared to the elegant yet simple views of The Persian.

"I heard what they planned to do to you," he added more quietly. "There is much barbarism to these people, despite all they have done to pacify and extend the trade routes."

"Yeah, there is," I agreed, thoughts on the battle in the city. "What makes you stay with them to document their history?"

"I am a scholar. My heart is in knowledge, in exploring the unknown." He offered a small smile. "I also defied my cousin, who is destined to be a prince ruler and am living in exile. The Empire does not discriminate. If you have a skill they value, they will adopt and reward you for service. There were no written records before the great Genghis, but the Empire wishes its history of taking over the world to be known forever. They value those who can write their stories."

I didn't expect the honest response. He was friendly, if a little reserved, which seemed pretty common for many of the people I'd met. As much as I didn't want a connection to anyone here, it was also nice to really talk to someone.

"My uncle requests you," Khulutei called to The Persian.

"Please excuse me," he said and stood. "God willing, we will speak again."

I watched him go, warmed some by the short talk with someone who appeared almost normal by my twenty first century standards.

Then again, the last time I found someone normal, he turned out to be a time traveler like me. My smile faded. Uncertain what to think, I turned my back to the room and focused once more on not letting the pain cloud my mental thought process.

At some point, I dozed off and awoke some time later, curled on my side by the wall of the tent and covered by a blanket. My head wasn't yet right, and the pain of my arms was warm and throbbing.

The forms in the tent were passed out sleeping around the fire. Not only that, but wind pushed the entrance flap open enough to show me the sky was beginning to lighten with sunrise.

Dammit. Overslept. I rose and took a moment to balance before walking around the snoring, sleeping men who appeared to have drunk themselves unconscious. With any luck, Chaghan was among them and wouldn't wake up any time soon.

Stepping into the pre-dawn morning, I paused to orient myself. There was a chill in the air, along with a current of warmth that told me it was going to end up a nice day. The tent's entrance faced east, which I took as a good sign, considering the river was to the east as well. There were dozens of tents standing between me and the river, but the encampment appeared quiet, as if the celebrations last night of their victory meant everyone was sleeping in.

I wasn't fully steady on my feet, and anything more than a walk jarred my arms painfully. Wrapping them around me, I hurried towards the east, hoping to beat the sun's ascent to the horizon. The white-yellow strip preceding dawn lined the sky, and night was beginning to make way for day.

What I took to be a couple dozen tents turned into close to a hundred. I wove among them towards the sunrise, my step quickening as fast as I could tolerate. Not more than fifteen minutes later, I broke free of the tents and reached an open space filled with thousands of horses along the river I could barely see through their bodies. At any other time, I would stop to pet every single animal I ran across.

But today, I didn't have time. If I stopped to admire their soft fur or rub their foreheads, I'd end up dead. I did, however, trace my fingers along the backs or rumps of those I passed and admired them. The steppe horses were closer to the size of ponies, hardy and muscular with long, tangled manes and tails. They appeared to be well socialized; none of them freaked out or startled when I passed, and two started following me towards the river.

I was holding out hope for a boat or bridge or something, but the minute I reached the riverbank, my heart sank.

There was nothing. It wasn't just this that left me upset; it was the width of the river. I didn't know enough about where I was to identify which river it was, but it was *huge.* Slow moving and far too wide to swim. Already, I was mentally going through the dangers of attempting to cross it. Potential undercurrents, fatigue, becoming tangled on the loose debris floating in it. For all I knew, there were piranhas or alligators or other animals that might smell my bloody arms and attack me.

I sighed deeply, and tears stung my eyes. I had a couple of choices. One was to turn back and try to reason with a madman. Another was to throw myself into the river and hope I didn't die. Maybe it would take me downstream … I looked in both directions. There was nothing out here. Smoke rose to the sky from the direction of the burning city, and I saw no villages or anywhere I could hide downstream.

It'd be suicidal. Yet I was doomed to die anyway if I stayed.

Thus far, I'd been lucky enough to survive my adventures. I could pray that my luck held and simply … go for it.

Heart hammering, I slid my slippers off and stripped down to a single layer of the silk gowns. The tiara I kind of liked and thought maybe I could sell if I had to, so I left it pinned in place.

"What do you do, goddess?" Batu's voice made me jump.

"Don't scare me like that!" I snapped automatically, my whole system jolted. He was the last person I wanted to see at the moment. "If you're here to take me back so your uncle can bleed me to death, I won't go!" I started into the river, pausing when the chilly water reached my calves.

I really didn't want to do this. My instincts were screaming at me.

"My uncle is wrong."

I hesitated to go further, eyes on a dead animal or something floating down the river.

"You seek to take your life?" he asked almost curiously.

Twisting to look at him, I was surprised to discover he wasn't wielding his sword and ready to drag me back. He was seated on the bank, elbows draped over his knees, dark gaze on me. He seemed curious rather than concerned despite claiming to be my guardian.

I did *not* get this guy.

"What do you care?"

He tossed me something.

I caught it. It was a small, sheathed knife.

"Death is assured with a knife," he said.

I pulled it free and gazed at the short, fat blade. No part of me could stomach the idea of cutting myself. I'd never been suicidal, never thought twice about stabbing myself. The only reason I'd put my life in danger now was because I'd rather do it myself and risk getting away than face Chaghan again.

"I'd think it'd be painful," I said with a shudder.

"You will die faster this way."

"Wait a minute. Do you *want* me to die?" I demanded.

"I respect your wishes."

I faced him, glaring at him. Batu was relaxed, dressed like a warrior rather than a prisoner. He didn't seem at all concerned, which left me baffled after the effort he went to in order to find and save me in the castle.

"Aren't you supposed to protect me?" I asked him.

"I am. I dishonored you by leaving you with my uncle. If this is what you must do to restore your honor, then so be it."

I rolled my eyes. "I wasn't … I don't … I mean, I won't *purposely* kill myself. Your uncle is an asshole. He did this." I held up my arms. "He was going to do worse today. I figured I'd come to the river and … escape." I gazed around me again. "Somehow. And if I drowned in the attempt, then I drown."

"You do not wish to die, ugly one," he said. This time, there was amusement in his tone. I didn't know what he found funny about this.

"How would you know?" I grumbled. My feet were cold enough that I wanted out of the water, yet leaving the river felt like a defeat in the strange game I was playing with Batu.

He indicated my shoes and pile of silk dresses. "Men who wish to drown keep their boots on for added weight."

I almost sighed. He was right. Even believing I could possibly throw myself to my death, I was subconsciously working against the idea. "So maybe I'm not the kind of person to risk it," I allowed. "Do you want to kill me quickly instead of turning me over to your uncle to be bled to death?"

"Give me the knife and we will find out."

I froze. I instinctively knew taking my shoes off would help me survive, and I instinctively hid the knife behind my back rather than obey.

Batu laughed at me. "Again, Moonbeam, I ask. What do you do?"

"I don't know," I admitted miserably. "I don't know what to do."

"Then let me help you."

I frowned at the man I'd seen kill dozens in the span of a half an hour. "You'd defy your uncle? Khulutei wouldn't."

"Khulutei is not your guardian. My duty is a sacred honor granted by the great Khan alone and cannot be revoked. Come with me." He stood.

"I've seen what you do to those around you. No one is left standing. Your speech about wolves eating lambs didn't help, either. Why should I trust you?"

"Because you do not want to die, and I do not currently wish to kill you," he replied. "What other choice do you have?"

I glanced downstream once more. *I'd never survive that.* Yet I didn't think Batu was helping me out of the goodness of his heart, either. I did have the sense he didn't want me dead, or he wouldn't have stood between the palace guards and me the day we met.

"What is your plan?" I asked and folded my arms across my chest.

"To take you to my *ger* first, so he cannot find you. Then I will confront him."

"And if he insists on bleeding me?"

"It will not come to that."

I wasn't entirely convinced he'd sway or keep his uncle at bay. But, given my circumstances, I didn't seem to have much choice anyway. I needed a much better plan than this one. Hiding in his tent would give me more time to think.

"I'll go with you," I said grudgingly.

"Very wise, goddess." The way he said it made me think he thought the opposite.

There was something really vexing about Batu. I didn't understand his manner of thinking or why he seemed like the happiest, most murderous Mongol I could imagine.

He started away from the river.

With some reluctance, I left the water, gathered my things and trailed. His tent wasn't too far from the horse herd. Not that I was able to tell any of the mushrooms apart, but it was in the second row from the horses.

Smaller than his uncle's, it was nonetheless cozy, warm and rendered comfortable with rugs and pillows on the floor. A collection of weapons lay on one blanket near his bed, as if he'd been cleaning them.

I dropped the mess in my arms on the floor near a pole. Standing, I stepped back, not expecting him to be in my space already. He moved quietly despite his size, and I had a flashback to the castle, when he'd overpowered me with little more than a pinky.

Unaware of my thoughts, he took one wrist and flipped it towards the ceiling. He began to unwrap the bandages. He was close enough for me to smell him once more, and I recalled with butterflies in my belly the way he'd brought me back from the brink in the castle.

"What're you doing?" I asked.

"Assessing what he has done to you." He tossed the bandages into the fire and studied the inside of my forearm.

I didn't want to look. Images of them sawing off my arm after I contracted gangrene from the poor sanitary environment flashed through my head.

"They are not deep," he said and lifted my arm.

I winced and peered at it. Stripes three inches long marred my arm every inch or so. The cut in the palm appeared the deepest and angriest.

Okay, so I'll only have my hand sawed off. The thought made my breath catch. I tugged my hand away and stepped back.

Batu snatched it back.

"I don't want to assess the damage!" I told him.

"It must be done, if I am to request permission for punishment."

"What're you talking about?"

He eyed me and took my other wrist, unwrapping the bandages. "The punishment for hurting or stealing or other crimes against another in the Empire is nine times the crime. You are given special protections. To punish a man of my uncle's standing, I must know exactly what to request."

"So you're going to ask for permission to knife him?" I asked.

"Yes."

"You killed forty people without permission!"

"They were not Mongol."

The simple logic rendered me speechless. It never occurred to me they had *rules* in a society such as this or that, having rules, they'd follow them.

He glanced at me, and there was a sparkle in his dark eyes. He found me funny. Or maybe he laughed at everything. I didn't know him well enough to know. I wanted to think being so close to a barbarian like him was causing my stomach to churn but … meeting his gaze, I began to think there was some other reason I was distracted by his scent and low, gravelly voice.

Aware of his long look, I kept my gaze on my arm.

It's not possible for me to like someone like this. I had seen him lop off ears and heads with no more concern than someone peeling bananas. This world … it could never become mine. *What if I don't have a choice?*

The reminder that I had no way home, no way to communicate with someone who could help me, rattled me.

"You were going to swim with no clothes but a crown," he observed.

"I *like* the crown."

"It suits you." He flicked the pearl on my forehead with a forefinger. "Every goddess should wear a crown."

"I'm not a goddess, but I'm keeping the crown after all this."

"You speak your mind freely."

Looking up at him, I searched his features, wanting to know if this was a bad thing or not. Carter had given me very general information about social norms and protocols for this time period and said not much else was known, specifically about how women were expected to act. After seeing Ghoajin smack down her husband a few times, I figured there was more leeway here to speak my mind than there had been in the eighteen forties.

But I didn't know for sure. The answer wasn't on Batu's features, though I realized somewhat uneasily if he wanted me to act a certain way, he had the muscular body and ferocity to make it happen. I didn't always check my speech, because I was from a time and place where I was accustomed to saying what I pleased to whomever I wanted.

"This one is deep." He rested his hand on my forearm.

I jerked.

"Be still, goddess." He rolled my arm over. One of the stripes went all the way around. Shallow on the top of my forearm, the two edges of the cut didn't meet on the soft underside.

"Is that bad?" I asked.

"It will heal quickly."

"No, I mean, is it bad I speak freely?"

"As long as you know to hold your tongue when it is wise."

"Like dealing with your uncle."

"Yes."

"And when talking to you?"

"You amuse me, goddess," he said with a faint smile. "You are honest like a horse and delicate like a flower. It is a good combination."

I didn't know how to respond. I'd never thought twice about a horse's *honesty*. But I imagined animals didn't hide things the way people did. He was right about me; I was candid, outgoing and open, for the most part. I liked adventures, or did, until Carter.

He was probing my elbow with his thumbs before sliding his hand to my upper arm to check for wounds. The lightness of his touch was in stark contrast to how he handled his enemies. I didn't yet know how such brutality and gentleness existed in one person or how to handle his closeness.

I shouldn't … I couldn't be attracted to him. I'd barely lost Taylor. It wasn't possible for me to start to like anyone let alone a massacring monster.

He released my wrist and slid a hand around my neck, nudging my chin up into the air so he could see the damage the choker and leash had done.

I flinched when his thumb brushed one side of my neck, the side opposite that which Chaghan had been standing when he yanked me the hardest. The pain wasn't the only sensation I was aware of. Batu was standing close enough for me to feel the heat rolling off his thick form while his touch was light enough to be a caress.

"Very well," Batu said and stepped away. "I see no more blood. Any pain elsewhere?"

I was about to ask if he had x-ray vision to see through my clothing when I glanced down and realized the layer of white silk I wore was completely sheer. I started to laugh, a little embarrassed but more amused than anything.

"No pain," I said. "Sorry about …" I waved to my body and bent down to grab one of the heavier layers from the pile.

"Dressed as such, you can speak to any man any way you please, Moonbeam," he said.

I shot him a warning look, and he smiled.

There was something about Batu I kind of liked. More than I should have. The sense of familiarity I experienced with Carter and Taylor wasn't there, but neither was the threat of danger. I wondered again if part of my empathic memory chip remained active, because I should've feared Batu after the show he gave at the castle.

But I didn't.

"Is Flowers … Monkey safe?" I asked.

"She is. She is close."

"Close enough I can see her?"

"In time." Laid back and allegedly a sworn guardian, he was also not about to trust me with the location of the girl he thought was keeping me here.

What a weird dynamic. To be nice and smiley – but secretly distrusting and occasional of unspeakable brutality. I didn't know his intentions or even if what he said about being my protector was true. I gazed at him, concerned I was starting to rely on someone I shouldn't.

Again. Like John, Nell, Carter and even Taylor. I was too trusting when I left for my first adventure. At least now I was questioning whom I chose to trust.

"What concerns you, Moonbeam?" Batu asked. He was rifling through a pouch on the table near his bed. Retrieving bandages, he returned and knelt beside me.

"I'm not concerned."

"You are a poor liar." He sat back on his heels, eyes on my face.

Ugh. I had grown some during my time in the Old West, but I hadn't yet mastered the ability to mask my true feelings. "I don't belong here, which shouldn't surprise you," I replied.

Batu slowly began wrapping my arms with bandages once more. "You left once before, many years ago, after blessing my grandfather," he stated. "Why have you not returned to the sky if you feared my uncle?"

"It's complicated," I murmured. "And your uncle destroyed my ability to leave."

"How?"

"I had a … tool. It let me do things that might have helped me leave. He destroyed it."

"This is good."

I looked at him, startled.

"The Eternal Blue Sky sent you to us. You are meant to be here," he reasoned.

"But …" How to explain to him I was from the future … did I even want to go down that road with someone I had no intention of connecting with? "I want to go home. I know you understand that. You want to return to your home on the steppes."

He paused in the wrapping of my arm to gaze at me. "I do understand."

I waited for more. He was pensive. His thigh was pressed to mine while his wide hand all but swallowed mine. His other hand was on my thigh in a move I took to mean he was either comfortable with no personal space or absentmindedly possessive.

"You said you cannot return home," he added and resumed wrapping my arm.

"I can't stay here."

"Where else would you go?"

The question floored me, not because I hadn't thought about it, but because it really hit me that I was homeless, lost in time. Without waiting for me to respond, Batu quickly bandaged my other arm.

"You have no home of your own. I'll take you to mine," he said firmly.

I blinked out of my stupor. "Thanks, but I do have a home," I said.

"You cannot return to it. I am going home, and you are coming with me." He rose. "What other choice do you have?"

None. It wasn't his fault I was stranded here, but I couldn't help begrudging him for pointing it out yet again. I almost wished he wasn't so rational or conversational, that he had slung me over his horse and taken me somewhere without shooting so many holes in the desperate logic I was clinging to.

He was different. I didn't know if I liked that or not about him.

"Remain here, goddess." He started towards the entrance.

"Where are you going?" I twisted, gaze settling on the wide expanse of his muscular back.

"To inform my uncle he can be expecting censure from the Khan."

That'll go over well. He left. Rather than wait for his uncle to storm the tent, I dressed in my layers of silk and slippers and dug around his belongings until I found a satchel in which I could store some items for travel. If he was lucky enough to return with his head, I didn't think I'd be so fortunate as to leave here with mine.

I packed the satchel with some bread, a bladder of water, the knife he gave me and sat back, satisfied I'd done well. Before I had a chance to assess my best plan for escaping, he strode through the entrance.

I had yet to see Batu in a bad mood, despite his prison stay and slaughtering everyone in the castle. The tightness of his features made me tuck the satchel behind me in case I pissed him off even more.

"It didn't go well," I assessed quietly.

"It did not."

"At least you have your head and … ears," I pointed out.

His gaze settled on me. His face was unreadable, and the fire of anger burned in the depths of his eyes.

"We're not reconsidering our duty to protect the goddess are we?" I asked uneasily and stood, ready to make a run for it, however futile I knew that to be.

"No."

"Oh. Why are you looking at me that way?"

"What way, Moonbeam?"

"Like the wolf is about to eat his lamb."

He snorted and shook out his shoulders before falling still once more. "My uncle has given me until twilight to turn you over to him."

"Ah." I gripped the satchel more tightly. "You, uh, planning on giving me a head start to escape?"

His attention sharpened as it went to the arm I kept behind my back. He approached and stopped within my space, reaching around me to grab the bag. "What do you do, Goddess?" he asked.

"I figured your uncle was not going to react well and started packing."

He gave me the wolf-about-to-eat-a-lamb warning look.

"If you plan on turning me over, why would I take you with me?" I retorted at the unvoiced accusation.

He yanked it free. "I am not turning you over, Moonbeam. You do not understand: this is my duty." He tossed the satchel onto his bed. "We will not need much more than water and my horses."

"We?" I echoed. "You're going to defy your uncle?"

"Your gifts are yours to bestow, not his to take."

It shouldn't have, but his words kind of made me feel like crap. I had the ability to heal through no logical explanation of my own and decided to run instead. Batu didn't seem to be judging me. Not that I cared if he did … although …

Stop it, Josie! There was no way I was going to be bled to death, no matter how almost decent the intentions of his uncle were! I hadn't survived this long and been through what I had to let some lunatic to torture me. *Unless that lunatic is Carter.*

I was a mess and needed a good cry.

"Why not just give me a horse and tell him I escaped?" I asked. "Then you don't have to upset him."

"I would rather suffer the penalty for defying my commander than let it be known I was defeated by a lamb."

Asshole. "I'm not a lamb or a goddess or ugly or anything else you call me," I said. "What is the penalty for disobedience?"

"Death."

"If you go with me, you're in trouble."

"Only until the Khan's closest advisors are made aware my uncle is dishonoring the Eternal Blue Sky."

I watched him. He gathered up his weapons and rolled them into linen before strapping them to his back. What possessions he chose to take were few: a box the size of my palm, bandages, water bladders, three tiny pouches and a few other items that all went into his pockets.

He was serious. He was going to leave his uncle, under penalty of death, to help me escape alive. Why did it bother me? Why did I not want the massacring Mongol to die on my behalf?

"Batu," I said and took his arm. Turning him to face me, I

frowned at him. "You don't have to do this. You don't have to risk your life. I'm homeless and lost, but you don't have to be."

Rather than appear grateful or understanding like I expected, he gave me an odd look, as if I'd told him my favorite food was elves.

"Do you not have duty and honor where you come from?" he asked.

"Don't overcomplicate this! It's far easier just to set me free."

"How will you survive a world that is foreign to you, goddess?"

"I can manage."

"How will you hunt? Or find water?"

I sighed.

"Which direction will you go?" he persisted.

"Batuuuu!" I whined. "Why can't you –"

"And bandits? How will you defeat them? What if your horse runs free of you? Do you know how to catch it?"

I groaned. I felt like I was in grade school again being lectured for texting during class.

"How will –"

"Stop!" I said and gripped my head. "I don't know those things! But my point is that you shouldn't be forced into a position where you can get hurt or killed because of some lost goddess."

"You have no point, ugly one."

I met his gaze again, ready to set him straight when I saw the twinkle in his eyes and registered the nickname he used when teasing me.

He was *teasing* me. Did he take nothing serious, not even his life?

"Your concern is misplaced," he added.

"Can you just say thank you? Thank you, Moonbeam, for being concerned for my life?" The moment the words left my mouth, I realized they were wrong. So wrong. I wanted no connections or personal attachments, and I'd admitted to being worried about him.

Granted, he was risking everything for me, a complete stranger, out of some zealous devotion to duty. It didn't make me any less responsible for what happened if he left with me. It did mean I was failing miserably to keep my distance.

The same had happened in the Old West, except I was far less cognizant of becoming part of that world. I planned on fighting it tooth and nail this time, mainly because of how hurt I was from the first adventure.

"It is an honor for a goddess to be concerned for my life," he said and bowed his head. "Now we go."

He swept up saddlebags and slung them over his shoulder, then strode out of the tent.

I wanted to kick something out of frustration. He was right; I had no sense of duty so deep, I'd leave my family and risk my life for a stranger. It wasn't my way, but it was so entrenched in his mind, I wasn't able to protest it.

With a deep breath, I decided to go with it and stepped out of the tent and almost collided with him.

"Ah, goddess."

I froze at the voice. *I knew we weren't going to escape the madman.*

Chapter Six

Batu's arm was extended to keep me behind him. His uncle stood a safe distance away, a crescent of warriors flanking him while Batu's cousin, Khulutei, stood grimly farther behind the group.

Batu was tense like he had been at the castle before he started his mass murder spree. His weapons were sheathed, still, which was good. He was a badass in every way, but even I didn't want to see him take on an entire army.

"Do you accept my challenge, Uncle?" Batu asked in a hard voice very unlike the one he used with me.

It struck me how dangerous he was. How I managed to forget, or maybe block, what happened at the castle and mouth off to him left me wishing Carter had implanted a cultural sensitivity chip in my brain along with the others. I could've been dead a million times over at Batu's hands. He was serious about his duty.

"No one has defeated my champion, Batu," his uncle said. "You are my sister's son. I do not wish you dead."

"But you wish me dishonored?" Batu returned with no sign he was considering turning me over.

I didn't fully comprehend what they were talking about but didn't ask. It was one of the times he mentioned where wisdom prevailed over candidness.

"Very well," Chaghan said with some resignation. "Are you prepared to face him?"

"I am."

Chaghan studied his nephew for a long moment before his gaze slid to me. I held my breath, praying he decided to let us go after seeing the dedication of his kin.

"Tomeid, fetch our champion. We will meet at my tent," he said. "I trust you will come without an escort, nephew."

"I will," Batu agreed.

My heart sank.

Chaghan and his entourage left. Khulutei remained behind.

"What just happened?" I ventured.

Batu faced me. "This is good."

"When you say that, you mean the opposite."

A flicker of amusement softened his features. "He has given me the chance to defeat his champion rather than condemn me to death. When I slay his warrior, we will leave, with his blessing."

I listened. "And if you don't win?"

"It will not come to that."

"You said the same about him being open to reason about not killing me."

"You are funny, ugly one." He clasped my neck with one rough hand briefly. "I have a plan if it comes to that. You will ride east. There is a crossing point upriver and a village two days beyond. Travel light, do not stop, and remember to take four horses so you do not tire one out too much."

It didn't make sense to me that he was so calm discussing what happened if he ended up dead. It was even less logical that he thought I could escape an army if he couldn't, not to mention hunt animals or fight off brigands. Hell, I didn't even know which horses in the herd of thousands were his.

Twisting, he waved his cousin forward. "Khulutei will accompany you."

"You are wise, Batu," Khulutei said and approached. "I've prepared your horses. Should the match not go in your favor, I'll do what I can to help the goddess."

"Hang on. You're talking about *dying*," I said, staring up at Batu's strong features.

"Only if I fail to win," he replied.

"That doesn't disturb you?"

"Why should death disturb me, goddess?"

He was serious. He didn't fear death. I was unable to understand this mentality, either.

"Ah, *you* fear my death," he said with a small smile.

"I don't fear your death." Hearing the words, I felt my face warm. "I mean, I don't want you to die, especially not for my sake, but it's not *your* death. It's anyone who dies on my behalf."

"I am honored, Moonbeam." He was amused again. "Come, Khulutei! I have a champion to slay."

The two of them started away.

I stared after them, flustered that he thought once more I was concerned about him. I sort of was … and fighting it hard, because it made no sense. While true I didn't want anyone anywhere ever dying for me, I also specifically didn't want *him* sacrificing his life because he considered it honorable.

It wasn't. It was stupid to get into a fight instead of running away.

"Do you come, Moonbeam?" he called over his shoulder.

I followed, dreading whatever was about to happen.

They led me back to Chaghan's tent in the center of the army. Two neighboring tents had been moved and lines drawn in the dirt to create a space the size of a boxing ring. Warriors already bunched around the place eagerly with the commanders in fur towards the front of the crowd.

The men parted for the three of us. I moved closer to Batu and Khulutei. One corner was designated as his. The Persian caught my eye and nodded his head. Before I could wave of make my way towards him, Batu rounded on me and took my arms. He bent until his face was even with mine.

"Listen, Moonbeam. If this does not go in my favor, you must leave before I am dead," he told me firmly. "Khulutei will take you somewhere safe. You cannot wait for me to be declared dead before you flee."

The gravity of his expression alarmed me. "Batu, I don't like this."

"It is not to like or dislike, goddess. It is to survive. Do you understand this?"

I nodded a little uncertainly. I definitely didn't want to witness someone's death.

Not again. Not after watching John, Nell, Fighting Badger …

Taylor. He walked into his death the same way Batu was: with his eyes open and his heart seemingly at peace with it. The parallels between this moment and the last I spent with Taylor rendered me speechless. My stomach was twisting, my body tense. I wanted desperately to block the memory of Taylor and to escape before I had to witness Batu's death, too.

"Do not mourn. I am not dead yet, ugly one," Batu teased.

"I don't want you to die," I told him truthfully.

"If I have your favor, I have the Eternal Blue Sky's. I am not afraid." He moved away.

Unable to shake my darker thoughts, I struggled to focus on the present. Khulutei joined me, tense and serious.

Cheers went up as a man larger than Batu made his way through the crowd. He reached the corner opposite us, and I gasped. Batu was large; this man was a tree displaying the scars of previous battles.

"Can Batu win?" I asked Khulutei uneasily.

"All things are possible."

It wasn't exactly a ringing endorsement. I glanced at the quiet man beside me then at Batu. My champion was stripping off his tunics and over shirts down to his pants. He had the body of a large cat: powerful muscles moved beneath a thick layer of skin, wide shoulders and chest that slimmed down to narrow hips, a flat stomach and long, lean thighs. His torso bore multiple scars in different shapes and was bow legged, probably from riding horses. He was large, strong and fearless.

Impressed, I caught myself staring at his exposed back. He was hairless except for the darkened patch filling in his baldhead. Like Taylor's lean frame, Batu's body wasn't molded in a gym but from constant battle and everyday survival. He just happened to be much bigger than everyone around him, with the exception of the giant champion he was facing off with.

One of the warriors teased him about his baldhead. Batu rubbed it and smiled in response. I didn't understand how he was so easy with men who would kill him at the drop of the hat if his uncle ordered it.

"Do they use weapons?" I asked.

"No. It is a wrestling match," Khulutei explained. "One must kill the other with his bare hands."

Barbaric didn't begin to explain how crazy that sounded.

The two men went to the center of the ring, and the crowd fell silent. Chaghan rose from his position seated on the ground with his back to his tent. He looked over both men and then gave a solemn nod of his head before returning to his seat.

The two faced off, bowed and then lowered themselves into low stances.

I didn't want to care about what happened. But I didn't want Batu to die, either. He shouldn't become the next name on the list of people around me to suffer, and I wasn't looking forward to another layer of guilt.

I didn't deserve to have someone fighting for me. I had done so much harm in my first adventure …

My thoughts were soon dashed when the giant landed his first punch against Batu. The solid smack of fist on flesh made me flinch. I had never seen a fight, aside from glimpsing UFC matches while flipping through television channels. There was a reason I never stopped to watch; I didn't care for violence, especially something this brutal.

I was soon immersed in the battle before me. It stretched longer than I expected, with the two men sometimes locking up in wrestling moves before one of them broke free and they began beating on each other with such ferocity, I started to feel sick and couldn't always look. Batu was as quick to react as he was thick, which seemed to be his only real advantage, aside from apparently taking a beating pretty well. Every time the giant knocked him down, he bounded to his feet as if he hadn't just been smashed by a three hundred pound rock.

The giant went down less often, but when he did, struggled to recover. Batu was more of a gentleman and let his opponent get to his feet before continuing. At first, I thought this considerate in his unique way, until I realized one of them had to die before this was over.

Tense enough for my neck and chest to ache, I watched the giant draw first blood while Batu landed more direct punches. They locked up in mid-grapple on the ground once more, both of their chests heaving. Sweat and dirt coated their bodies. The men around us were cheering, some for Batu and some for the giant, while Khulutei remained stoic and tense beside me.

"Batu is hurt," he said for my ears only.

I peered more closely at my guardian, unable to see what Khulutei did. "They're both bloody," I said.

"Batu is favoring his right arm. It is likely broken."

"Broken?" I identified which arm was his in the tangled limbs of the warriors. It looked fine to me, and it was currently wrapped around the giant's neck. His expression was that of someone in extreme concentration, not pain that I could tell. The blood of both men was mixed and smeared everywhere, though I didn't see anything like a bone piercing his skin. "Are you sure?"

"Be prepared to leave."

I crossed my arms, fear shooting through me. "He'll be okay," I whispered, unable to bear the idea of Batu being killed over me. *Come on, Batu. I can't lose anyone else.*

Khulutei said nothing. I had the feeling he'd yank me out of there fast if the battle passed the point of no return for Batu. I wasn't schooled enough in this kind of barbarism to identify that moment. Even if it came, I'd rather stay here and face my fate than run away and live with Batu's death on my conscience.

Batu's grip around the giant slipped, and the larger man rolled free. The two launched to their feet and another brutal round of punches, grabbing and kicks. I still didn't see what Khulutei did; Batu didn't seem to be pulling punches the way I expected someone with a broken arm to do.

Khulutei shifted his weight between feet beside me, the only indication he was worried. I glanced at him and swallowed hard. I was starting to like this world even less watching how they settled disagreement. It didn't seem likely that any of them had made it this far.

"Good," Khulutei murmured.

I focused again on the battle, frustrated I didn't understand the battle like Khulutei did. Batu had just been thrown off the back of the giant, who was staggering. All I could think of was that Batu did something before being tossed onto his back. He rolled and hopped to his feet, a little more slowly this time, but still bright eyed and focused.

The giant, however, was shaking his head and stumbling.

"Finish it, cousin," Khulutei said under his breath.

As if hearing him, Batu pounced. Any mercy he had shown the giant in letting him stand whenever he fell appeared to be gone. He smashed one of the giant's knees and sent the man crashing down with a cry of pain.

And then he began to pound his fists into him. Over and over, until the giant fell onto his back and weakly tried to fend off Batu's blows.

Batu didn't stop and continued to beat the man's face and neck. Blood sprayed everywhere while the men around us cheered more loudly.

Sickened by the sight of a man being murdered, I closed my eyes and ducked my head, seeking my happy place.

The sense of detachment stirred and tugged me away from reality and consciousness. The scary world outside vanished, for which I was grateful.

See me. Hear me. Touch me.

This time, I fought the attempt to bring me back. My senses, however, disobeyed me, and I gradually became aware of Batu's body pressed to mine, his arm around me, the scent of his sweat and blood as I was held against his chest.

"... wrong with her?" Khulutei's words were alarmed.

My eyes fluttered open, and my nose wrinkled. Batu's blood and sweat smeared my cheek and hands. I drew my face away from his chest in disgust.

"She is not of this world," he explained.

With a sigh, I looked up at his strong features. His face was bloodied, one eye and his lip swollen already. His right arm hung at his side limply, and he was breathing hard. The image of him beating a man to death was at the back of my mind. Combined with the blood marring my skin, I had the urge to run far away until someone from the future found me.

I pushed at him.

"You are back, goddess." His voice was strained, though he appeared steady on his feet. "Cousin."

Khulutei looped an arm around me. I struggled, but he was as solid as Batu. Resigned to being in his arms, I watched Batu wipe blood from his face with one of his tunics.

The crowd was dispersing. Their uncle was gone from his place of honor, while the body of the man he slayed remained in the ring. I looked away from the bloody mess quickly.

"It would be wise for you to leave soon," Khulutei advised. "Our uncle is angry. He will honor your victory for now, but when night falls, much can happen."

"I suspect the same." Batu gazed at the tent. "I will need a healer before we go. May I see your wife?"

"We can go there now." Khulutei released me and started away.

I wobbled. Batu instinctively steadied me, and I shifted out of his reach, freaked out by his brutal displays of violence.

"Do not run, lamb," he warned, as if aware of the thoughts racing through my mind.

"I won't," I replied. *If only because I have no idea where to go.* "Are you hurt?"

He shrugged.

I sensed a warrior of this time did not express pain or emotion unless he was on the verge of death, if then.

"You are not pleased your guardian is victorious?" he asked, studying me.

"Death disturbs me, Batu. Violence, too."

"This world of yours … it is unusual."

I started to laugh, once more on the verge of hysterical, and stopped, aware of how inappropriate it was at the moment. "Let's get you patched up," I said instead. If I didn't stay focused and busy, I was going to have a meltdown.

Despite the savagery of what I had just witnessed, I was also thrilled Batu was still alive. *One less person on my list of people who died because of me.*

He began walking. He was moving slower than usual. With no limp and no outward sign of pain, I had no idea what was wrong. I didn't want to ask, though, not when I was experiencing profound relief that he had survived and was mostly okay. I didn't want to feel anything towards him, even the same general concern for his life I experienced about everyone in the world.

Watching him fight for my freedom …

It bothered me on a level I didn't want to acknowledge. "Thank you for fighting," I said awkwardly. "But please don't do it again."

"You are my commander now, ugly one?" he asked.

"You're sworn to obey me, right? So you have to listen. I don't want you fighting for me."

"I'm sworn to protect, not obey, whether or not you wish it."

It was a fruitless discussion. I heard it in his tone. Duty yadda yadda. I was edgy after the battle, not only from watching him do what he did, but because I really didn't want to be here or responsible for the life of someone else.

What choice did I have? For all I knew, I was trapped here for good.

Khulutei's tent was large and close to his uncle's. We entered, and Batu sat at the fire in the center with a grunt of pain. Two women were present, along with Khulutei, and they immediately went to Batu's side with baskets filled with apothecary supplies.

I sat down on the opposite side of the fire.

"Goddess, these are my wives, Jichin and Bayarjin," Khulutei said.

The two women glanced my way, bowed their heads and returned to working on Batu.

"You have two wives?" I asked, surprised.

"Three," he replied. "Two are adept in the ways of healing."

"Three wives. But … how?"

All of them looked my way at this. Batu appeared amused, his cousin confused and the women uncertain.

"Moonbeam does not understand our world," Batu explained. "Khulutei is a wealthy man. A wealthy man takes many wives. The more wives, the wealthier he is. It is our way, goddess."

"Do you all live here?" I asked, unable to comprehend how three women could live within hearing range of their husband making love to one of them.

"We each have our own *ger*, goddess," one of them answered with a smile.

"Oh. That's good." *But crazy.* "How many wives do you have, Batu?"

"None."

Why did that answer relieve me? Because I didn't want to make a handful of women widows?

"It is forbidden for a guardian of the goddess to take a wife until he reaches forty seasons. A new guardian is appointed at this age," Batu explained.

"How many wives will you have?" I asked.

"I do not intend to live that long."

"Why?"

He eyed me. "I have known you two days, goddess, and been in two battles."

"You will need several guardians," Khulutei said with a trace of a smile.

I really didn't like this joke. I wasn't worth killing for and definitely not dying for.

"Are you hungry, goddess?" one of Khulutei's wives asked.

"Yes."

"Milk?"

"Do you have real food?"

"The Goddess of the White Path consumes more than milk?" Khulutei asked.

"Um, yes. I eat what you do."

He exchanged a look with the wife who asked me. She rose and went to a low table with jugs of water and wrapped food, returning with dried cheese that crumbled like feta and a small chunk of cooked red meat.

I ate both happily. Batu's broken forearm was set and bandaged with long pieces of timber inside the linens to keep it straight. They dressed the wounds on his face, hands and wrapped one ankle as well.

He was quiet throughout it all, allowing the women to work their trade. I found myself puzzling over him, unable to understand how he could beat anyone to death. I couldn't fathom doing such a thing to a mortal enemy who murdered my family. The violence gene passed me by.

He met my gaze. He was relaxed, his powerful body giving him the appearance of someone always ready to spring into action. There was nothing in his face or eyes I was able to read; he seemed content to study me.

My thoughts were not so simple. I was struggling with the emotions from my first adventure back in time. I had hoped they'd leave me alone or I could lose them in the whirlwind activity of this new place and time. If anything, they were stirring stronger and stronger. The more I interacted with someone like Batu, the more I felt Taylor's loss and the trauma of living through the deaths of so many people I had cared about, despite learning who they really were.

I didn't know the real Batu and was still concerned for him. He didn't know me and was laying down his life at my feet. There was so much wrong with these scenarios without taking into account the brutal world I had been thrust into.

We need to have a real talk. I decided. I needed him to know I wasn't magical or divine or worth his life. I didn't necessarily want to know more about him, though, even if I needed to know if he'd turn out to be like the traitorous Nell, who I trusted with everything, or John, the man who murdered his own daughter yet pretended I was her.

I had run into too much craziness in my first adventure. I had to keep my distance and make sure no one else ended up dead – or uncreated – like Taylor.

Averting my gaze, I ran my fingertips over one of the bandages on my arms. It was just my luck lately that I could heal others – but not myself.

Heal others. I considered Batu's broken arm. I was feeling guilty about him being hurt, but I didn't need to.

"Batu, why didn't you ask me for …" I waved at my arm, not

wanting to finish the question.

"It is yours to give, goddess. I do not ask for your favors."

I rolled my eyes. "I do not understand you. May I have some wine?" I asked one of the wives. "And a knife."

She brought me both. I hesitated. This knife was much larger than the one Batu gave me. I wasn't able to consider cutting myself with the pain of my other wounds still throbbing. I gazed at the sharp blade squeamishly.

I stood and circled the fire, kneeling beside Batu. I held out both to him. "I can't do it," I said.

He held my gaze a moment before accepting the offerings. He took one of my hands.

"Just don't ... make it bad," I said nervously.

Sensing I was ready to bolt, he tightened his grip and deftly positioned the blade of the knife near my thumb. I closed my eyes and braced myself. The sharp prick made me gasp once more. Assured it was over, I opened my eyes.

The black specks remained in my blood. There were fewer, though, and I suspected the preservation or cryo agent or whatever it was gradually was being cleaned out.

Batu released my hand, and I squeezed droplets into the wine with a grimace.

"How did you come by this gift?" Khulutei sounded unsettled.

"By accident," I replied. "I was asleep for at least seventy years. This ... black stuff is what kept me sleeping and healthy."

The look he gave me was one of unease.

Batu was peering into the goblet as if uncertain he wanted to drink it. "You beat a man to death with your hands and are afraid of a little blood?" I asked him, surprised.

"Blood is sacred, goddess. Normally, offering your blood to another in such a way binds your spirits to theirs," one of the women explained. "It is a way for non-kin to become kin, for strangers to become brothers."

"Ah. Makes sense." I had no clue about their customs or traditions. I started to move my hand so the blood wouldn't drip onto my white silks when I noticed the delicate layers were already soaked through from Batu's blood. "Is it too much to ask for new clothes?"

"Would you trade?"

I glanced up and saw the envious way one of Khulutei's wives was eyeing the silk. She settled beside me and quickly wrapped my bleeding thumb.

"Yes," I said without hesitation. "Um ... do you like this dress?"

She nodded with a smile. "Come with me to my *ger.* You can choose what you wish."

I stood and trailed her to a neighboring tent. In this one were two children under the age of five who appeared to be sharpening knives and arrowheads. It was definitely a different world, if children this young were comfortable with weapons.

I changed out of the ruined white silks into a sturdier, more comfortable linen tunic, loose pants and wool over-tunic that reached mid-thigh. She took the white layers and carefully folded them before we returned to the other tent.

Batu was on his feet when we entered, testing his body. The wine goblet was empty. He wore a tunic and had replaced his weapons. His face was beginning to swell, giving his features a lumpy appearance.

"You are prepared to leave, goddess?" he asked.

I nodded. "Are you?" I looked at his broken arm.

"I have traveled with far worse," he assured me.

"Okay then."

He clasped arms with his cousin, spoke a few quiet words and then strode out of the tent.

"Thank you for your hospitality," I said to the women.

They both smiled.

I trailed Batu into the morning. Six horses awaited us, two with saddles, two with supplies and two bareback.

"Can you ride, goddess?" he asked, pausing beside a grey horse.

"Yes." I stopped beside him, admiring the pretty creature. I rubbed its forehead.

He took the reins. "Then let us ride."

I mounted the horse. The wooden saddle was less comfortable than I imagined though it felt sturdy. He adjusted the stirrups with no sign his arm was bothering him before mounting his horse.

Wheeling his to face the east, he wove his way through the encampment and the herds of ponies between it and the river.

We headed upstream, to the north, after reaching the river. I glanced back towards the burning city several times, plagued by fear and doubt. My last known location was the city. I had assumed if Taylor's people found me where Carter originally dropped me off, then someone could find me again, no matter where I was.

I hope.

Chapter Seven

We rode north until it was sunset, passing over low hills and through patches of forests until we reached an area of rolling plains. There was no road, and we ran across no one, once we left the river. I wasn't sure what I expected – maybe a rudimentary form of hotel? – But it wasn't to see Batu unloading one of his horses in the middle of a field.

"We're stopping here?" I asked.

"We are."

I climbed off my horse and grimaced. My legs were sore and my ass hurting from the day on horseback. Not much of a fan of camping, I watched Batu begin to build a fire with grasses, small branches and what looked like dried cow poop.

I sat opposite him with a groan.

"Can you hunt?" he asked.

"No."

"Fish?"

"No."

"Shoot a bow?"

"No."

"Cook over a fire?"

"No."

He glanced at me then the horses. "Can you manage to take their saddles off, ugly one?"

"Yes." I was almost relieved he wasn't upset that I had no real value whatsoever in this place. "How is your arm?"

He shrugged.

I rolled my eyes and got to my feet. Limping to the horses, I stripped off their saddles and bridles with no grace. It was hard enough trying to remain on my wobbly feet. I wasn't able to lower anything to the ground without my legs feeling like they were going to buckle.

The horses moved away and began munching on grass. Batu had stopped near a stream, and one headed to it for water.

"Will they run away?" I called to him.

"No. They follow me wherever I go."

Like really big puppies. I wasn't totally convinced animals I knew to be pretty independent were going to remain, but this was his world. In the morning, he'd be healed anyway, so he could chase them down.

I went to the stream and knelt beside it, loving the peaceful sound of rushing water. I rinsed my face but feared drinking from it without asking Batu about its quality. Tugging off my over tunic, I shivered in the cool evening breeze and peeled off my bandages to clean my wounds. After my first adventure, I'd learned to be a little less prissy. I could bathe with a bowl of water or a stream. There were no copper pots out here for bathrooms, and I guessed I was about to become a little less prissy than before by going to the bathroom in the wild.

My arms didn't seem infected in the last light of the day. They hurt, though, and I had a stress headache.

"I will not hunt today," Batu said, joining me.

"Fine with me. Is this water safe to drink?"

"Yes."

I drank my fill and sat back on my heels. Stars were brilliant on the side of the sky opposite of the horizon, and the moon was a sliver.

"The night I came here, the moon was like this," I murmured, a pang of longing in my chest.

Already I saw more stars than I ever had in southern California, and the sun wasn't fully gone yet. This world … Batu's world … was raw, unspoiled, beautiful.

But I didn't feel part of it. I didn't know if I ever would. If I spent too much time thinking of the aunt and uncle who raised me, of Taylor, of how this might be penance … I'd cry.

I wasn't a crier. I didn't like feeling sad or down or depressed. I had a sunny disposition, although, since arriving here, it had been more like this twilighty time of night, a combination of dark and light where there had only been sunshine before. The loss of Taylor was forever on my soul. This much I knew.

What would Amy Pond do? I asked myself, thoughts on one of my favorite Doctor Who companions. *She'd believe the Doctor could find her and trek on until he does.*

Carter was my Doctor Who. I didn't care that Taylor's people had found me. It was possible I leaned towards Carter because I had met him and experienced a sense of kinship, however weird and improbable that was. Moreover, I knew how smart he was. He had done the impossible, according to Taylor, albeit, somewhat imperfectly.

I touched the back of my head, where I imagined the microchips were implanted by Carter. He had almost mastered technology an entire agency of time travelers viewed as impossible.

If he did this, he could find me.

Do I want him to? I couldn't trust him or his intentions. He also claimed not to be able to return me to my time. Confusion jammed up my ability to reason, to identify what I really wanted – and what was possible.

Maybe it's better I stay lost in history.

But *here*?

"I miss home." I sighed. "I don't think I'll ever see it again, Batu."

He was quiet, gaze on the sky.

"If you couldn't go home to the steppes, what would you do?" I asked the warrior beside me, genuinely curious to hear his grounded take on reality.

"I would make a life wherever I was," he said simply.

"You wouldn't try to go home?"

"I would, unless it was impossible."

He spoke to my situation, not his. There was no impossibility large enough in a world this small for him not to return home. I had nearly a thousand years of time between me and my home. He just had to travel for a few weeks on horseback to get anywhere in the known world at this time.

The breeze tickled the back of my neck. I picked up my over tunic and pulled it on.

"What if you weren't convinced it was impossible?" I asked.

"Then I would try until I succeeded or until I knew it was not possible."

There was tightness around his eyes that warned me his well-masked pain was wearing on him after the long day of travel. I was still uneasy about being around him but finding it difficult to recall him as the monster I'd seen him become when we were close like this and he seemed so … normal. Pleasant almost.

"The fire will keep wolves away," he told me and got to his feet.

I trailed him to the small bonfire. He had stacked the saddles and his belongings neatly on one side of the fire. He had put up a pup tent-sized shelter consisting of a felt wall connected to the ground on one side and a boulder on the other. It was going to be a tight fit … unless it was for him and I was on my own.

Sitting with another grunt, I sighed when I was down and my leg muscles could relax.

Batu passed me dried cheese and meat, along with milk. The meat had no flavoring but was tender.

I ate what he gave me and gazed into the fire, feeling a little lost in my thoughts. He tossed me a pouch, and I blinked. It landed in the grass beside me.

"What is it?" I asked and plucked it up.

"I carried these since I was a child."

I dumped the contents of the pouch into my hand. "Moldavite," I murmured and leaned forward until the fire turned the dark chunks of glass a familiar green.

"I was born near where you fell from the sky," he added. "My bloodline supplies the guardians. We all carry these to remind us of the sacred honor. They came with you, did they not?"

"Yeah," I said, smiling.

"Does this remind you of home?"

I considered how to answer. Not of home, but it was a connection to my time. As a hobby geologist, I had a fascination with the green glass before leaving on my adventure and awoke in the eighteen forties surrounded by it, and again seventy years ago when Carter dropped me off in the steppes.

"It helps," I replied, touched by the thoughtfulness of someone who beat his opponent to death barehanded not twelve hours before.

"You can fashion a new crown." His eyes went to the delicate silver ring around my head in amusement.

I had forgotten about it and touched the filigreed silver. I always wanted to be a princess when I was little. Maybe a goddess of sorts was close enough. "Can I keep one?" I asked and studied the murky green glass.

He hesitated.

"Or … maybe I can see them whenever I'm feeling homesick?" I added, realizing how important the fragments of Moldavite were to him if they represented his family honor.

"I like this better."

Replacing them in the pouch, I tossed them back to him. "Thank you, Batu."

"I understand." He shrugged.

You are so weird. Sweet in one instance, collecting human ears in the next … I didn't understand what I was dealing with, because he was too foreign to the kind of people I'd met thus far in my life.

"When you are ready to sleep, we have shelter," he said and motioned to the pup tent.

"I'm ready," I said, exhausted by my day. "Will we both fit?"

"We'll make do, ugly one."

Whatever. I still didn't get his sense of humor. I went to the tent and saw he'd put down one blanket on the ground, and there was another rolled and waiting. He didn't follow me, for which I was somewhat grateful. I was tired enough to tell him this sucked, and I didn't think it was the right emotion considering he didn't have to help me survive out here at all.

I crawled into the pup tent. The felt blocked the breeze. While nowhere near as comfortable as a bed, it had to do. Resting on my side, facing the felt wall with my back to the center of the tent, I closed my eyes.

I think I do want Carter to find me. But I wasn't sure. What was worst about everything I'd been through: the helplessness of knowing I could do nothing to change my fate? I was either being manipulated by others or ... lost.

I slept deeply at first, until I rolled from my side onto my stomach. Pain from my hands and arms shot through me, and I jerked awake.

"Owww," I muttered and delicately shifted off of them once more. My lower body was so stiff, it trumped my arm pain, if only for a moment.

"What is it, goddess?" Batu's sleepy voice came from beside me.

My back was pressed to his once I straightened. He was warm and solid. I stifled tears of pain and released the breath I was holding.

"Nothing. My arms hurt," I answered him.

"Mine does not."

"Good for you!" I snapped, irritated once again my magic worked on everyone but me.

He chuckled. His breathing deepened, and he slid back into sleep.

I rolled onto my back then side then back. *Everything* hurt now that I was awake. My thighs, my ass, my hips, my arms and hands. There was no comfortable position on the hard earth.

Shifting onto my side once again, I flexed my hands to test them. They hadn't healed at all, or at least, they felt as raw as they were when Batu's uncle cut them.

I moved to my back and stared into the darkness. Batu moved beside me.

"Be still, Moonbeam," he grumbled.

"I can't. Everything hurts!"

He shifted onto his side facing me. Seconds later, his arm went around me, and he pushed and pulled me until my back was to him. Draping his over tunic over me, he pulled me into him.

I wriggled away. "What're you doing?"

"A shepherd does this when a lamb is fussy." His arm locked around me.

"I'm not a lamb!" Trapped inside his shirt, with his ungiving frame behind me, I ceased struggling not long after I started. His scent was strong, his warmth stronger, and both began moving through my system to relax me.

"But you are fussy."

There were moments when I really hated his observations. He jostled me more to slip his arm beneath my neck. He wasn't the first man I'd slept with like this, but he was definitely the strongest. It was a little unnerving to have his powerful body at my back.

"Shall I sing to you?" he asked.

It's not really singing. I was too irritated to want to explain how different his singing was from what I knew. "Maybe."

"What song? Sky? Grass? Water?"

"Water." Not that I remotely understood the difference between them.

The low growl emanating from his chest began. His chest rumbled at my back, and the vibration entranced me before the second layer of higher pitched notes came from his mouth and nose.

The non-song was as unusual as it was soothing. As with the first time I heard him sing, I was very quickly taken away from my own thoughts and plunged into a near trance by the droning.

My eyes drifted closed, and I felt my body relax under the influence of his song and heat. Seconds before I fell asleep, his singing drifted off, and his breathing deepened once more. He fell asleep. Drowsiness soon softened my pain and pulled me the rest of the way under.

I slumbered soundly in his arms and dreamt of the night Taylor was erased from the universe.

"It is time, goddess." Batu's words woke me.

I lifted my head.

He was shifting behind me. The sudden absence of his body heat woke me fast as the predawn chill crept in. Batu left the tent.

I sat and blinked, shivering. "Time for what? It's not even dawn."

"We must leave soon. But first, you learn the bow."

It didn't really sound so great. I was sore and craving coffee. Deciding I might need to know how to shoot someone if I was truly stuck here, I forced my achy body to move and left the warmth of the tent for the chilly, dark morning.

"I am fully healed," he said from the fire, pleased.

I'm not. "Good," I murmured. "In case we run into another battle today."

"It is possible." He stood. "You have no survival skills, ugly one. I will teach you if I can, if you are able to learn."

"I can learn," I said, somewhat taken aback. "It can't be that hard."

"Steppe children begin learning when they are three seasons." He waved me towards him and held out a bow. "They ride a horse first and then learn the bow."

"Three?" I echoed. "It can't be that hard if you teach three year olds."

"We shall see."

I approached and waited.

With no sense of personal space, as usual, Batu took my shoulders and turned me around then stepped into me until his chest brushed my back. He held the bow in front of me with one hand and took my other hand with his.

He placed both my hands on the bow. "Can you draw it?" With his hands hovering, he waited for me to try.

Determined to prove I could do what any toddler could, I braced one sore hand on the front of the bow and started to pull the taut string back.

Or tried. It didn't move more than an inch. Squaring my stance better, I tried once more.

"Is this a trick bow?" I asked, puzzled.

He took it from my hands and drew it effortlessly, even with me standing between it and him.

"Maybe I can learn something else."

"The knife or sword?"

I grimaced. I didn't look forward to stabbing anyone. "Or … I can take care of the horses and you can kill people."

"You are too delicate, ugly one. I may not always be around to protect you."

Frowning, I took the bow and made another attempt without getting much farther. "Are you sure children can use this?" I asked.

"They have bows made for their size. I will have one made for you. It will be slightly bigger than that of a child of five seasons."

"Really?" I twisted in his grip. "I'm that bad?"

Batu flicked my braid over my shoulder, his features not yet visible in the dark morning. "You will learn, Moonbeam."

A little too close for comfort, I stepped back. His arms dropped.

"You really think I need to know?"

"You will be hunted."

"Why?"

"For your blood. For your blessings. For many reasons," he said.

I shuddered, and this time, it wasn't the morning chill.

"Do not be scared, goddess," he reassured me. "I am here." He moved away, towards the six horses grouped together a short distance away.

I watched him go, not at all convinced he could stand between me and armies of those who sought me. Of all the places to be lost …

I was starting to stress out. Bad. "Batu, I need to … stretch." His uncle had clearly never heard of yoga, and I doubted Batu had either.

"What is this?"

"I'll be by the stream." With some resignation, I chose a boulder to use as cover while I went to the bathroom and used leaves for toilet paper. I once thought peeing in a bucket was bad, but it now seemed like a luxury.

The lack of modern amenities added to my frustration and fear. I went to the stream, washed my hands, discarded my heavy over tunic and began a slow yoga routine to help my poor aching muscles as well as my frantic mind.

The bubbling brook distracted me from my misery, along with the gentle routine I used to perform with my aunt in her backyard. She had been a diehard yoga practitioner. I started out doing it to help me recover from hangovers and ended up taking a class four times a week the last two years of college.

College. What a waste. At least I don't have to worry about repaying my student loans.

Pushing the thought aside, I concentrated on my practice. I was pleased my body cooperated and closed my eyes. The first rays of dawn soon warmed my face. I continued with one of my one-hour routines, needing the temporary escape from my situation.

I still didn't understand Carter's purpose in sending me to the Old West, aside from un-creating Taylor. The importance of Flowers in history was also lost on me, and I hoped she was doing well. Batu seemed to think she would be safe, though I wasn't certain yet I trusted him with everything. He took my physical safety to heart but I had no other real influence on him. For all I knew, he took her somewhere and killed her the way he had everyone else we'd met.

It was scary not to know much about my fate, my purpose. I had once considered not knowing my major in college a crisis, but that was a joke compared to the life I lived now.

The rising sun began to push back the chill of morning. I finished my routine and opened my eyes.

I was facing the small camp, which Batu had packed up. The horses were saddled and waiting. He sat on a boulder nearby, watching me and chewing on a chunk of meat. While still hurting, my lower body was definitely moving better off after the yoga.

"What is this you do?" he asked again. Unlike his uncle, he didn't accuse me of a magic spell.

"It's called yoga," I said and swiped my tunic from the ground. "It helps me focus my mind and helps my hurt body."

"It is a dance?"

"Not really. It's … kind of how like you sing. It's an interpretation of nature."

"It is quite beautiful to see."

Of all the potential comments I'd expect, this was not one of them. I looked up to see if he was teasing. He didn't seem to be. His dark eyes were on me, and all traces of his wounds from the day before were gone. Warmth rose to my cheeks, and I was momentarily quiet, unable to figure out why butterflies leapt to life in my blood from the knowledge he had watched me – and found it beautiful.

"Thank you," I said at last. "Everyone does it where I am from."

"Your people dance from place to place and mine ride." The corner of his mouth pulled up in a half smile.

I rolled my eyes at him.

He stood and motioned to my horse. "Are you prepared?"

"Ugh, no. My legs and ass hurt."

He laughed.

I got the feeling sometimes women – or maybe people of this time in general? – didn't talk the way I did around him. I climbed onto my horse reluctantly. My butt was tender, and I settled into the hard saddle with a hiss.

"How does your magic heal me but not you?" he asked as he mounted.

Rub it in, jerk. "I don't know," I said through clenched teeth. "I'm not supposed to be able to heal anyone."

"Then how can you?"

Because some madman dropped me into a coma that lasted nearly a century. There was no way to explain it that wouldn't sound stupid aloud, even to my ears. But I sought some response.

Batu led us to the northeast once more. He slowed until I drew abreast of him and handed me a chunk of dried meat and a bladder of milk. I ate and sipped, putting together the least crazy story I could about why I could heal.

"I met your grandparents and then was put to sleep for seventy years," I began. "To keep my body … alive and unhurt during the time, someone put the … uh, magic in my blood. It's slowly leaving my body now. Soon, I won't be able to heal anyone."

He listened while his restless eyes took in our surroundings. "Who is Taylor?"

Jolted by the name, my breath caught.

Batu glanced at me. "You spoke to him in your sleep."

My jaw clenched. I stared at the sky without really seeing it for a long moment, my emotions churning. "What else did I say?" I asked tersely.

"Not much. You said, *Forgive me, Taylor,* over and over."

My heart ached in response to the sorrowful sentiment.

You made a difference, Josie. Taylor's final words killed me to recall. I did make a difference – but an awful one I'd do whatever I could to fix, if I ever had the chance.

Batu took the milk back. I shifted, returning to my physical body.

"I don't want to talk about him," I said. "Please."

"He is dead."

I didn't respond.

"You were too sad for him not to be."

"Batu!" I snapped, trying his grandmother's way of dealing with a warrior since asking him nicely didn't seem to work.

"Very well, goddess."

We rode in silence until the weather grew warm enough for me to shed my outer layer. Batu appeared to know the direction despite there being no road or trail guiding us. The hilly plains were beginning to level out, though patches of trees, streams and ponds continued to punctuate the landscape at intervals. We were never far from water, and it dawned on me he was using the water sources as his guides.

"You said something about herding last night," I said, breaking the quiet. "Did you herd sheep?"

"I was raised in a war camp. Every child of the steppe is taught the skills of our forefathers: the bow, horses, herding and hunting. The army travels with its own herds of horses, sheep and goats. Children take care of them until they are old enough to learn to fight."

"You were serious last night about a fussy lamb," I said. I was almost disappointed not to have been … special for a moment. Did he really think of me as a sheep or some other animal?

"If a lamb is lost or left by its mother, the herder must find it and care for it. Placing it here helps." He patted his chest. "It appears to work on fussy goddesses as well."

"I wasn't *fussy*." The image of him caring for a lamb and then loping over the horizon to collect ears almost made me smile in bafflement. "You are nice to a lamb but you kill everyone else."

"Lambs provide wool when they are older."

"True. So the kids in a war camp take care of animals, learn to fight and are taught survival."

"Yes."

"War is awful."

"It, too, is necessary. The Eternal Blue Sky has declared all four corners of the world are ours. We must ride out and claim them."

"You really believe that?" I peered at him.

"It is true. Look what we have done in a hundred years. We claimed the east and west and everything in between."

It doesn't last. I didn't know much about this time period, but it was no great leap to assume time wore away the Mongols' hold on the known world the way it had every other great civilization.

"You are a good warrior," I observed, somewhat disturbed to recall how good he was.

"I am my clan's champion. Only the greatest warrior is chosen as a guardian."

"I know it's an honor but … wouldn't you rather be at war with everyone else?"

"Father Sky has blessed me with this fate. I am grateful for it."

He wasn't like me. He didn't question *why* things unfolded the way they did.

"Although …" He trailed off.

"Although what?"

"I have no wife. No sons."

"Do you want a family?"

He gave me another of his odd looks. "Do you *not*?"

"I don't think so."

"Warriors do not generally live long. I chose to become a guardian instead of marrying," he explained.

"I understand that. You're always at war," I said. "So you worry you won't have a family."

"At times."

I wasn't expecting his candid response. It left me feeling a little more … confused about who he really was or rather, how he could have such extremes.

"Taylor was my husband," I said quietly. "I was married to him for a few days before he died. I don't think I want a family. It's too easy to lose someone, and it hurts when you do."

"It is the nature of things, goddess," he said.

"Well, I don't like it. I won't be married again."

"Neither will I, as long as you are alive."

"Sorry, Batu."

"I have no regrets, ugly one."

"I'm not ugly!"

"I know." He smiled without looking at me.

I wasn't certain how to take his response. Part of me wanted to double check and make sure I'd heard him right while the other part of me screamed about not getting attached or involved with anyone in this world.

Deciding to go with silence, I slid back into my thoughts for a while before turning my attention to my surroundings. The four horses trailed us the way he said they would, and we traveled from water source to water source through green grasses towards snowcapped mountains in the distance.

"What season is this, Batu?" I asked, struck by the notion I had no clue what day it was let alone the time of year.

"Late summer. The nights will start to become too cold to sleep without a fire."

I recalled when I landed originally in the Mongol Empire. It was so cold, breathing hurt. I assumed it was winter.

"Where are we going?"

"To the steppe where I was raised."

"Why there?"

"Because it is home."

"No more wars for you?"

"My time will be spent watching over you, goddess, unless you choose to vanish once more."

"Which I can't do."

"My home is far from the wars and the men who will hunt you. To reach us, they will navigate territory that does not welcome strangers and pass through many steppe people."

It was a smart plan to place layers of protection between anyone like his uncle and me. It seemed to fit Batu's desire to return home, too. At the heart of the Empire, no one could reach me.

Except maybe Carter.

Chapter Eight

WE RODE THROUGHOUT THE DAY, STOPPED FOR THE NIGHT IN A thatch of forest, and continued for another two days.

On the fourth day, we continued past night fall. I expected him to stop in another field or at the edge of a forest or somewhere similar, but he continued. Soon after dark fell, a clump of around five buildings came into view. One was far larger than the others, and light and sound spilled from the windows.

"What is this?" I asked.

"Traders' post and inn." Batu glanced at me and then leaned over to tug up my hood. "Keep your face hidden. You draw attention."

I pulled it the rest of the way. The closer we got, the less I liked the idea of a hotel of this kind. It was very … rough. Not only did it smell of waste and unwashed bodies, but the mix of people weren't what I expected. Mongols I recognized by their clothing, though some appeared European or Chinese, but it was the men who looked like bandits or scruffy, shifty-eyed thieves who concerned me.

"Are we staying here?" I asked when Batu stopped at the stables beside the post.

"We are," he confirmed. He dismounted and handed over the reins to a stable boy. "There is little crime here, goddess. The Khan's code is enforced strictly."

I didn't ask, but I suspected the punishment for every infraction was probably death. Dismounting, I bit back a groan of pain after the day on the horse and limped to Batu.

"We will eat here," he said and began walking towards the loud inn. "I have a trade to conduct and then we will rest."

The moment we set foot in the inn, I decided there was nothing on the planet that would dissuade me from his orders this time. The roughened crowd was eating stew or meat and drinking wine and ale. Boisterously drunk or busy eating, the place reeked of humanity, and everyone was armed. I crowded Batu as he wove through the men towards an unoccupied table in corner.

Sitting, I huddled more deeply into my hood and gazed around.

"Wait here," he told me.

I watched him navigate the crowd to the window of the kitchens. Batu returned a few moments later with bowls of stew, bread and wine. He set them down and sat, eating quickly, his eyes never still as he observed the people around us.

I ate more slowly. The stew meat was tough and chewy though there were some unidentifiable spices in it. Batu wolfed down his food and sat back with a glance at the food I'd barely started.

"You do not leave your seat, Moonbeam," he told me firmly.

I nodded. Without another warning, he stood and strode to a doorway leading past the open floor of the dining area into the hotel part of the inn. He disappeared, and I paused in my eating, not liking the fact he was gone.

Shaking out my concern, I picked up the warm bowl of stew with both hands – they didn't have spoons – and sipped the broth. Where the meat was better off swallowed than chewed, the broth had a good flavor. The bread was basic and a little stale while the wine was stronger than I was accustomed to.

All things considered, it wasn't a bad dinner. I sat back to watch the rough world around me. No women were present, which I was guessing was probably a good thing. This crowd didn't seem like the kind to deal well with women.

The men at the table beside me rose, and my attention shifted to them. They wore a mix of clothing, the heavy wool of the Mongols mixed with faded silks and furs. They appeared to be wealthy traders, and the gleam of one's silver belt sparkled in the light of the hearth and torches. Several pouches dangled from his belt, weapons and …

… A cell phone.

I blinked and looked again. It looked a lot like a silver iPhone.

Jarred by the idea, I sat up straighter to get a better look, but he had turned away and started towards the hotel side of the inn. He and his companions didn't look any different than the others around me.

Neither did Taylor. My short-lived husband had fit in perfectly with the rest of the men from the eighteen hundreds.

The man with the phone disappeared down a hallway. I stood, adrenaline pumping and Batu's warning in my head. After a brief hesitation, I started through the crowd. I was small enough that most people didn't notice me, and those that did looked away after a glance in my direction. Tugging the hood forward, I sneaked peeks at those around me while hurrying as fast as I could to the entrance into the hotel area.

Stepping into a wooden hallway, I saw the man with the phone disappear into a room towards the end of the corridor, accompanied by the others. I hastened down the hall and paused outside the open door. They had stepped into a private meeting room, complete with another roughly hewn table and chairs, a hearth and pitcher of wine.

I ducked behind the doorway and stayed out of sight, listening closely in case they were time travelers talking about their adventures.

If they were, they weren't discussing it. Their conversations centered around trade. One man was displaying goods the others were negotiating for. Some of my conviction began to wane, and I frowned. It was always possible only one of them was a traveler like me and was there on business.

"Who are you?"

I whirled and stared at the man before me. His eyes were narrowed, his hand on the hilt of a dagger.

"No one," I murmured. "I was lost." I stepped away.

At the sound of my voice, his gaze sharpened. He snatched my arm and hauled me into the room with the others, all but slinging me onto their table. I caught myself with my injured hands and suppressed a groan at the streak of hot pain.

The others stared at me then the other man, surprised. One of them yanked my hood back, and that seemed to unfreeze them.

"What is this?" one asked and wrenched the tiara off my head. "This pearl is of great quality."

"She's dressed like a Mongol," another said.

Several other made cruder comments, and I straightened and took a step back. "Excuse me. I did not mean to intrude."

"You speak when spoken to, whore!" The man nearest me snapped and slapped me hard.

Startled, I rested a hand against my stinging cheek.

"Who do you belong to?" another demanded.

"No one." I backpedaled, only to run into the man who tossed me into the room.

He closed the door behind him, and I started to suspect this was not going to end well. Cursing myself silently, I debated what to say or do.

"By all rights, she is under my roof and therefore mine," an older man who looked to be in his sixties declared and stood. "But I will sell her for a fair price."

Sell?

At first, I thought the men were as taken aback as I was. They were quiet for a long moment, exchanging looks, before one slapped a hand on the table containing misshapen silver coins.

"Broghun, tie her up!" the owner of the hotel ordered.

The man behind me grabbed me.

"No, wait! I'm here with –" I objected and yanked away.

He slapped me, this time hard enough to make my head spin.

And then the sense of detachment crept upon me.

Not now! I ordered my tired mind. I started to fade … and struggled to concentrate on my senses the way Batu told me to. Stuck in my internal war, I was vaguely aware of having my hands tied and my mouth gagged. I couldn't utter a single word anyway, not when I was in this horrible stage of detachment.

"You cheat!" one of the men shouted and smashed his fists into the table.

His outburst pulled me out of my mind, and I took in what had happened during the moments I was indisposed. I was being held by the man named Broghun. His back was to one wall and his arm around my throat while he watched the bidding war. The rag wrapped around my head for a gag tasted foul.

"I am not a cheat," another man said calmly. "I only say I think this one is poison. This" he held up my crown "is not a trifle given to a man's favorite concubine. Someone will be seeking for her, and any man caught with her will likely be punished."

All of them fell silent and looked at me. Rather than desire for a new toy, they regarded me with wariness.

"Her body turning up in the morning in the stable will keep her from identifying us."

I strained against Broghun. The man with the phone seemed on board with this, and I reached for the gag to scream for Batu.

Broghun shoved my arms down.

"Then I will sell the right to kill her," the hotel owner reasoned. "Or you can take your chances with her master."

"I'll kill her for free!" one said and approached me.

"And I will tell her master who did it. One of you will pay me for the privilege, or all of you will face his wrath. Whoever kills her, keeps this." He held up the tiara.

What a jackass. I'd never heard of people paying to off a witness. The old man was crafty – and doggedly opportunistic.

"Five silvers!" one spat and threw the coins down.

"This pearl alone is worth five times that," the old man said with a frown. "Look at it. Look at the woman that's yours for the night. As long as she ends up dead in the morning, what does it matter what happens to her?"

What kind of logic was this?

They began passing the tiara and its teardrop shaped pearl around so everyone could debate its quality. Just like that, I seemed to be forgotten. At least, for now. I twisted my wrists to test the bonds and tried once again to yank the gag out of my mouth with no luck. Broghun was keeping a tight watch on me.

Starting to panic, I silently swore never to leave the spot Batu sentenced me to again, if I found some way to escape this time. My heart was pounding, and I looked once more in the direction of the man with the phone.

He wasn't even bidding on me. I had no idea what to do, if I was dragged out of here by some other asshole who wasn't going to be reasoned with the way I might a fellow time traveler.

There was a knock at the door.

"Private trade!" the owner shouted.

The person knocked once more.

Broghun motioned for the man nearest the door to answer it. He did so, and my heart sank even further when I heard the quiet voice on the other side. I wanted to be rescued – but I didn't want to witness another massacre.

"Batu!" I tried to cry through the gag.

He was already headed into the room. Before he crossed the threshold, the man who answered the door was on the floor, bleeding. The men in the room stood, and the sounds of swords scraping scabbards filled my ears.

Blood sprayed me, and I closed my eyes, not wanting to see the bloodshed. Last night, I had convinced myself yet again Batu was kind of a cool guy.

Every time sword sliced through flesh, or someone screamed, I flinched and reconsidered my opinion of the Mongol warrior. Warm droplets of blood landed on my face and exposed neck and hands. I tried to block out the sounds of murder, of men dying, and focused instead on not passing out.

Broghun threw me to the side. I hit the floor and smashed into a bucket of excrement and god knew what else. My eyes opened, and I almost puked at the lumps and dark matter before me. Shaking off my hands, I didn't dare risk getting the filth in my mouth by pulling off my gag.

Someone almost stepped on me, and I scrambled out of the way to the side of the brick hearth to watch.

I had never seen anyone move like Batu, and I doubted anyone else in all of space and time did. Power and agility, extreme focus combined with instinctive action. He mowed down the first four men in the room before one of them had a chance to strike him. The fourth and fifth made valiant attempts, but it was child's play against a master or … lambs fending off a hungry wolf. Limbs and heads went flying. This time, I couldn't look away, no matter how much blood sprayed the ceilings and walls.

I owed him my life, and I had to get out of here. Away from a man who could not only stomach committing such brutality but joke around about it.

When no one was left standing, he straightened from his position and gazed around.

The spell broke, and I realized the man with the phone was on my side of the table, although he seemed to be missing his head. I cursed myself again. I should've tried to save his life somehow but I was enthralled in the horror of the massacre.

Batu bent over the man nearest him. With no more thought than he gave saddling his horse, he began what I assumed was the Mongol method of double-tapping – making sure the enemy was dead by a shot to the head, or in this case, offing his head.

Inching forward, I gripped a knife that had fallen near me. I flinched at the sound of his sword cleaving meat and bone but focused on sawing through my bonds. They came off easily, and I pulled the disgusting gag from my mouth.

I bent over the body of the man with the phone and tugged at his belt to get to the device.

And then I sat back, dismayed.

It wasn't a phone at all. It was a silver box whose front was dented up and back was lacquered, resembling a phone case.

Am I that desperate? I had risked my life and Batu's for … a jewelry box. I hadn't doubted it was a phone, hadn't thought twice about what it was I saw. I lunged after it with the desperation I'd been keeping a close lid on for so long.

I gazed at the dead men around me and blinked back tears. I had been on the verge of breaking down and weeping since Taylor disappeared, but now didn't seem any better of a time than the other moments of weakness.

Batu met my gaze from the corner of the table. "There you are, Moonbeam." He wasn't at all concerned about the carnage or destruction around him.

His calmness and the violence of my surroundings scared me, the way it always did. I rose and turned away, needing air, to flee, to escape him and this world I didn't think I'd ever adjust to.

I can't do this. I started towards the door.

"Do you think it wise to run, lamb?" His voice lowered into a soft growl.

My hand dropped from the doorknob. I braced myself to have another knife thrown at me or for him to grab me.

Neither happened. I remained where I was, about to flip out, but afraid of what he'd do if I did. I was too aware that I caused this massacre because I had mistaken a jewelry box for a phone.

What was wrong with me? One moment, I didn't think I'd want Carter to find me. The next, I was following strangers into a room where no one could hear me scream, chasing some mirage of a phone.

Batu's body heat reached me, and I realized he was standing quietly behind me, as if waiting to see what I'd do.

"I'm sorry, Batu," I murmured. "I don't know what I was thinking."

"Was it worth it?"

I twisted to gaze up at him. "Was what worth it?"

"Whatever it was that drew you here. I know they didn't force you this far." His dark eyes were on me. He had a way of peering into my soul without judging me, of making me think the man capable of massacring a room full of people wasn't going to hurt one hair on my head. His weapons were sheathed, his breathing hard and even. If anything, he appeared concerned.

"No, it wasn't," I said, thoughts on the slain. "I made a mistake. I don't know what's wrong with me."

I really didn't, except that I was shaken by the thought of spending the rest of my life here.

Batu reached around me to open the door. Without speaking, we left the men where they'd fallen and emerged into the dining area once more. Rather than stop for more food, Batu continued out the door and into the night.

"We aren't staying?" I asked as he strode towards the stables.

"It's not wise when you've just slain the owner, ugly one." He pointed out.

I was surprised he wasn't angry with me or upset my foolishness had made him kill a room full of people.

Moments later, we were leaving the trading post, headed into the night. The hand that got the full dose of the shit bucket was stinging. I unwrapped the bandages, doubting the filth-soaked linen was remotely good for my open wounds.

I was hurting and not just physically. If anything, the traveling and wounds in my hands and arms were wearing down my ability to manage the sorrow, confusion and ache of losing my world, my family, my life.

Desperation it is. It was creeping up on me, perhaps spurred on by exhaustion and the quiet days of travel. I slid into the deep, dark thoughts I'd been fighting since I left the eighteen forties.

We rode for quite a while. I was guessing he wanted to put distance between us and the trading post, in case someone came after us. The night was cool, but I was soon shedding my over tunic, hot despite the breeze of early fall that tickled my hair. I threw my head back to gaze at the diamonds glittering in the black silk of a sky above. It was beautiful, raw.

"What do you do, Moonbeam?" he asked curiously.

I blinked and lowered my gaze from the sky. My horse had stopped, and I was leaning back precariously on its back. "I'm not sure." I straightened. The pain in my arms and legs was gone, except for the cut in my hand that had been soaked with filth. I lifted it to my eyes, amazed by the stardust around it. Too hot, I fumbled to peel off another layer – and stopped.

"Batu."

He was already headed back towards me. I struggled to focus on him.

"You are not well," he observed. His features were blurry.

"I think I have an … infection."

With little finesse, he hauled me off my horse onto his. "We cannot stop here. I know a place where we'll be safe close to here."

"Hot," I complained and shifted in front of him.

"No fussing, lamb," he said, amused. He rested one hand on my clammy forehead. "You are fevered."

"Don't cut off my hand," I whispered.

He said something else, but it slid through my thoughts and out. My eyes closed. I was overheating and beginning to shiver.

This can't be how it ends.

Chapter Nine

I WENT IN AND OUT OF CONSCIOUSNESS, RESTLESS SLEEP, VISIONS of Batu leaning over me and fevered dreams. The dreams were always about Taylor or growing up in the house of my aunt and uncle. Adopted by them when I was young, I had been a member of their family as long as I could remember.

I missed them. I missed Taylor.

They might as well have never existed.

My hand blazed with fiery pain, eclipsing the rest of my aches and pains a hundredfold.

Stuck in the misery, new thoughts overtook me when the fever dreams finally receded. I witnessed Batu slaughter the men in the room over and over, envisioned Carter the night he sent me back in time. My mind was too jumbled and taxed to form any other coherent thought but this: for whatever reason, I was meant to be here. Whether or not I ever left wasn't something I controlled or could count on, and I definitely couldn't dive after every man wearing a jewelry box I mistook for a phone.

Batu was right. One day, he might not be there, and I'd be killed in the drop of a hat.

My future was therefore clearer: it was to survive the day to day of a world I couldn't quiet grasp.

This all slid away when genuine sleep claimed me. I sank into it gratefully and awoke when an evening breeze tickled the skin of my exposed arm.

I was weak, hungry and fatigued. Sitting up, I registered the sound of a stream or small river first and the felt walls of the tent second. It was raining outside though the interior was dry.

I absolutely *reeked.* The scent came from my clothing, left over from the refuse in the bucket at the trading post.

"You are alive." He sounded upbeat.

I sat and gazed at my injured palm. It was still puffy and red but not alarmingly so. Doubting they had any sort of antibiotics in this time period, I studied it, puzzled. "How did you stop the infection?"

"Urine."

I looked up at him. "What?"

He gave me another odd look.

"You peed on my hand?" I stared at it, horrified.

"It will stop an infection. How do you not know this?"

I couldn't take my own smell or dwell too long on the idea he'd been peeing on my hand. Something within me snapped.

Close to tears, I crawled out of the tent. I wore a tunic that reached my knees and nothing else, but I didn't care. Half walking, half staggering through a chilly sheet of rain, I made it to the cold stream and waded in until it reached my waist. Flinging off the smelly tunic, I sat. Cold water covered my shoulders and lapped at my chin.

"Can't take this," I whispered and began to scrub at my hands and arms, wanting the refuse and filth off me. "Can't get home." Rain and tears blurred my eyes. I was nearly too weak to stand. For the first time in my life, I considered how much easier it'd be to float away than spend another day struggling with my world and thoughts.

I dunked my head and scrubbed at my scalp and hair without being able to clear my nose of the smell or my heart of the fear.

I'm never going home. I had considered the possibility before. With my body and mind fatigued, the thoughts were able to penetrate any sort of denial or hope between me and the reality of being stuck here, of never seeing my family again. The cage where I trapped my emotions for Taylor was cracked as well.

I was never supposed to go home or be happy, not if Carter had his way.

Then why did I want him to save me when I knew very well he wasn't going to? I was better off starting a new life here, accepting the fact I'd never see my aunt again or join her for yoga and coffee on Saturday mornings.

I was never going home. Ever. Not in any scenario, no matter what Taylor's people promised me or how many pills Carter sent me to swallow. Taylor was gone, and so was my life.

I didn't have a chance to grieve for him. It suddenly seemed selfish not to have shed a few tears for the man who wanted to spend his life with me, who helped me when I needed it and forgave me knowing what I was going to do to him. After all, no one else but me would mourn him – and he deserved to be remembered.

The emotions I'd been avoiding since I began my adventures washed over me, overwhelming my fatigued mind, and I began to cry. Sensing I wouldn't be able to fight the onslaught of grief, I scooted back until I was safe on the bank, folded my arms around my shaking legs, and sobbed.

Aware of Batu, I wasn't able to push him away when he scooped me into his arms and walked through the rain back to the tent. I huddled and cried, shaking from cold and emotion.

Moments later, he wrapped his arms around me and pulled me into him, draping his tunic over me the way he had the other day. Instead of holding me between his inner and outer layers of clothing, I was in direct contact with his warm skin. I pushed my face into his chest, uncurling from my ball, and clung to him, sobbing my heart out.

I fell into another, shorter fevered state complete with crazy dreams. It didn't last long, and I awoke in the morning, possible a day or two later, weak but also far more energized than I had been the previous time. Pushing myself up, I checked my hand. It was bandaged, and I wore another long tunic, this one clean. My hair was in my face, and I nudged it back, too exhausted to braid it.

Sun shone outside the tent. It was cool and bright with the scent of wet earth in the air.

Batu wasn't around. I was almost grateful; I wasn't sure how to explain my breakdown. I rifled around until I found pants and my boots then left the tent. The horses were near the stream, though Batu wasn't within sight. A fire had burnt out nearby, and his bow and arrow were seated on a tree stump.

The sight of it reminded me of a newly formed resolution I made some time in my fevered state. I was going to try to make it in this world, which meant being … useful. My twenty first century skill set and Internet finesse were wasted in a time when survival was the main focus. I hadn't ever been camping before this or started a fire or hunted or done anything remotely helpful to me here.

"At least I can speak languages." It was my greatest asset to the thirteenth century, though in all honesty, it didn't do me much good wandering the wilderness with Batu. I wasn't helping him any.

I had to prove to *me* my life was worth saving.

Approaching his weapons, I picked up the bow again and looked it over. There had to be something I was missing about how to use it. I would've given anything for a Wikihow video or Wikipedia article on the mechanics of using a bow and arrow.

I lowered it and gazed around with a shiver. What if he didn't come back one day? How the hell was I going to survive this place?

Clenching my jaw, I lifted the bow. "If a three year old can do this, I can," I muttered. I positioned it the way he showed me and tried to draw it once more.

In my weakened condition, I didn't even make it the inch I had last time. I relaxed, repositioned my feet and then sucked in a deep breath, pulling with all my might.

It was useless. *I* was useless. Frustrated, I picked up an arrow and tried again.

"What do you do, goddess?" Batu's quiet voice came from behind me. I didn't hear his silent step and turned to see he had a quail and three rabbits strung together and hanging from his waist.

"I need to learn to do things here," I said.

He lifted his catches. "Can you skin animals?"

The sight of blood, and the dead animals, dismayed me. I was an animal lover. I ate meat but I didn't think I could get through skinning a rabbit without breaking down into tears. "I can try," I said with a half-hearted shrug.

Batu laughed.

"There must be something I can do," I said, searching his features.

He tossed the animals beside the fire and approached, reclaiming his bow and the arrow I'd attempted to notch. "You are not meant for such labors, goddess."

"How will I survive? What if something happens to you?" I searched his face, frowning. His dark eyes took in my features. He reached out and tilted my chin to peer into my eyes then lifted my bad hand to inspect it. "I can't take care of myself the way everyone else here can."

"Everyone has a skill," he stated and released me. He appeared satisfied I was no longer ill. "Not everyone hunts. Not everyone tends the fire."

"You can do it all."

"I'm a warrior, ugly one. You are not."

I breathed out a puff of frustrated air. Batu stepped out of my personal space and went to the tree stump to sit and skin animals. "Then what is my skill to help us survive?"

"You entertain me."

"No, really, Batu!"

"We will discover it."

He didn't know either. I should've known this, but it still hurt a little to think he thought so little of me. "I'm totally lost."

"You are right here. How can you be lost?" With his back to me, I wasn't able to tell if he was messing with me or not.

"Because I don't belong here. I feel lost in every way."

"Then I will find you and remind you of where you are." This time, I heard the humor in his voice. "You cannot be lost if someone finds you, Moonbeam."

His logic defied me sometimes. I circled him to see him yanking the skin of rabbits with ease that left me a little sick to my stomach. It added to my sense of helplessness to control my fate or even whether I lived or died on a daily basis without his help.

"I can't stand it, Batu!" I nearly shouted.

He looked up at me.

"What am I supposed to be doing? Aren't I supposed to be … useful?" I demanded, uncertain how to explain I was having an existentialist crisis.

He lowered the rabbit in his hands. "I do not understand what you seek, goddess," he said, studying me. "You are angry, and I do not understand why."

"Because I feel … helpless. Useless. I'm not part of your world, Batu, and I am unprepared to be here, but I realize now I'm here for good. I can't go back to my home. I don't want to be a burden to you, and I don't want to die. So I'm stuck in this weird place."

He tilted his head to the side. "This is madness, goddess! Why does the lark sing or the deer leap?" he asked. "It is in their nature to do so, and we do not ask them why. It is not in your nature to hunt or skin animals or draw a bow. You are still part of this world. You should not question yourself this way. You are no burden to me."

He meant it. I didn't know how I was anything but a burden to someone like him, but his features were clear and dark gaze sincere. If anything, he was amused by my crisis.

His answer soothed me some. I sat down on the other side of the fire. He returned to his skinning and gutting, and I watched. He led a fairly simple life. He never asked why something happened or failed to roll with the punches. His outlook was grounded and very much in the present, while I felt like I had to find the deeper meaning in everything or uncover how today fit into the big picture of the overarching plan for my destiny.

I preferred his perception of the world. Grateful for today, unconcerned about tomorrow, Batu was the epitome of how my yoga instructor said we all should be.

Aside from the killing and the fact he's not vegan, I added mentally.

He had a way of calming my anxiety and grounding me, too, and he was definitely not bad to look at.

Maybe … he was what I should be like. Maybe I should notice the gorgeous stream or the grassy steppes stretching out to meet the sky and how far I could see instead of the internal agitation that had me running in circles tormented about why here, why now, why me.

Which wasn't like me. Before my first journey through time, I was very laid back and capable of going with the flow. The Old West was eye opening in so many ways, a growing experience unlike any I had been prepared for.

I wanted to let go of all that, though, the emotions and doubt and fear and everything else that sent me into a tailspin or prevented me from moving forward.

"I have languages," I murmured.

"A great skill indeed. You can barter with traders, command our enemies to submit, and speak to all of the Empire's peoples."

"Yeah." It was a lot. I didn't see how it tied to survival, but Batu was probably right. Maybe everyone had a unique contribution to the Empire, as he said. Mine wasn't physical or part of the day-to-day but equally important. *At least, I hope so.* I didn't want him or anyone else getting sick of me and tossing me out to survive on my own. Because I knew I wasn't going to make it long. I didn't have the survivor's instinct.

"Do you feel well enough to travel?" he asked.

I nodded.

"My mother's clan is near here. We will seek refuge with them."

"Is your mother there?"

"She died when I was young," he replied.

"Oh. I'm so sorry, Batu."

"It is the nature of things."

Nothing fazed this guy, for which I was grateful, because I'd been an emotional mess since we met. I started to relax again, assured of my safety and companion in a way that flew out the window every time he drew his sword and started slaughtering people.

I had to stop questioning who he was as well, if I wanted to stay sane. The day-to-day approach was going to be the only way I'd make it here. This was to become my new home; I had to accept that and make it work.

He finished with his chore and tossed the meat into a small pot. Starting the fire once more, we sat while he boiled the meat. We ate a cup of soup before he drained the water and packed up the meat in a bag.

I tried to help get the horses ready, only to end up taxed and dizzy. I sagged against my horse.

"It is good you try," he said and took the saddle from my arms.

"Omigod! That's the worst thing you've said to me yet," I said with a tired sigh.

He smiled and saddled my horse before lifting me on top of it. His strength left me stunned once more, and I wasn't about to think about how much he did for me when I was unconscious or fevered.

"Batu, thank you for taking care of me when I was ill," I said, realizing I hadn't bothered to acknowledge all he'd done.

"Do not thank me for my duty, goddess," he said, uninterested. He mounted his horse. "Though had I sold you to the trader at the post, I might be home by now."

"*Sold* me?" I repeated, startled. "Were you shopping around?"

He turned his horse away before I could glimpse his face. "I had several offers."

It took a moment for my shock to wear off. Nudging my horse forward, I drew abreast of him and stared at his features. "You weren't considering it, were you?" I questioned.

"You would command much more at the Imperial City."

I grumbled at him under my breath but really didn't fault him too much. If he'd known I was going to get sick, he probably would've sold me.

He glanced at me, and I saw the sparkle in his eyes.

"You are not funny," I told him.

"I do not try to be, ugly one. I did receive offers, and you would fetch more at the Imperial City. But I do not wish to sell you."

"Because I amuse you? Or was it your honor that demanded a higher price?"

"Honor has no price. You are also beautiful, and you have a good heart, even if you are confused."

I started to respond and then stopped. Did he compliment me or insult me? Or was he being … him and speaking his mind without intent to do either?

"If you decide to sell me, will you tell me in advance?" I asked.

The corners of his lips quirked up in his half smile. "So you can run, lamb?"

I hate that tone. The low growl, the one that told me was pretty serious about sinking his teeth into me, was nothing short of terrifying. "Maybe I'll try to kill you instead. I've seen you chop off enough heads I might be able to do it."

"You cannot skin a rabbit, goddess. How will you harm a man?"

I couldn't. I knew it. He knew it. "You won't sell me, will you? One day I'll be too old to be beautiful and too bitter to make you laugh."

"No, Moonbeam. Even then, I would not sell you."

I couldn't figure this guy out. His teasing was almost too subtle for me to catch it, and his dedication to duty and honor so singularly focused, it didn't seem possible. How did someone obsessed with honor slaughter everyone who came within arm's reach?

"At least you admit I'm not ugly," I said, taking what small victory I could with the perplexing man beside me.

He smiled without responding.

We rode for most of the day. I didn't make it to noon before exhaustion overtook me. It then became a challenge to stay awake, despite the relative discomfort of being on horseback and sweating in the late summer sun.

So entrenched was I in not falling off my horse or dropping into the sleep beckoning me that I didn't notice the city of mushroom tents until we were nearly upon them. Startled at how dulled my senses were, I blinked to make sure I wasn't hallucinating. They were really there. Several hundred tents flanked on three sides by herds of animals. Someone I took to be a guard rode out to us when we were half a mile away.

"Batu!" he exclaimed when close enough.

I focused on the mane of my horse, not feeling well enough at all to care what they spoke about. A real bed was my only concern. That, and not embarrassing myself by falling off my horse before we made it to the tent town.

The rider returned to the tents, and soon, several people were gathered at its edge. I didn't feel up to greeting anyone and sighed. It was past sunset, though plenty of light remained. My legs were shaky, my hand throbbing and my skin clammy.

But I wasn't going to tell Batu I was weak.

We reached the people, and he dismounted, cheerfully greeting several men and two older women. I waited until everyone's attention was elsewhere before dismounting and leaning against my horse.

How was it possible I felt worse on the ground than I did in the saddle? I leaned for a long moment, closing my eyes and breathing in the scent of leather and horse. Gathering what strength I had left, I straightened, resolved not to appear weak to the hardy people of the steppes.

Several more people had joined Batu, who appeared to be telling a story by the grin on his face and his expressive hand gestures.

"Moonbeam?" The voice was ancient, thin and papery.

I faced the old woman who looked like she was over a hundred. Wrinkles engulfed her feature as she smiled. White hair was piled on top of her head, and she was hunched over a cane. Her dark eyes were bright, and she wore a white feather in her hair.

White feather. Like that worn by the spry young woman who helped me when I first landed in Mongol Empire before the pills.

"Ghoajin?" I asked hesitantly.

She laughed, the sound coming out mostly air.

"Omigod!" I was on the verge of squealing but didn't, not wanting to draw more attention to how different I was. I did, however, hug her gently.

"I told … Batu … to find you or not … return," she told me in her ancient voice.

I laughed. "You've lost none of your edge!" Leaning away, I was careful not to disrupt her precarious balance or mine.

"You have not … aged, Moonbeam," she said, squinting at my features. "What happened … to you?"

"Well, it's a little difficult to explain," I started. "I was put into a deep sleep for a very long time."

She nodded, though I sensed she didn't understand. I didn't know how anyone could. "It is good to see you, Moonbeam. You will … come to my *ger.*" She turned and started away. "Batu!" she belted.

I stifled a laugh. My suspicion that Batu was constantly being yelled at by someone in his family seemed to be correct. I already knew how fierce his great grandmother was and was pleased to see she'd lost none of her edge. I didn't know why I was so happy to see her, unless it was because of how little I connected to this time. She was a small anchor, one of the first people I met when I landed in a crater.

She was also a reminder of what Carter had done to me, of how Taylor's people had found me in her tent and forced me into the future a few decades.

I really didn't know what to think sometimes.

Not wanting to draw the wrath of the hundred-year-old dynamite of a woman, I trailed her as she walked slowly with the help of a boy around the age of thirteen or so.

Batu soon joined us and swept his great grandmother off her feet to carry her. I heard her grumble at him, and he ignored her.

It was hard for me to come to grips with the idea they had families, love, and somewhat normal lives when I also knew the boys and men around us were headed to war. The duality of this world stumped me, despite witnessing how Batu balanced being dedicated and lethal.

I followed them into a large white *ger* that appeared to be the same I had stayed in for a night seventy years ago. Pausing in the entrance, I looked around, a little unnerved at being once again where Taylor's people had grabbed me. I didn't see the massive, cloaked and masked figure who threatened to kill me last time I was here. I wanted to think he was dead by now.

But I knew better. He had been in the Old West with me and again in the tent of Ghoajin. He was a time traveler with his own mission, one I wasn't able to identify by his random interference.

"Moonbeam." Ghoajin had seated herself by the fire. She waved for me to join her.

I did so and slid into the space between her and Batu. Family members began scurrying into and out of the tent, laying out food for a large feast around the fire. I turned to speak to Ghoajin only to find the elderly woman nodding off. Taking pity on her, I glanced at Batu.

His eyes were on a woman across the tent, one who was staring back at him briefly until she noticed I was looking at her, too. Young and pretty, I sensed there was or had been something between them.

"You know her?" I asked, curious about the side of Batu that didn't involve war and survival.

"Yes." His gaze dropped to the fire. "She was to be my wife, if I had not chosen to become a guardian."

"Oh." Why did I feel a small twinge of envy? Or was it jealousy? "Maybe she will wait until you are forty seasons and marry you."

He snorted. "She married another." The words were casual with no sign of suffering, yet I sensed there was more to the story or at least, emotions he was glossing over.

My Batu was not as simple as I thought.

And I really was jealous. I had no idea why, though. He had never shown interest in me, and I certainly didn't gravitate towards someone who was violent.

"I'm sorry," I said. "I took you from her, didn't I?"

"I chose duty," he replied with a shrug. "I knew what that meant."

"But that doesn't mean it's easy."

He met my gaze. "You are right, Moonbeam. It was not easy, but it was right."

I wished I could think of Taylor in that light. His loss could never be right or necessary.

Batu and I looked at each other for a long moment. The exchange felt … intimate, two people who understood loss and the suffering that followed. I dropped my gaze to the fire, not liking the way my blood often stirred when we gazed too long at one another.

"Moonbeam, where did Batu … find you?" Ghoajin asked, awake once more.

"Tell us a story, Batu!" one of the children exclaimed.

A chorus of others joined in.

Batu rose, and they fell silent. "Are you prepared for a tale of adventure, battle and magic?" he started solemnly.

The *ger* was silent. The woman preparing food smiled at one another at his dramatic start, and the children all gathered around the feast.

Someone set a wooden plate of food before me, and I ate.

Batu stepped away and began a ridiculously melodramatic re-enactment of being captured by the Arabs, tortured in their dungeon and then breaking free to rescue me and battle free from the soldiers at the castle. He mixed humor and hyperbole, brandishing his sword to fight off imaginary attackers and pretending to stroke his hair whenever he mentioned me.

I found myself laughing along with the others. I already knew he had a sense of humor, and seeing his one-man play helped me appreciate his view of the world even more. I wasn't accustomed to being the serious, pensive one, but between the two of us, I was.

The children cheered when he reached the end of his tale, and he bowed to them. Batu sat at the feast down the table. The space beside me had been taken by an older woman.

Too exhausted to do more than eat, I listened to those talk around me and answered the questions Ghoajin directed my way. This felt like a welcome home party for me as well as Batu. It was an odd sensation, one I wasn't sure was appropriate. It wasn't my homecoming, or wouldn't feel like it, if Ghoajin wasn't present and hadn't given me the seat of honor at her side.

My gaze drifted more than once to the pretty woman Batu had wanted to marry. She had three kids of her own hanging around her, all under the age of five, and was cheerful and outgoing. It was a good thing, except I could tell by Batu's occasional glance in her direction that he bore some sadness about his choice.

I understood regrets in a way I hadn't when I went on my first adventure. It was heavy knowledge, and I didn't like it. I had the feeling Batu saw what I did when he looked at the woman he wanted to marry: the opportunity to be normal that he passed up.

Neither of us was going to qualify as normal people in our lifetimes, no matter where or when those lives occurred. As he often said, it was the nature of things.

The party continued into the night, until my recovering body began to slouch of its own accord. My eyelids grew too heavy to keep open, and I rested my elbows on my knees and struggled not to fall asleep in my plate. I was full and comfortable, warmed by the fire and cheered by the happy people around me. Seeing Ghoajin was an unexpected morale boost. I wiped my face and drank more water to help me stay awake.

"You need rest, goddess," Batu said from behind me.

Blinking, I twisted. I hadn't noticed him move from his spot down the table, but I'd stopped noticing much of anything. "I don't want to offend Ghoajin," I murmured.

"She is asleep. She cannot be offended."

I looked at her and saw she was indeed out cold, her head resting on the shoulder of the woman beside her. I smiled and made it to my feet.

Several people called out to him as we left the feast while the others seemed content to eat and talk. The night chill helped my senses awaken some, and I hugged myself, following Batu through the tents.

He ducked into one, and I followed, pausing inside the entrance. "Whose *ger* is this?"

"My mother's. She had no children but me. They leave it up for when I visit."

"Do you visit often?"

"When possible."

"I can't believe Ghoajin is still alive." The words sounded morbid aloud, and I glanced at him, rushing on. "That came out wrong. I'm sorry."

Batu was peeling off his weapons. "She is the oldest living member of any steppe tribe. You are right to be surprised, ugly one."

I smiled, dwelling on how much time had passed with some disbelief. I could've played it off as not happening if I hadn't met her when she was young. Carter's brilliance – and the idea I could've been stored like wine in someone's basement for seventy years – never ceased to terrify me. It was also amazing to have passed through time as I had and had met Ghoajin on either end.

"What do you do, goddess?"

Blinking out of my thoughts, I moved away from the entrance to the fire, where it was warmer. "Thinking about how I was asleep for so long. Where was my body while I slept?"

"It is not known. Some say you were buried with the Great Khan, Genghis. Some said you went back to Father Sky." He shrugged. "The Arabs found you, but I know not how. When I heard they had found you, I came after you."

If you hadn't killed Mahmood … I didn't let the thought stick around. It was likely I would never know for sure where I ended up sleeping away seventy years.

Batu approached me with new bandages the way he had since finding me. He unwrapped my hands and arms, inspected them and then rewrapped the bad hand and opposite forearm. "The others need air," he explained and tossed the used bandages into the fire.

Peeling off his tunics and boots, he dropped into the bed opposite the door, his bare chest drawing my attention.

"There's only one bed," I complained, looking around.

"We have slept together since meeting, goddess. Why does it bother you now?"

I rolled my eyes at him. "We had no choice in the wilderness."

"Then sleep by the fire. I am in need of a real bed." He rolled his muscular back to me.

I guess it doesn't matter. It just seemed weird to sleep with him when we weren't trapped in a pup tent built for one. But I wasn't about to sleep by the fire as he suggested. I, too, needed a real bed and a good night of sleep.

Stripping off my boots, I snuggled into bed with him. He was right; we had been sleeping together for a few days at least. One more wasn't going to matter, and … I kind of looked forward to his warmth and strength at night. In a world that scared me, he left me feeling protected.

Pressing my back to his, I couldn't help wishing I could wake up to a hot bath in the morning to soothe my aching legs.

"Batu, do you regret not staying here and marrying the woman you wanted to?" I asked drowsily.

"I do not regret any choice I have made."

Of course not. What an ass. "I saw how you looked at her."

"What purpose does regretting a choice serve, goddess?" he responded. "It cannot be changed, and I made it with honor."

"But don't you *feel* anything?" I asked in irritation, sitting up to stare at him. "You cannot go through the world without feelings. It's not possible." He had issues expressing his emotions; this much I knew.

"I *feel,* ugly one. I do not let this control me." He twisted to see me. "You feel too much."

"I do not."

"It controls you, does it not?"

"It didn't use to." I shook my head. "You're right, I think. You're always right. I don't understand how it's so easy for you to just … live."

He chuckled. "What else would I do if not live?"

He was either being dense or didn't understand what I was trying to say. Either way, I was done for the night. "Sleep well, Batu." I settled back into the bed, my back to him.

"And you?" he asked, shifting. "Do you regret Taylor?"

"No. Yes. I don't know."

"You are peculiar, Moonbeam. How do you not know your own mind?"

"It's complicated."

He wrapped an arm around me, the way he had since the first night in the pup tent. I started to object – but liked being there too much to tell him to back off. He was warm, solid, and strong. He grounded me when I was tired, sick or scared of my new world. Relaxing into him, I lifted my head for him to shift an arm beneath my neck.

I liked it when he held me.

"How so?" He sounded drowsy. He pulled me into his heat.

"I don't regret meeting him. I regret the circumstances that placed us together, and I also regret …" *making him cease to exist.*

"These are not things to regret," Batu said. "This is –"

"- the nature of things. I know."

"You have a delicate heart. If you killed him, this regret I would understand. But you are not capable of taking a life."

I was quiet, staring at the fire in the middle of the tent.

"Moonbeam?" There was an odd note in his voice. "Why do you choose to be quiet now?"

"Because I'm tired."

"You did take his life."

"Good night, Batu!"

He pushed himself up on his elbow, removing my pillow. Batu pushed me onto my back. He gazed down at me, surprise on his features.

"You, Moonbeam, murdered your husband?"

"I did not murder him," I snapped and tried to push him away.

He captured both wrists in one hand easily and pinned them to my chest, unconcerned with any attempt I made to escape. He was too strong to be remotely fazed. "But you had a hand in it," he said, reading my features. "You were involved somehow."

I sighed, resistance deflating with the aid of exhaustion and sorrow. "Yes, I did," I admitted. Lying took energy. I sucked at it to begin with, and I had no energy to spare. Batu was too relentless to let me lie to him. "Someone used me to get close to him then killed him."

"But it was not your sword," he pointed out. "Why are you guilty for an act that was not yours?"

"I don't want to talk about it." I tugged at my hands.

He smiled, aware I wasn't going anywhere until he got what he wanted.

"You can be a real ass, Batu," I muttered. "Why do you care?"

"Because you do not wish me to know. It is important to you, so it is important to your guardian."

I was too tired to debate his logic. "Taylor knew he was dying. Before he did, he forgave me for my involvement in his murder and told me I had … made a difference in his life. Everyone around me died, Batu. Not just him. I was the only one who survived, and that feels … wrong. His kindness in his last moment feels wrong. Telling me I meant something to him despite what was going to happen …wrong." I clamped my mouth closed, close to tears. "I shouldn't have survived and he shouldn't have died. If we had never met, he wouldn't have."

Understanding crossed Batu's features. He released my hands.

The truth was out. There was no need to fight him anymore. I wiped my eyes quickly and sighed, struggling for control of my emotions. "That's why I'm sad," I said tightly. I rolled onto my side once more, hoping he took the hint to leave me alone.

For once, he did. Batu lay down once more, resuming his position holding me. He had to have noticed my irregular breathing as I worked on composing myself once more, but he was mercifully quiet. If anything, he held me more tightly, and his body against mine soothed the emotions I couldn't control.

While I appreciated his silence, it also bothered me to think he might be judging me for the first time.

Eventually, I fell into a deep, dreamless slumber.

Chapter Ten

I AWOKE ALONE THE NEXT MORNING AND WAS SOON COLLECTED by Ghoajin for a tour of the encampment. We walked among the members of her clan for most of the morning. She proudly introduced me as the goddess she had told everyone about and explained to me everything we saw, from how the women trained the children to ride horses, shoot bows, and maintain weapons to which principal members of the clan had how many herds of goats, sheep and horses.

We were followed by a trail of women and children, along with some younger boys who had not yet been sent off to the war camp nearby for further warrior training. Women ran the encampment, she told me, and what we saw seemed to support this. Aside from Batu, the only men of fighting age present were wounded, slaves, or men there for the protection of the camp.

I had run into the concept of slavery in the Old West. It made me extremely uncomfortable, but what I saw here was a little different than I expected. The slaves were expected to serve the families that owned them but were also free to intermarry with the Mongols, buy their freedom by volunteering to fight, or provided accommodations if they had special skills. Some were adopted, others rewarded with horses and others strung out in the sun with whip markings as a warning against stealing or disrespecting their owners.

It was another display of the world that bred a man like Batu: barbarity and generosity side by side with loyalty trumping pretty much everything else.

And then there was the harem. It was contained in a large tent and owned by one of Ghoajin's nephews, who was the chief of the clan. No one was permitted to enter without his permission or paying off someone.

We didn't go inside, for which I was grateful. It was hard enough for me to put aside my twenty-first century American morals and perceptions without being confronted by the existence of sex slaves. Ghoajin assured me the women were treated well, but …

It didn't sit right. In the Old West, there had been a brothel that fascinated me, but a harem sounded a little more sinister to me. I was working on not judging the culture or the people around me for living the lives they thought were natural.

We stopped at noon to give Ghoajin a break and sat down in the shade of a tree for a light lunch with several of her great grandchildren and the children of Batu's ex, who accompanied us, along with several other women. I watched the kids play with a smile.

"I am glad Batu brought you back," Ghoajin said. "When he was six, his mother died. He left his father's clan and … disappeared." She paused to catch her breath. "For ten years. He was gone. And then he came back, to us, his mother's … people. He knew how to fight and was determined … to become a champion warrior."

I listened, fascinated by the story about a man I barely knew.

"He was consumed by the need to prove himself," his ex, a woman named Suvdin, added.

"He was," Ghoajin agreed. "He never spoke of ... what happened when he left. But he came back ... with fire."

It was difficult for me to imagine a child of six surviving this brutal world on his own. Then again, I could almost believe it about Batu.

"He is fire," Suvdin said. "He consumes or is cold. He does nothing or he conquers all. He is much like the tales we heard of Genghis."

Ghoajin nodded proudly.

I detected some ... wistfulness or maybe regret in the soft tone of Suvdin. Batu claimed not to be dwelling on his choice of duty over the woman he cared about, but she seemed to be. I shivered at her description, able to understand how right she was about Batu. His fierce devotion and loyalty, coupled with his athletic prowess, was a combination that would be explosive in a real relationship. She was right; he would burn up the woman of his focus with possessive passion.

Hearing her talk about him made me feel awkward around her, a little too aware that I slept in his bed, albeit platonically. He wasn't mine, and I had no intention of ever marrying again, but for the sake of his people's customs, I was the woman at the center of his world.

Two girls sat down behind me. "Moonbeam, can we touch your hair?" one asked.

"Yes," I said with a smile. They'd been eyeing me for most the morning.

One pulled out the pins holding it up in a bun, and they both gasped when it spilled down my shoulders. The two immediately began whispering and alternately braiding or twisting my hair. It felt nice to have someone mess with my hair the way my aunt used to every once in a while. Content, I gazed out over the encampment below the hill we sat on.

This … this was my new life. It was foreign, scary and very different, but it was where I had landed and where I'd remain. I wanted to be more like Batu, to let go of the decisions of the past and live for today. It was going to be a struggle to learn their world and customs, but I also had a great deal of time.

Batu was wrestling with boys in their early teens just outside of the tent city, teaching them moves and correcting their forms while they practiced. I watched him without the ability to understand the emotions that often stirred when I spoke to him or spent the night in his arms. Whatever they were, they were gradually becoming stronger – and they weren't bad, which I think surprised me more than anything else.

"Suvdin," I started quietly. "Can you teach me to shoot a bow and arrow?"

She appeared pleased. "Of course, Moonbeam. This is a great honor."

I wasn't certain what to say. They had some weird deference for me, despite me telling them repeatedly that I was a normal person.

Normal people don't reappear seventy years later without having aged a day. I tried to dismiss this thought, wanting to fit in and become what they viewed as normal around here.

"Do you wish to start now?" Suvdin asked.

"Yes, that'd be great," I said. "If it's okay with you, Ghoajin?" I asked uncertainly, not wanting to abandon my hostess.

"I am surprised Batu has … not taught you," she replied. "He is a good boy, but he has … always been different. I will … remind him to respect … those he should respect."

I started to laugh but stopped, seeing how serious she was about yelling at her great grandson.

Suvdin smiled and shooed away the two little girls who had put random, lopsided braids in my hair and waited for me to rise. We walked down the hill, towards the area where the children around seven had been taking an archery class earlier. A barrel filled with practice bows of different sizes was present at one end, targets at the other.

Suvdin sized me up and selected one, handing it to me. Not wanting to embarrass myself by failing to draw it, I waited for her instructions.

She chose another and motioned for me to line up behind a rock demarking the area where shooters stood. With simple instructions and many, many corrections, she began to teach me. To my delight, I was able to draw the bow she chose. It was hard but nothing like Batu's.

Everything seemed to be going well, until I shot my first arrow.

It landed two feet in front of me. I groaned. My right arm was sore already. It was harder than it looked to hold back the bowstring.

"You must hold your form," Suvdin said, trying not to smile. "Nothing moves until the arrow is gone." She adjusted my form. "Try again."

I lifted the bow and notched an arrow. This time, Suvdin kept one of her hands under my right elbow to prevent it from dropping before I fired. With the other, she braced the front of the bow, taking some of the strain off me.

This time when I shot, it landed five feet in front of the target. "We did it!" I exclaimed. "We got close!"

Suvdin nodded and ducked her head.

"Fine. Laugh," I said. "Batu said three year olds can draw a bow better than me."

"I would say children of five seasons," Suvdin replied kindly.

"Thanks." A little embarrassed, I was also proud for having done this well. "Again!"

She helped me five more times before stepping back to watch me fire on my own. I did worse without her help but not as bad as the first time. I tried a few more times, excited I was at least shooting in the right direction. Mostly. Everything I shot went left.

"What do you aim at, goddess?" Batu's voice was amused.

"Isn't it obvious? The point five feet in front of the target," I retorted.

Suvdin did laugh this time. "Her aim is better than yours, Batu."

"So I see." He circled us, trailed by two younger boys I took to be cousins. He was scrutinizing my form with intensity that left me warm and self-conscious.

"Suvdin says I shoot like a five year old, not a three year old," I added, somewhat satisfied.

"She is being kind," he replied, eyes sparkling. "Let me see. Shoot at your target." He crossed his arms.

I lifted the bow and arrow, rejuvenated after the brief rest and with newfound adrenaline pumping through my veins. I hit my usual target – a random spot five feet before the box I was supposed to hit.

"It is an improvement," Suvdin said.

Batu approached. He stood in front of me, close enough for his body heat to reach me. "Show me again."

I lifted the bow. He tilted my right elbow up a little more then rested his hand on my left elbow and lifted a few inches. Content, he stepped back.

"Take a deep breath and release."

I did as he said. To my delight, my arrow reached the target this time, though it was nowhere near the dot at the center.

"She can be taught," he allowed.

"She shows promise, Batu," Suvdin chided him gently. "It is clear she has never held a bow. She will progress, perhaps as far as a child of ten seasons."

"Nine."

She smiled.

"Thanks for the vote of confidence, both of you," I said, too cheered by the fact I did it to care if they didn't think me capable of outlearning someone half my size. "I'm ready for war."

Batu chuckled. "No, goddess, you are not. You will not see war." The edge in his tone wasn't one I had heard before.

Glancing at him, I thought I saw a shadow cross his features. It didn't seem possible Batu had even more depth than I suspected last night. I was more curious about him after his great grandmother's tale about his disappearance.

Catching myself staring, I left the barrel to retrieve my arrows. I collected them all and returned. Suvdin's attention was on Batu; his focus, however, was on me. They were talking quietly.

Ghoajin appeared from behind a nearby tent, trailed by her entourage. "Batu!" she barked.

"Yes, grandmother," he said, a trace of a smile on his features.

I grinned, loving her abruptness with the men of her family.

"We must talk."

He moved away from Suvdin to attend his grandmother.

"I love Ghoajin," I told Suvdin. "She yelled at her husband like that, too."

"She is a strong woman," Suvdin agreed. "Are you comfortable here? Batu has said this is not your world and the bow seems to frustrate you."

"I am, thank you. I want to fit in."

"The Empire welcomes everyone. You do not need to change who you are, Moonbeam. Your gifts are such that they support the Empire and its people."

Every once in a while, when someone said *Empire*, I envisioned spaceship battles from Star Wars. This empire seemed more forgiving than Darth Vader or the Emperor, though I suspected life as a slave wasn't the greatest.

"Batu says you are to stay here for a short time. You will be welcomed to return at any time."

"Thanks," I murmured. "I don't know what his plans are. It's apparent I can't go anywhere without him." I waved towards the targets. "I'd starve in a day."

Suvdin ducked her head with another smile. "He will take care of you. He is a good man." The wistfulness was back. I applauded her silently for not seeming jealous, though maybe she understood my relationship with Batu wasn't what hers would've been, had they married. I was a ward, not a wife. "It is time for Ghoajin to rest."

Suvdin moved away from me, towards the gaunt, tiny figure lecturing her much larger great grandson. The families were close, loyal and interconnected. I imagined the probability of survival was higher in a community such as this. It was different than the more independent way of life I was accustomed to. There was no driving out of town to visit friends or family without knowing how to hunt or fend for myself during the time I was gone.

I was slowly puzzling through how to make it here. A tremor of fear and uncertainty slid through me at the thought of never seeing home again. It was a lot to let go of, and I didn't know exactly how to release my past or my hope of seeing home one day.

Be like Batu, I told myself. If I narrowed my focus to today, I'd survive. I had to stay occupied and continue learning.

Not yet fully recovered from my own ordeal, I was almost grateful to see Ghoajin and Suvdin move away with their entourage. I needed a snack and a nap. One glance around was enough to tell me I had no clue which of the identical mushrooms was the tent I could rest in.

Replacing the bow in the barrel, I walked to Batu. "I'm not sure which one is ours," I admitted. "Can you take me back to the *ger*?"

He turned away and guided us through the maze of tents, ducking into one. I trailed him and sighed upon entering, beat from the hours I spent on my feet learning about the camp. The fire at the center was out, though the tent remained warm.

"You are well?" he asked.

"Yeah. Tired." I sat down beside the fire. My legs were stiff from horseback riding, too. I was a mess. "Suvdin is really nice."

"She is."

I glanced at him. As if expecting me to watch his reaction, he gave a half smile.

"My little lamb is trying to be clever," he said. "I prefer you honest, goddess. Too many men and women are foxes."

"It's not my concern how you feel about her after all this time," I said. "I guess I'm curious."

"I am happy, ugly one." He sat down opposite me. "This is not what concerns you."

"No." I hesitated. He was easy to talk to, more so than anyone else I'd ever met. "It's not easy to give up something you care about. I'm not sure how I can let go of my world, my family, my friends."

"You think too much."

I rolled my eyes at him. He was probably right, but it was still irksome for him to say such a thing aloud. "Okay. Then I'm taking a nap," I said and rose. "Leave me alone for a while."

"Do you wish me to sing you to sleep?"

Flinging myself into bed, I considered his request. His weird singing did have a tranquilizing effect, one that cleared my busy thoughts. "Yes."

The low rumble began, and I closed my eyes.

Within seconds, I was out.

It was dark when my nap was over. I crawled out of bed and stretched. Batu was gone, though his gear was present. I tugged on my over tunic and left the tent. The night was not quite cold enough to see my breath but close. The temperature extremes here had to be close to thirty degrees over the course of twenty-four hours.

Making my way in the direction of the bow practice area, I paused to listen to what sounded like another feast coming from the opposite direction. I didn't feel up to people tonight, which was unusual for me. I was normally pretty outgoing. The nap helped clear my mind though I was still more emotional than usual, given my situation.

I went to the bow and arrow area instead. It was dark, except for the brilliant starlight and the warm glow of mushroom tents around me. Sorting through the bows, I tested three before identifying the one I thought I'd used earlier with Suvdin.

"Okay," I murmured, mentally reviewing what she'd taught me. I took a breath and followed her instructions. My arms were a little steadier after rest, and I aimed carefully at the target.

Releasing the arrow, I frowned. It landed in the same area as earlier, to the left of center, five feet in front of the target.

I tried again.

And again.

"If nothing else, I'm nailing that spot," I said and lowered the bow. I rolled my shoulders, at a loss as to how to fix either my aim or distance issue.

"You favor your right arm and left eye."

Turning at Batu's voice, I frowned at him. I wasn't surprised to see him there; he had a knack for finding me, which I attributed to the fact he was obligated to protect me and knew I was helpless. "What do you mean?"

"They are stronger." He plucked a bow from the barrel and stood in front of me. "My right arm and right eye are stronger." He demonstrated by closing his left eye and pretending to aim. "Your eye and arm are mismatched." He closed his right eye this time.

"Oh." I fiddled with the bow. It was awkward to close my right eye and aim. "There's no fixing that, is there?"

"You can switch arms."

It took me a moment for my body to obey the command to swap. The new position was even more awkward than closing my right eye, my left arm considerably weaker.

Lowering the bow, I gazed up at him, disappointed.

"Or, you leave the bow to me," he said and took it from my hands. "Your skills lie elsewhere."

"I don't *want* them to," I said and snatched it back. "Where I'm from, I'm completely independent. It seems … wrong to depend on you or anyone else for surviving every day."

Batu considered me. "You will have to train your left arm or right eye."

"Let's do that."

He shifted to the barrel and retrieved a different bow. "This one is lighter." He swapped the one I held for the new one. "Left arm."

I lifted it. It was all kinds of uncomfortable.

Batu circled behind me to position and brace my elbows. His body heat was a pleasant contrast to the chilly night, and I shifted closer. Any qualms I had about personal space were mostly gone with him after all he'd done when I was fevered and our nights together, but I had to admit – I kind of wanted him close, too.

I aimed and let the arrow loose. To my delight, it hit the bottom center of the target. "I'm doing it!"

Batu chuckled. He bent for another arrow and handed it to me before returning his hands to my elbows.

"Do you think I'll be as good as you one day?" I asked and focused on notching the arrow.

He was quiet.

"Batu?" I looked up at him over my shoulder. "Is silence your way of saying no?"

His gaze was on the target, and there was a trace of a smile on his features. "Do you prefer I lie to make you happy or tell the truth?"

I gave an exasperated sigh.

"Which one?" He nudged me with his hips since his hands were supporting my arms.

"Truth," I grumbled.

"You are better served learning a different skill."

I released the arrow. It landed beside the other. "At least I'm consistently bad."

He dropped his hands, and I turned to face him. There were moments when I found myself breathlessly intrigued by the exotically different man before me, and this was one of them. The starlight and darkness of night rendered his masculine features mysterious. His muscular frame was relaxed, his dark eyes on me as I watched him. His shaved head was shadowed from several days of growth.

He was attractive in a similar fashion to his world: raw, untamed and unnerving with relentless intensity. If Batu was a fire, this place was an oven. I didn't know where this sudden tension between us originated or why I hadn't noticed it before. It was not out of the picture to find him sexually attractive or to want something more, if I was stuck here. I had gone into my marriage with Taylor with too little care. I never planned on getting hitched again, but a lifetime without sex wasn't on the table, either.

Just … it was Batu, my guardian. If things went sour, we were stuck together until one of us was killed off. It didn't seem smart to dip my toe in the pool, yet the connection between us was too intense to deny it existed.

Unease stirred as I thought again of Taylor and my promise to myself never to connect with anyone or anywhere again. I had all but ditched that at this point, resolved by the fact I was stuck in the thirteenth century. But I didn't quite feel ready for anything more than what I had with him, either. The lesson I learned in the Old West was far too powerful: people around me died. Batu was in a position of irrefutable danger as my guardian.

I couldn't take another heartbreak. I didn't care how long I was in the Mongol Empire.

"I think I'm hungry," I said and cleared my throat. Stepping away, I crossed my arms. "You?"

He replaced the bows and arrows. I was no longer cold; the heat of awareness was skittering through my blood, heightening my senses, and leaving me too eager to experience the heat of Batu's body once more.

Rather than return us to our tent, he led me to Ghoajin's, where a boisterous feast was in full swing again tonight. We were warmly greeted, and I took a seat beside Suvdin.

We stayed into the wee hours of the evening before the wear and tear on my body dragged me close to a doze once more. Batu escorted me back to our tent, and I tugged off the over tunic, followed by my boots, the moment I stepped foot inside. Hoping the awkwardness from earlier was gone, I stumbled into bed and sighed.

"Suvdin is going to see if I am better suited towards any other skills tomorrow," I told him, eyes on the ceiling. "When I'm not translating, I want to be useful."

"You are determined, ugly one."

"I want to contribute, Batu. Is that so hard to understand?" I listened to the sounds of him undressing while forbidding myself to look. I already knew he had an incredible body, and I was working on suppressing the warmth of desire heating the base of my belly.

"No, goddess, it is not. You should not force it. Your skill will find you."

"Maybe. I need to keep occupied as much as possible, too."

"To take your mind off your home."

He read me way too well. I twisted my head to look at him. Shirtless, he was arranging his clothing and weapons on a blanket near the door. I watched the muscles of his chest and back slide beneath thick, smooth skin. "Thereabouts."

"Thereabouts," he repeated, amused, with a glance at me.

I wasn't certain what he found funny this time, either. While Batu wasn't complicated, he was too different for me to understand him at times. "Are you laughing at me?" I asked and sat up, wanting to know once and for all why he seemed so entertained by me.

"No, goddess."

"I swear, once a day at least, you look at me like you're laughing at me."

He shrugged. "You are different. I am trying to understand."

"Hmm. That's good."

He straightened from his chores and gazed at me, waiting.

"I don't understand you either," I told him. "You run around chopping off limbs and heads and then you hold me at night with such gentleness …" *Bad example.* My cheeks were warm. "You're so honorable, except when you're at battle."

"You do not believe battle to be honorable."

"I do not believe *killing* to be honorable."

"Ever?"

"No."

He studied me. "You believe me to hold no honor."

"No," I said quickly. "I don't believe that at all. I believe our worlds are very different, and I am trying to understand yours. You are very honorable in this world, but where I come from, it's … not like this. At all."

"You were raised to believe one way and now must adapt."

"Exactly."

"It is good you seek to adapt and not reject where you are."

"Thanks." *I think.* "I am trying to let go of where I came from, who I was there. It is a challenge."

When I looked up, he was smiling.

"What?" I demanded, exasperated. "Why are you laughing at me now?"

"I do not laugh at you, Moonbeam," he said and approached, dropping into the wide bed beside me. He rested on his back. "You are so grave about so many things."

"This is a very grave concern. How should I be?" I asked, confused. I shifted back to give him some room. My gaze instinctively went down his body, from the thick chest to his flat abs and narrow hips.

"You should trust you are where you should be."

"You have everything figured out," I said somewhat enviously. "How do you do it?" I stretched out on my side, head propped up and gaze on his features.

"See, hear, smell, feel."

I sighed. "I know. You don't dwell in your mind like I do. It's not that easy to turn off."

"It is."

"For you, maybe! I'm not some warrior brute who –"

He cupped his hand at the back of my neck and brought my face to his. His warm lips pressed to mine, and at once, my senses were flooded by the scent of his skin, the pressure of his mouth, the heat of his skin and solidness of the chest I braced myself against.

My thoughts vanished, sizzled away and replaced by my senses.

His kiss was gentle. At first, I was too surprised to move away, but shock melted into the tension between us, and I had no urge to leave his body.

I started to respond, felt what I did, and pulled away to stare at him.

He released me and returned the long look.

"You're right. It worked," I said, embarrassed by the lowered timbre of my voice. "Good night, Batu." Twisting, I lay down on my side, my back to him. I felt like running but had the sense he'd pursue if I did.

My pulse was roaring, the warmth at the base of my belly blazing.

"Good night, Moonbeam," he returned softly. He rolled onto his other side and pressed his back to mine. "We named you Moonbeam. Do you have a different name in your world?"

"Yes."

"What is it?"

I hesitated. My old mantra of not getting attached no longer mattered now that I was stuck here. I stared at the felt wall a few inches in front of my eyes. I now had confirmation of the mutual attraction between us. But I didn't know what to do about it. It seemed dangerous if there was emotion complicating our protector-goddess relationship.

I shouldn't tell him my real name or encourage the bond between us.

But … I did. It only seemed fair after all he'd done for me. "Josie."

"It is a peculiar name."

"No more peculiar than Batu would be in my world." I smiled. I liked Batu – a lot more than I should.

I also couldn't help thinking of Taylor once more. While it was true we were married for mere days, and he was dead, I experienced a flare of guilt at kissing Batu when I didn't feel over Taylor yet. It was more than the guilt of him being uncreated; this felt more like I was cheating on his memory.

In truth, I didn't know what I owed him. He had made my life better while I was in the Old West and helped me cope. In turn, I helped make him cease to exist.

I don't want that to happen to Batu. Maybe this was what bothered me most. I cared about Taylor and lost him. I cared about Batu, too, and didn't think I could go through such loss again.

Chapter Eleven

THE NEXT DAY WAS HELL. SUVDIN RAN ME THROUGH EVERY CHORE, task and skill in the entire camp, or so it felt like. Exhausted, thoroughly defeated, wanting to cry, I returned to the tent I shared with Batu just past sundown.

"What did you learn?" he asked from his position sharpening his arrowheads near the fire. He didn't look up, but this time, I *knew* he was laughing at me.

Biting back tears, I flung my over tunic down. I was drenched and still smelled of sheep urine, goat blood, leather tanning oil … and everything else I'd gone through this day. "I can't do anything," I said, voice quivering. "The animals hate me. I threw up when I tried to skin a rabbit and the wool spinning made me sneeze until I couldn't stand up. I can't shoot a bow or heft a sword or …" I started crying out of frustration. Swallowing the tears, I continued. "I can't carve wood to save my life or track prey or figure out how to carry those water buckets on my shoulder. Batu, I can't even put up a tent!"

He was laughing.

Struggling for my composure, I took a deep breath and wiped my face. I had reopened the wound on my bad hand and sat down to change the bandage. "I even messed up bandaging the injured warriors," I added.

Batu was laughing harder than I'd ever seen him.

"Would you stop?" I snapped and flung a wad of linen at him. "Someone told you I failed at everything, didn't they?"

He wiped tears from his eyes and settled, though his grin was huge. "Yes. The children were eager to share."

"The whole camp knows I'm useless!" I said miserably. I dropped onto my back and sighed. It felt good after my arduous day. "I could be a whore. That's the one thing I didn't try."

"That you cannot do," he agreed, still far too amused.

"If it's all I'm good for, then I can."

"A goddess does not whore."

"How do you know? Have you met any other goddesses?"

"No other goddess has a guardian who will put a sword through any man who gets too close." He laughed again.

I've seen him do that already. My eyes closed and I relaxed onto the ground. At least the day was over. If nothing else, I had made the people of the encampment laugh with my clumsy attempts to take on their everyday chores. If not for my language skills, I'd volunteer to let them trample me with horses, which was supposedly an honorable way to punish someone deserving of death.

"I just want to be part of your world," I murmured.

"Patience, ugly one." He stirred and knelt beside me, his scent and heat sending spirals of excitement through me.

I sat up. "I can do it," I said, too aware of his muscular form and the kiss we shared last night.

He ignored me and took my wrist gently. Batu wiped away the

blood before bandaging my palm once more. I didn't look at him when he sat so close. What had been a comfortable distance yesterday morning was nothing short of flustering today.

"You have said nothing about last night."

I really hated how he seemed to read my mind. I sought the right words and then gave up. I was never good at hiding what I thought or felt, and he'd know if I tried. "I don't know what to think about it."

"More thinking," he grunted and sat back on his heels.

"What do *you* have to say about it?" I challenged and met his dark gaze. I held my breath without meaning to, nervous when I shouldn't have been.

"It did not displease me, ugly one." His eyes sparkled.

"You're doing it again, Batu. Teasing me."

"I fear honesty would confuse you when you are already confused."

Wow. I didn't expect this response. By the intent look on his face, he was saying exactly what I was reading between the lines. And he was right: I wasn't ready for his complete honesty. Not yet. Not when I had no place in my new world and felt afloat. He was my anchor, and I feared losing that.

Which sounded selfish and confused me further.

"You're right," I said. "I'm not ready for honesty."

As usual, he appeared unfazed. "This is good," he said and stood, returning to his side of the fire.

"How so?"

"Because there is something worth being honest about."

I flushed. Taylor had made me feel special; Batu made me feel …

I didn't even know. Exhilarated, terrified, ecstatic and uncertain, all at the same time. I was on a rollercoaster with him and had been since we met. They weren't emotions I could free when I didn't know how I fit in.

He began sharpening arrowheads again, content with our almost-discussion about our almost-relationship. He had nothing to worry about; those that didn't know to fear him or his claim on me lost their heads. He had all the time in the world to wait for me to be ready.

"Moonbeam?" The tremulous voice came from outside the tent.

Standing, I opened the flap, and my gaze dropped to the little girl. "Flowers!" I exclaimed and knelt.

She threw herself into my arms, and I laughed, startled and delighted to see the little girl who had shared in my first adventure. Two Mongol warriors who looked the worse for wear, as if they had traveled quickly and fought their way through an army, stood nearby.

Batu opened the flap of the tent and greeted them, welcoming them inside. The two entered, and I released Flowers from my hug. We walked inside, hand in hand. My curious gaze found Batu.

"I sent for her," he said nonchalantly, as if he didn't know how important Flowers was to me when I knew he did. His attention went to the men who brought her.

Flowers clung to me. I smiled down at her and knelt once more. "You're safe," I told her. "Are you well?"

She nodded.

"You look exhausted." I brushed hair from her face.

"We did not stop traveling for two days."

"Do you want to lay down and rest? Then we can find some food?"

"Will you lay down with me?"

"Sure." I stood. It was a little awkward to take a nap with the three men in the center of the tent, but I was gradually becoming accustomed to the community way everything was done here. Taking her hand, we walked to the bed at the back of the tent. I lifted her onto the edge and tugged off her boots and then unfastened her cloak.

She rolled back into the bed and gave a sigh of contentment. Smiling, I crawled in with her and wrapped her in my arms. Flowers smelled of dust and horses and was soon fast asleep.

I was too hungry to be tired after my day but waited until certain she was out before leaving the bed. Batu and his guests had already left. Sitting by the fire, I watched the dancing flames, poured myself a goblet of milk, and returned to the fire to wait for Batu. Another deficiency to add to my ever growing list: I couldn't find my way around the encampment if I were being chased by bandits who wanted me dead and I had to find him to save me.

Talk about getting lost in the parking lot.

Flowers began to snore. I glanced over with a grin. If nothing else, having her here meant I couldn't have too much alone time with Batu. There'd be space between us to alleviate the tension so I could think.

I still didn't know why Taylor's people wanted Flowers saved. Grateful Batu hadn't taken her away and secretly killed her, I was at a loss to explain the significance of her survival. She was going to be in the same boat I was: learning to adapt to a new culture and society. If nothing else, she was young enough to learn to use a bow, which defied me at this point.

"Moonbeam?" Suvdin's soft call came from the entrance.

"Come in!" I stood.

She entered, trailed by Batu. "I heard you have a guest in need of a home." She smiled.

I glanced at Batu. "I thought she could stay with us."

"She'll be safest if she remains here with Suvdin," he replied.

For the first time since we'd met, anger stirred. I wasn't about to make a scene in front of Suvdin – but I wanted to. "She's sleeping," I said instead. "She'll be frightened if she wakes up to strangers."

"This is wise. Do you wish to bring her to me in the morning?"

Suvdin asked.

"Yes," I said, albeit unhappily.

Suvdin either didn't hear my reluctance or was graciously overlooking it. She smiled and left.

I crossed my arms and glared at Batu. "Why can't she come with us?"

"She is safer here, goddess."

"She's safer with you to protect her!"

"You are angry." He appeared interested.

"Of course I am! You didn't even ask me before you gave her away to someone else. She's my responsibility."

"What would you have me do, Moonbeam?" he asked and approached, standing close enough that my anger began to slide into another warm emotion. "To protect you, I cannot have distractions. We may not be long in any one place. Here, Suvdin has agreed to adopt her as a daughter. She will be safe and have a family. It is a rare kindness and honor."

But I want her with me. I bit my tongue and absorbed his words. He made sense. He always did. He understood this world better; I trusted him with my own safety.

Turning to face Flowers, I still hesitated. "I would've preferred that you ask me first," I said finally. "I don't disagree with your decision. But I want to be informed."

"Very well, goddess. I did not mean to cause you distress."

I didn't know why it upset me so much. It was partially because Flowers had originally been under my protection, and I deserved to be consulted before he made decisions about her welfare.

But there was more. I just couldn't figure out what. Flowers, like me, was an outsider, and it was nice to have company.

"Suvdin has three children. She's okay with a fourth?" I asked him.

"She is. I provided the means to support her for her life as well."

"What does that mean?" I faced him curiously.

"I gifted Flowers a thousand horses. They become her new father's."

"So you bribed them."

"What is this?" he asked, head tilted. "It is honorable, goddess."

"Sorry." I drew a breath. "I'm still learning. Do you have a thousand horses?"

He chuckled. "I have a thousand and forty."

"That doesn't leave you many, comparatively speaking," I said. I had no clue the worth of a herd of horses, but I could guess a thousand of anything was a big deal, especially in an era like this. It was a large amount for a girl he knew nothing about and even more impressive when he appeared to be giving away nearly all of his wealth.

"She will be safe, as you wish," he said, not at all concerned about the loss of horses.

I suspected he wasn't doing it for her. He did it for *me*.

"Thank you," I said, anger melting. "You didn't have to do this."

"I did," he countered. "It was honorable."

And you are an honorable person. Even if his quick sword rattled me. It dawned on me, not for the first time but more insistently, that he had sacrificed a lot for me, even before we met. His way of life, his chance at a family, his horses and money. It seemed like ... more than duty to me. I didn't know him well enough to believe with certainty this was true.

The warm emotions blooming in my chest and rattling my thoughts rendered me silent.

I watched him check on Flowers.

He chuckled. "How does someone so small take up so much room?"

I smiled. I was confused again without really understanding why. He had never hidden who or what he was. There should be nothing about him that baffled me.

"Batu … when you kissed me last night …" I paused, collected my thoughts, and continued. "Did any part of who I am bother you? I don't fit in. I'm not tough or strong like your women. I proved today I can't do anything productive in the camp. Did you think twice about who I was when you kissed me?"

He was facing me, taking in my words with intentness. "Why do you think I kissed you? Because you are beautiful?"

"Well … yes."

"You are peculiar, ugly one. I kissed you because of who you are."

I had kind of hoped he would say something different.

"If I wanted beauty alone, I would visit the harem," he added.

"Ugh!" I groaned. "You were doing so well! If you had stopped speaking before *harem …*"

"You value honesty." He gave a half-smile. "There are concerns where I cannot be honest with you, and thus I will always be honest when I can."

Batu had secrets?

"I am heading to the war camp," he added. He bent to wrap his weapons.

The idea of him in war made me uneasy. "You're going into battle?"

"Not battle. There is some strife among the clans allied to my uncle. I go to speak to them and ensure they remain loyal."

"The uncle who wanted us dead?"

He nodded.

"Hmm. That's nice of you, considering he tried to kill us both."

Batu shrugged. "Loyalty, goddess. It is important."

Not to that asshole.

"We can talk about what is between us when I return, ugly one." The tease took the intensity out of his words.

Initially worried about him leaving, his declaration replaced concern with a surge of other emotions I didn't want to acknowledge. "When I'm ready," I reminded him. "Not that there is anything."

I didn't want there to be.

Batu ignored me. He read me too well. "Stay with the wolves, little lamb," he reminded me.

I really hate that tone.

I watched him leave, dreading and thrilled about the idea he, too, sensed something between us. He was too candid to let it fester, but I didn't feel anywhere near capable of discussing something so serious when my world was still so fragile.

Chapter Twelve

Exhausted, I nonetheless had trouble falling asleep. It wasn't just the fact Flowers kicked in her sleep, either.

I was dwelling over what Batu said and what I really wanted to happen in my new life here. My future – specifically a family, husband – had never crossed my mind until my first time travel adventure, when I'd thought I was stuck in the past with Taylor. In college, I wanted to make a name for myself in some career path before I considered settling down. In hindsight, the plan was kind of vague. I didn't have any idea what I'd be doing if not wandering through time. I had trouble choosing a major in college, because I liked too many different things. Having graduated before these adventures started, I was planning on interning somewhere, maybe in the marketing department of some huge company, to see if I fit in and if not, trying something else.

They weren't solid plans, not like spending my life in the Mongol Empire. I didn't need a career here, aside from being a translator. But

... it wasn't fulfilling to think of my life as being on call to help bridge languages in between figuring out how to survive the day to day.

It seemed like there should be more, yet there wasn't really time for more in the way I was accustomed to. I couldn't exactly have a long list of hobbies like I did in my time. I'd have to learn another, more practical skill as I adapted to this time. The community and family centric Mongols held similar perspective as Batu: they didn't ask why they were who they were or where they were – they lived. It was both a freeing and frustrating philosophy, one I struggled with despite deciding I wanted to live like they did.

Staring into the darkness above my bed, I had the sense I knew why: because I was still looking for a way out. Even telling myself I wasn't, even admitting it was impossible. I wasn't ready to fit in, because I didn't think I'd be staying.

Except when it came to the flutter of emotions I had for Batu. I hoped it was simply attraction, because he was strong and sexy. As with Taylor, when I looked at my future and the possibility of remaining here, I could almost see it happening when I considered Batu as my friend if not partner in survival.

Or ... as something else.

I had the sense if I told him to back off, he would. Batu had been straightforward with me since the beginning and humored the idiosyncrasies I didn't think existed in this time. What I had to figure out: if I really did want him to back off. If letting myself explore what we could be would somehow jeopardize the tiny part of me holding out for my return home.

Restless, I fell into a light sleep and awoke when Suvdin came to fetch both Flowers and me. We were led to the edge of the camp, where Suvdin placed Flowers with a group of children being taught to fire a bow and arrow. I watched the two of them interact, a little uneasy still by the deal Batu had struck. His logic was sound: if we left to wander the steppes for a while, Flowers should be comfortable.

This just seemed so permanent.

My gaze roamed with my thoughts, and I shielded my eyes against the morning sun to see Ghoajin atop a horse headed towards a tent located a quarter of a mile from the rest of the encampment. I watched her, puzzled as to why she went and why she was alone. She was so fragile at her age, hunched over the horse's mane.

"Where is she going?" I asked when Suvdin joined me.

"To care for the sick."

"I thought they were ..." I waved at the tents behind us, uncertain which side of camp the battle injured and ill were kept.

"Not these people." Suvdin's tone grew hushed. "They suffer the Great Plague. They cannot be kept close to camp, so they are tended until death in the *ger* there."

"Oh, wow." I searched my memory for what kind of plague it might be. It was in the early thirteen hundreds, by all accounts, which was about the time the Black Death wiped out half of Europe. "Are there doctors or ... uh, healers who help them?"

"No," she said grimly. "It wiped out many clan members and warriors several seasons ago. It returns to the steppes every summer to claim new victims, and remains a danger at the trading posts."

"We stopped at a post."

"Batu would only have done so if necessary. He knows to avoid such places during summer."

I frowned. I never did ask why we stopped there. He had business to conduct, but I fell to infection after and hadn't thought twice about the stopover. "But why does Ghoajin go alone there?"

"She is one of three who caught the Great Plague and survived. She can be around the ill without falling sick again. The others are with the army to tend any who fall ill there."

A memory stirred, one that made me pause to pull it from the depths of my mind. I swore Carter said something about the Black Death to me at some point …

You are immune to everything from the Black Death to diseases that don't exist yet.

It was too much of a coincidence to assume he was joking. I didn't know that at the time, but he had clearly planned on sending me to this era of time from the beginning, no matter how my trip to the Old West turned out.

"What is it, Moonbeam?" Suvdin asked.

For a moment, I debated what to say. I had no reason to distrust Carter's claim. He wanted me to survive, but the idea of facing something as horrific as the Black Death, something that wiped out over a third of the population of the world at this point in history, was kind of creepy. It didn't seem right that Ghoajin had to do it alone.

"I think I know a skill I can use to help out," I said slowly. "I can't get the Great Plague. I can help Ghoajin."

Suvdin hesitated. "Yesen Yeke is not likely to approve, Moonbeam. You are a gift from the Eternal Blue Sky," she said. "Our clan chief will not wish to put you in danger."

"But I won't be in danger."

"We can ask his permission. Besides, there is nothing to be done for those who catch it. We remove them from camp to protect everyone else, and all but one out of a hundred survives."

It sounded horrible to segregate the ill and leave them to die, yet I understood the rudimentary medicine of this era couldn't handle such a sickness. It was the men in the tent dying – or then entire camp if it spread. I was kind of grateful she doubted I'd be allowed. It was the skill I looked forward to the least, even less than skinning an animal, because of the horror stories that remained in history classes and literature about the plague.

"You can also swim," Suvdin pointed out. "Few of us can or will."

"How does that help you?"

"We will figure it out."

I sighed and prepared myself for another day of grueling manual labor that left those around me laughing and me less convinced I could ever fit in here.

The day went as I expected. Tired, sore and hungry, I joined the family in Ghoajin's tent for a feast after nightfall. I was too exhausted to ask her about the patients she treated in the tent, too tired to do much more than eat and offer Flowers smiles whenever she glanced uncertainly my way.

Suvdin showed me back to my tent and I started to get ready for bed – then paused.

Batu wasn't back yet. I had thought he meant to return today at some point. There was no sign he'd been back to the *ger*, either. I was looking forward to a night alone – but not if it meant he was in trouble or anything.

The man can handle anything. I reminded myself he was the champion of his people. If he got hung up somewhere, he was likely helping other clans take out their enemies or something, not lying in a ditch somewhere hurt.

Reassured, I stripped off my boots and clothing down to a tunic and climbed into bed, stretching luxuriously. Sleeping with Flowers was miserable, and, while I enjoyed being wrapped in Batu's arms every night, it was awesome to have a night to myself, too.

I slept the best I had since falling ill from infection. I didn't even hear Suvdin enter the *ger* or sense her until she shook me awake the next morning.

"Oh, damn." I pushed myself up groggily. "Am I late?"

Worry tightened the lines beneath her eyes and made her

forehead crease. "No, Moonbeam."

"What's wrong?" Not quite able to think straight so early, I found myself craving coffee as I stood and began to dress. "Is Flowers well?"

"She is. But Batu …"

I froze and straightened, alarm snapping me out of the post-wake up stupor. "What happened?" I demanded quietly. "Where is he?"

"He is ill, Moonbeam."

"Injured from battle?"

"No." She wrung her hands. "He is fevered. Ghoajin fears it's the Great Plague."

I stared at her. Last night, I had been debating whether or not I wanted to take a chance and explore a relationship with Batu, and today, the option might have been off the table. My chest was tightening, and a small voice in my head was trying to convince me I hadn't woken up, that this was a dream.

It wasn't.

"In that case, I will be helping him," I said at last.

"Yesen –"

"I don't care, Suvdin!" I snapped a little too harshly. "Batu has saved my life multiple times. If I can help him, I will. Where is he?"

"The plague tent."

"So even if he didn't have the Great Plague, he probably will now." I began to pace, my thoughts racing. I glanced at my bandaged hand. "Um, can you give me a moment to dress?"

"Of course." She left the tent.

With some queasiness, I knelt beside the weapons Batu left and drew a knife. I held my breath and poked the pad of my good thumb. Muttering a curse, I checked the blood.

No black dots at all this time. I squeezed more out, hopeful I'd find a quick cure to Batu's illness.

My blood was normal. Whatever had been in my system while I

was unconscious for seventy years was completely gone. Rather than be pleased by the absence of evidence of whatever weirdness Carter did to me, I was … scared.

I sat in silence for a long moment, fighting the sense of detachment that crept over me during moments of duress. Batu wasn't here to pull me out of it, and I recited his chant a few times to help me reroute my panic into focusing on my surroundings.

When the spell passed, I dressed quickly and fumbled to pull on my boots. I wasn't really certain what I felt about Batu being ill, except that he seemed too strong for this to be possible. The images of him fighting were in my head, the various times where he'd saved my life flashing so vividly, I began to think it was a joke a simple bug could take him down.

But no one was immune to aging or illness, especially not in an age when there was no modern medicine. We had gone to the trading post, and Batu was ill.

I wasn't going to let him be sentenced to the plague tent to be made comfortable with the assumption he was already dead. We had been through too much together, and he was my connection to this world.

I can't do another Taylor. The idea of losing someone else left me rattled and my breathing uneven.

"I'm ready," I said as I left the tent.

"You are certain you wish to go to the plague tent?" Suvdin searched my features. "Yesen Yeke will be displeased."

"He can come out and drag me back," I said with wry humor. "And yes. I am certain."

"Very well. I have some supplies you can take. Ghoajin will be out later." Suvdin appeared concerned. "Moonbeam, you will not fall ill?"

"I will not."

"If you are truly a goddess, then you must not let Batu go to the sky yet."

I offered a small smile, sensing her restrained emotion. There was a part of her that still loved Batu, and I had a feeling I was her only hope to help him. "I'll do what I can," I replied. *I really wish I was a goddess.*

She led me to the edge of the camp, where two horses waited. One was packed with food, herbs, milk, blankets and water while the other was saddled for me to ride. I paused, heart pounding as I gazed at the distance between me and the plague tent.

There was a chance, however slim, that I didn't survive this, either. What if the Great Plague and whatever Carter immunized me against was something different?

My entire life on the steppes with the Mongols had consisted of one near-death experience after the other. How civilization as a whole moved past eras like this and survived, I'd never understand. Reading about history definitely didn't convey the sense of danger people before the twentieth century faced every day.

"Take care of Flowers," I murmured and approached the horse waiting for me. "She's a good girl." I mounted. For once, my aching body wasn't at the top of my thoughts.

"She is already helping me with my younger ones," Suvdin said. "Ghoajin returns at night. If you do, will you come to see me?"

Carrying plague germs? I wasn't certain how half the camp didn't have the Black Death, if someone was going between the two points. "Sure," I said, not really concerned if I meant it or not. I had no intention of leaving Batu's side.

Too distracted by what lay before me, I left Suvdin without a farewell and headed toward the tent.

Its scent – of death and decay – reached me before I was close enough to dismount. I covered my lower face with one of the rags in the supplies and stopped outside the tent when I was close enough.

I had no medical training or sense. At all. I may have taken a first aid class at some point, but I didn't think applying a tourniquet or CPR was going to fix the plague. There was general medical knowledge I possessed that was possibly rare here: the need to wash my hands, how a virus or bacterial infection was transmitted, how to help regulate a fever …

I hoped … *prayed* … it was enough to make a difference. Leaving the horses, I opened the tent and almost threw up. The scent of refuse, vomit and sickness was strong. Ghoajin had tried to clean up, but she was too frail for the amount of maintenance an operation like this required.

There were three men within, each on a pallet with a bucket or two beside him where he could throw up or use the restroom. From the looks of it, one of them had given up or the bucket was full, because the area beside his bed was soaked with what looked like blood and food he'd vomited.

A fire burned in the center of the tent, and there were four tables and a bed present. I swallowed hard as I looked at two of the men, who appeared to be in advanced stages of illness.

"What do you do, Goddess?" Batu asked from the third pallet.

In twenty-four hours, he had gone from the strongest man I knew to someone who looked quite sickly. His face was flushed, his gaze unfocused and fevered, and he struggled to sit.

"Lie still," I told him and hurried to his side. I dropped to my knees.

Where he had once been the epitome of intimidating, I was able to keep him on his back with one hand pressed to his chest.

The change in him, the sight of his weakness, threw my thoughts into a tailspin.

Not Batu. I couldn't be here only to lose someone again. While true I barely knew him, he had voluntarily and without a second thought risked his life for mine on more than one occasion. Whatever I thought of his ear-collecting warrior duties, I also knew his lack of hesitation to place himself between me and danger spoke volumes about the kind of person he was.

He cared for me, and I cared for him despite the odds.

I blinked out of my thoughts. "Are you comfortable?"

"No." He chuckled. "Hot. Cold. Hot."

I felt his forehead. It was blazing. "I don't know anything about this illness." Worried, I rose and crossed to the man nearest him. He was covered in boils that rendered his appearance lumpy and bloated. Several were oozing blood.

"You should not be here, Moonbeam," Batu told me.

"I can't catch this illness," I replied. *Hopefully.* "Ghoajin can't handle this herself." I straightened, queasy and disturbed but aware there were three people who needed help. "And I'm not going to let you be alone and suffering with this disease."

"They can find you another guardian."

"You cared for me when I was ill. I will do the same for you."

"It is not your duty."

"Don't be stupid, Batu!" I snapped, irritated by his casual dismissal. "I am going to help you. Somehow."

"Very well, ugly one." He smiled tightly. His eyes were closed, his skin clammy and soaked through with sweat.

I left the tent and breathed in the putrid air outside of it. The place positively reeked. I was scared for him and struggling to figure out what should be done to make things better.

I really wasn't sure. Angry with myself, I began to unload the horse while my thoughts raced. I had no medical training, but common sense said their environment was an issue. I couldn't exactly create a sterile environment like that of a hospital, but I could take care of the disgusting conditions. It was a place to start and something Ghoajin wouldn't be able to do on her own.

Fire. "Ah, yeah," I murmured. Their clothing, the old rags piled under a table, anything that had been thrown up on ... I could burn that shit.

My makeshift mask slid off, and I gagged. It was even worse without it. I tugged it into place once more and eyed the tent.

In theory, I should be able to roll up its sides. There were leather straps dangling beneath the head of the mushroom, and the clean air would definitely make the place more bearable.

I circled the small *ger* and tested one felt wall. They were designed for quick erection and disassembly and to be carried in small wagons pulled by horses. The walls were in strips about ten feet wide and size feet tall. I had made an attempt to help someone put theirs up yesterday as part of my chores. Although I failed miserably to do it as instructed, I at least know how they were supposed to go up and come down.

It took some time – about two hours – but I managed to roll the first wall. Sweating when I was done, I stood back to assess my crude work with satisfaction. Batu had managed to sit and was watching, his muscular frame sagging and eyes glazed.

His weakness sent a streak of cold fear and despair through me.

Ignoring it, I went to work raising the other three portions of the walls. My sloppy work would never pass inspection of any eagle-eyed woman of the clan, but it served the purpose I needed it to.

Already the wind of the steppes was sweeping the smells away.

My second item of business: building a fire behind the tent to burn the nastiness within.

Batu had made an attempt to teach me to build a fire during our travels while another of the women had showed me again two days ago. I created a pit and filled it with some of the dried dung from the supplies and a few rags. There was enough flammable material that it was easy to take a flame from the existing fire and then just toss everything else into it.

Stretching out a blanket, I piled the dirty and spoiled rags into it.

Probably the material in the worst shape: the clothes of the men. Ghoajin wasn't strong enough to strip them down, and their tunics were soaked with sweat, blood and puss from exploding boils.

Peering at the worst of the three, I couldn't help thinking this was the most disgusting thing I'd ever seen. The man appeared to be barely alive, and my heart broke for him. I knelt beside him and gently began to pry off his soiled clothing.

"Batu, take off your clothes!" I called to him.

"Not my ... belt," he replied.

"Um, okay. You can keep that." *Like a belt matters right now.* But maybe it was like his Moldavite; it was for morale.

He grunted and did his best to maneuver out of his clothing. I watched for a moment, stricken again by how weak he had become in so short a time. He obeyed and stripped down until he was naked then rested back.

I didn't let my gaze stray where it wanted to. It seemed like something that'd send me to hell if I checked him out while he was on the verge of dying. Instead, I covered him with a blanket from the waist down and returned to wrestling gently with the worst off – a man I was nicknaming Lumpy, since I had no other way to identify him – and pulled off his clothing.

Lumpy and Grumpy – the second man who physically pushed back when I stripped off his clothing – were soon both covered with blankets in a similar fashion, giving me unfettered insight into how horrific this disease was.

Holding my mouth, I left and ran beyond the fire, not wanting to upset them when I vomited everywhere. I threw up last night's dinner and then sat back on my heels.

What the hell am I doing? The chances of any of them living were pretty close to zero, and I had absolutely no clue how to help. The moment I thought of Batu, I knew I had to try, though, no matter what the odds. He deserved it. He deserved for me to try to save him the way I hadn't Taylor.

Tossing my head back, I realized it was past noon, and Ghoajin hadn't yet ridden out. I could think of one duty I was dreading that I'd like to give the woman: cleaning Lumpy and Grumpy's bodies.

I wasn't entirely certain I was ready to handle this latest trial yet and remained where I was for several moments, lost in thought and dreading returning to the tent to see the suffering of others.

After a quick breather, I ate a little of the food Suvdin had sent with me and went back to reassess the three ill men. I had never felt quite so helpless before, as if I should know how to help them with my twenty first century knowledge – but didn't have a clue.

I could really use a history chip. Something to tell me how those who survived the plague did so.

With the fire burning off the filth, I sat by Batu and gazed at his strong features and the muscles of his exposed chest. It just wasn't right that someone like him could end up vulnerable and weak under any circumstances.

He was dozing, and I checked his body for signs of the boils. Some were forming on the skin of his upper arms, beneath the skin, dark splotches that looked like bruises but were round and raised.

"You can fight this, Batu," I whispered, troubled.

They all needed food and water. Or maybe, milk and water would go down more easily. Retreating to the horse, I returned with several bladders, half filled with water and the other half with milk.

"Goddess." Batu was awake.

"Drink some of this, Batu."

He accepted one bladder and propped himself on one elbow,

drinking obediently. I took it when he was done. His dark gaze remained on me, and I studied his features.

This couldn't be how it ended. This couldn't be how *we* ended.

"I am pleased you are here," he said at last and cupped my cheek with one hand.

I smiled. "When you're better, we'll plan where we're going next," I said with forced cheerfulness. I took his hand and held it in both of mine.

He said nothing. I pushed him onto his back.

"Shall I sing for you?" he murmured.

"Yes. A water song."

He began, and I listened, as intrigued by the man as I was his strange songs. With my stomach churning, I helped the other two men drink and began cleaning up their sores and boils. It took effort not to get sick, and I left twice to throw up where they couldn't see me.

At the back of my mind, I knew Batu was going down the same path these two had been down, but I couldn't let myself think about him in that amount of pain or his body covered with boils.

I had been through too much to let my mind trick me into a meltdown I couldn't afford. Nothing mattered – not the past, my confused emotions, my hope of returning home – except for helping Batu survive this.

Chapter Thirteen

THE NEXT SEVERAL DAYS WERE HELL. GHOAJIN CAME OUT FOR A few hours each day to help and to give me a chance to sleep while she tended the sick. She taught me about the medicinal roots and herbs they used to help soothe pain and aid sleep. When she was gone, I used the herbs she had prepared for the three men and stayed up most of the night to watch over them.

Lumpy passed on my fourth night, and I wept as I had never wept before. Not that I knew him, but because Batu's boils had spread, and I couldn't fathom the idea of living in the steppes of Mongolia without him.

Several of Lumpy's kinsmen came out after Ghoajin carried news back of the warrior's death. They built a funeral pyre between us and the camp, and Ghoajin and I wrapped Lumpy in blankets before hooking his pallet to a horse to be taken to the pyre. I dragged his body on top of it, and Ghoajin lit the fires, praying the entire time.

His death – while expected – still came as a blow. I had seen so many lives snuffed out while here through a combination of war and disease. The memories of all who died left me emotionally raw, frightened and once more questioning the greater meaning of life. Specifically, *my* life and why I was stuck here to deal with such sorrow.

I returned to the *ger* while Ghoajin spent hours beside the dead warrior's pyre. Smoke twisted and curled into the skies above us, and I sat beside Batu, my eyes almost too swollen from crying to see out of. Sliding my hand into his, I squeezed gently.

He was unconscious and had been for most of the day after throwing up blood several times in the morning. Ghoajin had knocked him out with some herbs. Boils covered most of his body, and I absently began cleaning his skin once more.

Grumpy was doing better than I thought he would. He slept most of the day, woke up to throw up once, then settled into a deeper sleep. His sores were beginning to heal over, even though his fever remained.

While I wasn't fully certain, I took the healing to be a sign he wasn't going to keel over and die next.

Several more days passed in a haze of exhaustion and worry. Every morning, I opened up the tent to sunlight and the winds of the steppes. I was getting better at rolling the tent flaps, though my work was nowhere near pretty.

The morning routine was the same: water all around, prepare herbs and milk for the men, wash them down and then wait for Ghoajin to relieve me. After a few hours of sleep, I'd drag the two men into the sun with the desperate hope that sunlight would help kill any additional bacteria and dry out their sores.

The longer I was present, the more convinced I became that I was the worst healer in the history of the world.

Blinking back tears, I shifted when Grumpy strained to sit up.

"You shouldn't be doing that," I warned him and sat beside him. I pushed him back down. "You're healing. You shouldn't tax yourself."

He grumbled something and remained where he was. I brought him milk. He was able to lift the bladder to his lips on his own this time. I considered every tiny advancement in his condition that he wasn't going to die, in the hopes Batu would soon show the same signs of recovery. Evaluating him once more, I was pleased to see the puffiness of his boils receding. The discoloring remained, and the few that burst were still of concern for infection, but the illness was retreating.

Grumpy was beating it.

Initially slow, his recovery sped up over the next five days. While Batu got sicker and sicker, Grumpy took enormous strides in the other direction. By the end of my second week in the sick tent, Grumpy was active for half the day, weakened, scarred and nowhere near healed, but fever free and healing. He became my helper and showed me better how to roll the tent walls, helped me move Batu into the sun, and generally assisted in cleaning up the *ger* during the hours when he had strength.

Batu's condition was critical. He had stopped speaking and was barely ever awake. I didn't know what made Grumpy recover and Lumpy die, and I didn't know how to do anything more to help Batu. I didn't leave his side, though, as the next week dragged on.

At the twenty-one day mark, Batu's fever finally broke. I was too tired to be excited, too fearful of a relapse to celebrate.

I awoke beside Batu after a fitful doze to find him resting peacefully. His skin was warm but not hot, and he wasn't muttering in his sleep or tossing and turning. As with Grumpy, Batu's boils were de-puffing. He looked like he'd been through a boxing match with a hundred different men; his body was black and blue from the illness.

Pushing myself up, I grimaced. I had a crick in my neck and tension ache from between my shoulder blades. I was an absolute mess.

"You are not eating enough," Grumpy said from nearby. He was prepping Batu's morning milk and herbs.

"It's hard for me to eat when I am worried," I replied.

"What does one have to do with the other?"

I snorted. He had Batu's simple logic. He handed me a piece of cloth with meat and cheese on it. Grumpy was almost fully recovered, though I suspected it was going to take him some time before his full strength returned. "How are you feeling?" I asked and nibbled on my food.

"Better. I feel ready to return."

"Good. You need a bath first."

"No bath."

I wasn't certain what it was about … ah. Somewhere in the back of my mind, I recalled they considered the streams and ocean to be the blood of the earth, and therefore, sacred. Ghoajin had also explained that a person's smell was part of his or her soul, and so to lose it in a bath was an insult.

"You have …" *germs.* He wasn't going to understand what those were. "… illness on your skin. It could infect others."

Grumpy looked down at his arms.

"Trust me," I said, amused.

"I do, goddess. You and Ghoajin healed me. If you say I need to bathe, I will." By his tone, it was going to be as trying of a task as healing from the Black Death.

You and luck are what healed you. I doubted anything I'd done here made a difference. The disease seemed to need to run its course.

"How fares Batu?" he asked and sat down beside his clansman.

He touched Batu's forehead. "He is better."

"He is," I agreed. "Hopefully he will recover as well as you did. Are you ready to return home?"

"I am," Grumpy said. "But I will stay with you until Batu is healed. It is only honorable."

These men and their bizarre sense of honor. But I needed the help. He had already rolled up the sides of the tent, a duty that drained me of energy. My gaze went to Batu, and I studied his bloated features. Of the few thoughts my fatigued mind had managed to form the past two weeks, life here without him was the one I couldn't comprehend. It was a different feeling than that I had about Taylor. Batu was a different kind of man, and the world here wasn't anything like the Old West.

I feared what my future held, but it seemed a little less scary with Batu at my side. I didn't fully comprehend my emotions for Batu except that I *needed* him to survive this with desperation that left me close to tears.

"Rest, Moonbeam," Grumpy said kindly. "I will watch over him. Ghoajin will be here soon, too."

I should have resisted, but I was exhausted. Standing, I crossed to the bed and dropped into it, soon deep in sleep.

Batu awoke the next day, and two days later, he was able to sit up and drink on his own. He didn't stay up long, though, and Grumpy and I worked to keep him stable over the next few days, while his boils disappeared and his skin began to return to a healthier color.

Another week passed. I began to eat normally again and slept curled up beside him. The morning I awoke with his arms around me, I knew the danger was gone. He certainly *felt* strong, even though he had a ways to go to recover his strength. I lay in his arms for several minutes, relieved and content. I missed this. Whether or not I should have, I wasn't certain. I hadn't spent any time on the conundrum of what I wanted to do about the man I spent a month caring for in a way I had never done for anyone else and risked my life to save. I hadn't thought myself capable of being a nursemaid to anyone. I had neither the skill nor patience, but nothing had mattered aside from seeing Batu recover.

Maybe that's my answer right there.

"How did you not fall ill, Moonbeam?" he murmured in a raspy voice.

I shifted, happier than I thought I should be to be in his arms once more. "I do not get these kinds of illnesses."

"You are fortunate. Next time, take off my head."

"Absolutely not. I'll always take care of you, Batu." I nudged him back. He rolled over obediently, and I sat to check his progress. "How are you feeling?" I lifted one arm to look at the discoloring. He was going to have scars in a few places from where the boils burst, but his skin was clearing up well.

"I am well, ugly one," he said, a thread of his former sense of humor emerging for the first time.

I hid a smile. I had the urge to cry again and this time, it wasn't because I feared for his life. "You need milk."

"I need meat," he returned. "I am not a child."

Grumpy smiled from his place prepping Batu's milk. "We have meat, cousin. If your Moonbeam approves, I will bring you some."

"Do you approve, my Moonbeam?" Batu asked and sat up, gazing at me.

It took me a moment to answer. His eyes were clear and bright, his face marred by several new scars, and his hair grown in enough to make his head fuzzy. The sense he was back made my throat tighten.

Unable to contain the swirling emotions, I hugged him around the neck. Batu embraced me and hauled me into his muscular frame.

It was so easy to forget he was weak from his ordeal. I had the urge to sink into him and stay, to sleep off a month of worry and fear.

His body was soon trembling from the effort to support us both. I eased back and released him. "You have a long way to heal, Batu," I told him, concerned. "But I think meat is fine."

"Good. I could eat a goat."

I sat back and watched as Grumpy – whose real name I had learned was Temujin – brought him food and water. The two interacted with familiarity that led me to believe they had grown up together. Batu's energy flagged after his meal, and he lay down for another nap.

It took another week before he was on his feet most of the day. As I noticed with Temujin, there were lingering effects, even after they appeared fully healed. Fatigue was one, and both men wore down more easily than before.

A full six weeks after I entered the plague tent, I returned to the main camp with the two men.

The weather had changed suddenly a week before, plunging us into a chilly autumn. Ghoajin had brought me extra coverings, but I burned pretty much everything before returning, so we came back in the bare minimum after all three of us had cold baths in the stream nearby. With wet hair and shivering, I stood aside as the two warriors greeted happy family members and received congratulations for being spared by the Eternal Blue Sky. I watched both for signs of fatigue or illness and was pleased both appeared to be healthy and upbeat, though I knew the road to full recovery was long.

It was decided there would be a feast in honor of the survivors this evening, and I walked away with Batu towards our tent. The only thing on my mind: sleeping. Hopefully for a week or so.

Entering the familiar *ger,* I found myself smiling as I looked around. If I had learned one thing from the sick tent, it was that I didn't want to take for granted that Batu was alive or that we were healthy and comfortable. There were no luxuries here, but I was learning there was something more important than material things: companionship, family and their link to survival.

He grunted as he sat on the ground beside the fire.

"What's wrong? Are you feeling ill?" I asked immediately.

"Be at peace, ugly one," he replied. "My body is healing. It will take some time."

I relaxed. "You sure?"

He met my gaze, amused. "As certain as I am that you need rest."

"I'm fine. My skill is immunity to disease," I said with no small amount of triumph. "It's the only thing I'm better than you at."

He laughed.

"But yes, I do need a nap." I crossed to the bed and dropped into it with a groan. "Oh, god! I forgot how comfortable anywhere but the ground is."

"Do you wish a song? Or a companion?"

I hesitated. My heart took off at his offer, and I didn't quite understand what had changed between the time before he fell ill and now that made him sleeping with me seem far less innocent than before. Nothing was different on the surface. I had had no time to explore my confusion or feelings to determine what I wanted in my new life.

But I also had no desire to be too far from him, to risk losing him again or failing to appreciate the small things that made life here so much richer than I had thought before. His family, the community of people who helped me save him – their warmth replaced the sparseness of their lives. I was starting to comprehend how he was so immersed in the day to day. He grew up knowing the danger that existed outside the encampment. Any time one of them left home, there was a chance he or she wasn't coming back.

Relationships, and the community, were more important than one person and his or her independence. It was an entirely different mindset for me, one I didn't think I'd ever fully adopt, but one I was also beginning to appreciate. And ... I was going to stop fighting the need to feel unique in a world that already accepted me as I was. It helped that I felt like I'd proven myself worthy to be here by taking care of Batu and Temujin.

"Yes," I decided. "Both."

Batu climbed into bed with me. He didn't ask or hesitate before wrapping me in his arms and pulling me securely into his hard frame. What happened in the plague tent brought us closer together. I experienced the sensation of belonging when I was with him. Not that I hadn't belonged anywhere before, just that this was ... deeper. We were so very different and yet bonded by the sense of intimacy our partnership created. It was comforting, gentle, and warm, like walking from a winter morning into a warm room.

I sighed, and tension melted out of me. The twinge of worry remaining from the plague tent wasn't likely to leave anytime soon. At least, not until I was convinced he was well. Exhausted, drowsiness swept through me the moment I closed my eyes.

"I think I can do this, Batu," I murmured sleepily.

"Do what?"

"I think I can make it here. Like, have a life and everything."

"Did you doubt this?"

"Yes. This place is so foreign to me. But I learned a couple of things while you were sick."

"Always thinking," he said and squeezed me to him harder. "What did you learn, ugly one?"

"That I'm stronger than I thought and that ... I'm not lost. You were right. I can and do belong here." It was mostly true. If given the choice of returning home or staying here, I would likely have a full-fledged meltdown. But since I had begun to accept returning home was off the table, I wasn't as scared or hurt as I expected. I suspected, but didn't want to admit yet, that the reason behind this was probably the man holding me.

"You wish to stay with me?" he asked softly.

"Yes," I replied then twisted to glimpse his face. "Why? Were you planning on selling me again at the next trading post?"

"No, goddess." He gave a half smile. "You seem at peace."

"Yeah." I settled back in his arms. "I feel that way, too." If anything, I should've been scared after realizing how delicate life was in this time period. But I didn't. I wanted to enjoy the moments I had with Batu even more after knowing how fleeting they could be.

"This is good. You are safe here with me. Rest."

It didn't take long for sleep to creep over and claim me.

Chapter Fourteen

I SLEPT FOR THREE DAYS. NEVER IN MY LIFE HAD I DONE something like that. Not as a child, not after hangovers or finals … my body appeared to be trying to catch up for all the missing sleep from the past six weeks at once. I woke up in the morning each day, decided I wasn't done yet and went back to sleep.

When I awoke on the fourth day, I felt almost normal. Batu was gone, which didn't surprise me, and I went through a quick morning routine. By the faint patter on the roof, it was drizzling. I hadn't quite figured out if there was such a thing as rain gear here and dressed in a heavy over tunic to venture outside.

The day was gray and chilly, and few people were out in the rain. I had no clue what duties and activities occurred on sunny days that might not on rainy days. With some uncertainty, I wandered through the tents, following a path I thought was familiar towards Ghoajin's *ger*. I had picked up another skill completely by accident from my time in the plague tent: identifying and using medicinal herbs.

Ghoajin had taught me during the long hours when we nursed the sleeping warriors.

I had learned to identify over a dozen different herbs by sight and smell, to combine them to form potent mixes in water or milk and to make at least one balm. I was eager to learn more from her.

Soon, I was pleased to confirm my sense of direction was correct. I reached her large white tent and stood outside the door. Thus far, people seemed to just wander into other people's *gers*, but I didn't really know if there was some sort of protocol I was missing or not.

I walked in.

Ghoajin was seated at the fire with two other women. She looked up, her smile swallowing her features. "I am pleased to see you well, Moonbeam," she said.

"Thank you." I sat with the others and watched. They were sifting dried herbs while one lady crushed some with a mortar and pestle. "I came to learn more about the herbs."

"Finally, you have found your skill, Moonbeam?" one of the women teased.

Aware my adventure was common knowledge throughout the camp, I nodded with a grin.

"It is a fine skill for you to master, since you cannot fall ill from disease," Ghoajin said. "You will do much good here, Moonbeam."

I hope so. I needed to feel like I was contributing to my new family, community and everyday life, even if I had learned they were willing to overlook my lack of practical skills because of my translating ability.

Curious about where Batu had gone, I was also a little grateful for some space. Sleeping in his arms had gone from a warm, comfortable situation into one that was charged with sexual energy I wasn't certain what to do with. It frightened me on some levels, a final sign of how permanent this world was. I was considering him as something more than a temporary guardian and lowering what flimsy guards remained around my heart.

I stayed with Ghoajin through the day and until the evening feast learning more about my new trade. It was beginning to feel more natural to be here, less like purgatory or a trial and more like a home.

I kind of liked that feeling. I had a home with my aunt and uncle, but it was different knowing they had three children of their own already. I always felt a little like I was on the outside looking in. Here, I saw more of an opportunity to become a true part of their world.

Batu came to the feast, and his presence warmed me in a way the fire could not. The idea he was alive, that I had saved him … I had never experienced the profound sense of relief that went through me whenever the thought crossed my mind. I shouldn't feel so strongly for someone who had a perspective of the world so different than my own.

I barely glanced his way when he entered with several other men, but I was so aware of him, I found food and my goblet slipping through my hands. I had grown suddenly clumsy. No one around me seemed to notice, and even Batu appeared too busy with others to spare a glance at me.

When alcohol had begun to muddy the minds of those around me, I slipped out of the tent into the rain. It was cold and wet outside, and the night glowed with mushroom tents. Compared to the uncomfortable warmth of the crowded *ger*, the coldness was a temporary relief, one that wore off soon after I began wandering through the tents.

During the daytime, I'd been able to use the colorful scarves or strips of silk that marked some of the tents to guide me. At night, all of the markers were … dark. The rain soaked them enough that I wasn't able to tell many colors, either.

One step forward, five tents back, I said to myself. At least I had found my way to Ghoajin's *ger* earlier in the day. It was half a victory.

I huddled into my over tunic and began to shiver, lost and cursing silently at my luck.

"What do you do, goddess?"

Warmth bloomed within me at his tone. "The usual. Getting lost."

"It is good I found you."

I turned to face him and tried to act natural.

Not that there was any reason to act *unnatural.* Except the fact my heart began to race when he drew near. I looked up at Batu without being able to identify his features in the darkness. Heat radiated off him, and I stood stupidly for a moment, trying to recall if I should move closer or hold my ground if I didn't suddenly feel so awkward around him. What did I normally do?

"This way, goddess," he said and started off in a direction I hadn't been going.

Somewhat relieved, I trailed him until we entered the familiar tent that was ours. "Where did you go today?" I asked and shook off the rain before moving closer to the fire.

"The clans are moving south. I was greeting old friends and family," he replied.

"Moving south … oh, for winter. How often do the clans move?"

"Every three to four full moons."

"Are we moving?" I stripped off my over tunic, got tangled in it and finally managed to pull it off, accompanied by one of my other tunics. I had three layers on, though, so missing one more didn't really matter to me.

When I tossed them to the side, I found Batu gazing at me, eyes laughing. He had managed to strip his over tunic with none of the difficulty I experienced with the heavy material.

"What?" I demanded.

He approached me and pinched the material of the second layer I wore. "This goes against your skin. This" he tugged up the undershirt I wore "goes on second."

"Oh." Ruffled by his nearness, I laughed. "So I was wearing my underwear all day long for everyone to see. That's just … ugh! Batu!" I groaned, my emotions skittering and evolving too fast to track. "I'll never fit in! They're going to think I'm crazy."

"They already do, ugly one."

I looked up at him, startled, and my breath caught at his strong features and nearness. "They do?"

"Unique. Mad." He shrugged. "Did you think you were not these things?"

I rolled my eyes at him. "I thought I could try to fit in."

"If you fit in, I would not find you so beautiful."

My face warmed despite my goal of not letting him know I was affected by him. "You like unique madwomen who wear their underwear for everyone to see. It would explain a few things about you." I started away, embarrassed but too … fluttery to give it much thought. In truth, I knew I did stand out. If I were a more emotional person like my delicate friend Kendra, I'd probably develop a severe insecurity complex. As it was, I was generally resigned to being a freak of nature here, but one everyone seemed to love. I could live with that.

"I brought you this."

I folded my overtunic and place it in a trunk I had adopted as mine before returning to him curiously. He held out a small, velvet jewelry pouch. I took it, and Batu moved away to sit by the fire. I opened it and dumped the contents into my hand.

Moldavite. Two pieces the size of my thumbnail. "Oh, Batu," I murmured, uncertain what to say. I studied the glass. He had possessed a few pieces in the bag he showed me. For a moment, I debated asking if these were his or if he had gotten them elsewhere. They were a symbol of his honor and his clan. It was a more thoughtful gift than I was expecting, one I sensed conveyed some sort of great … honor, even if I wasn't certain why.

They meant something to me, too.

A normal person, one who didn't try to categorize the shade of brown of his eyes or breathe in as deeply as possible to smell his scent, would ask.

"Are these … yours?" I asked.

He shrugged.

"Batu!" I snapped.

He glanced up from his spot at the fire without responding. The question made him uncomfortable. I could see it in his face. Curious about what he was doing, I sat down beside him at the fire.

"You can ignore me, and I'll tell Ghoajin you're being mean, or you can tell me!" I threatened.

"Do they please you?" he asked.

"Yes, of course." I gazed at the roughened chunks so green, they were nearly black. "Very much," I added, unable to help the emotion that emerged whenever I saw Moldavite. "But I know what they mean to you."

"They are yours."

"So they were the ones you showed me."

"Yes, Moonbeam."

I met his gaze, touched by the gift. "It wasn't because I helped you in the plague tent, was it? Because you know, that was my duty." I deepened my voice for the last few words and did my best impersonation of him.

"Do you mock me, goddess?" he asked, the corner of his mouth lifting.

"Yes, I do. You don't accept my gratitude for your duty. I don't expect yours."

"It's not for the plague tent."

My heart skipped a beat. It felt like we were close to something, and I wasn't certain I wanted to push through the veneer to find out what that was. I glanced at the glass and lowered my hand.

"You do not ask why," he observed and tipped my chin up until we were face to face once more.

"I might know why."

"Tell me."

"You sold me off to someone at a trading post and this is your farewell gift," I said, seeking the most outlandish explanation to ease the tension between us.

He grinned.

"How will I ever survive without you?" I assumed an exaggerated damsel-in-distress pose.

As with the first time he kissed me, he surprised me once again. Cupping the back of my neck, he brought my face to his and pressed his lips to mine. My world stopped, the way it had the first kiss, and within seconds, everything from his heat to his scent to his strength had filled my senses.

I expected some small, token effort of resistance from my mind, some tiny voice that screamed at me to stop and consider what I was doing.

Nothing came – except for hunger.

I eased closer and opened to him, leaning into him and knowing he was strong enough to support and protect me. His arms wrapped around me, his body enveloping me with heat and strength that made it safe for me to melt into him. The need rising from the furnace in my stomach was of a different kind than any I had felt before. I craved him with intensity that felt wild, raw, new, the kind that went beyond the physical desire screaming in my blood to the part of me I hadn't ever wanted to bare to anyone.

In that moment, I didn't care if his fire burnt me to a crisp. I wanted to be consumed by him – every last part of me.

"I am a wolf in every way, my lamb. Are you prepared?" His husky question sent a shudder of desire through me.

"Yes," I whispered.

He lifted me to my feet and kissed me once more.

His large, warm hand slid beneath my clothing to my skin. I shivered, amazed at how small and delicate his size and strength made me feel. His touch was firm, possessive, as he swept my clothing off with ease and quickness before stripping off his own. His hands swept over my body, but not for long. His urgency was as great as mine, and I felt it in the slight tremble of his fingers and the long, thick erection pressed to my belly.

Batu claimed what was his too decisively to tease or wait. He lifted me onto his hips and pierced me fast and deep. I gasped at the sudden sensation that was almost painful with his size and wrapped my legs around him. He knelt and lowered me onto my back without leaving my body. I let my palms skim the incredible strength of the coiled muscles of his back and ran my fingers through his hair. He kissed me breathless and began thrusting, hard, deep thrusts that were slow enough for me to feel every tiny, blissful sensation.

His warm skin against mine, his hands twisting in my hair or exploring my skin, his breath on my neck or mouth on mine, his erection piercing and rubbing me in all the right places as he moved …

I'd never been consumed by anyone like this, never experienced sex in a way where I felt like my partner had been molded just for me. With a warrior's aggression and stamina, Batu was going to be unlike anyone I had ever known, and I was already clinging to him, struggling to pull him into me, to merge our bodies in every way possible.

I wanted every part of him, wanted our skin to be in contact until I no longer craved his scent and strength.

Batu was unlike any man I had ever met, and before he brought me to climax the first time, I knew I wasn't just lost to history, I was lost to him.

Chapter Fifteen

THE NEXT TWO WEEKS – OR MAYBE THREE? – PASSED IN A BLISSFUL haze. I was rarely away from Batu. During the days, we sneaked in make out sessions between helping the arriving clans settle in for the winter. The nights were filled with passion and lust that lasted for hours, leaving us deliriously happy on most mornings, not at all concerned about the changing weather, the increase of people, lack of sleep or anything else that didn't involve us naked in each other's arms as soon as dark fell.

Batu was different than any other man I'd been with. Taylor had been a gentleman in bed and out, while the college guys I slept with before my time traveling adventures were well, typical college guys. More interested in getting off, in quick conquests or dating the girl who made them look good in the eyes of the other guys. I was the pretty, cheerleader type; I didn't usually run in circles where the guys were looking for depth, and I was okay with that.

But Batu … he was every bit the fire Suvdin claimed he would be.

Dominant, giving, determined to learn every curve of my body and then brand it with his mouth and hands. He was in control– and I *liked* it. He was as assertive and possessive in bed as he was dedicated to his duty outside. I had never considered a man like him to be the type I wanted to be with.

He was. I loved our give and take in bed, melting into his arms and knowing I was safe and protected, closing my eyes and letting him surprise me with what he did next. I loved feeling the difference between his warrior's frame and my smaller, feminine one. I loved how he made me feel special and delicate while also pushing me to new highs every time we made love. And I loved that when we were spent from sex, we talked and cuddled until one of us fell asleep.

My stomach fluttered as I thought of him, and I paused in my work crushing herbs beside the fire, lost in the memories of his skin and scent.

"My uncle is here," he said as he entered. He was accompanied by a cold wind that made me think winter was going to be unbearable.

"Your uncle?" I echoed, blinking out of my trance.

Batu's eyes went to my lips. He shifted his route from the weapons in one corner to me at the fire and dropped beside me. His lips found mine for a deep kiss, one that sent desire and fire streaking through my body.

He withdrew. "I cannot stay now, Moonbeam," he whispered and cupped my face. "The Imperial Court gave me permission to exact revenge upon him for what he did to you."

It took me a moment for my addled thoughts to return to the present. "Oh. That uncle."

He chuckled and rose, headed to the weapons.

I watched him for a moment before his words clicked. After all our days and nights together, I was abruptly yanked back to the reality of the side of him I'd never been comfortable with. I still wasn't certain how to view the violence with which he often committed his routine duties.

"What revenge?" I asked and stood.

"What he did to you, times nine, followed by his death."

What? It was hard for me to believe Batu capable of such a thing after how he treated me. And yet, I recalled thinking the same when I saw him behead and gut people that I couldn't imagine him being gentle with me.

He was both, and I still had no clue how to reconcile the extremes. "Batu, you can't kill him on my behalf," I started, struggling with the return of the confusion that plagued me the first few weeks here.

"It is an obligation, goddess. Duty."

"But it's not right. I don't want anyone else dying on my behalf."

He sat back on his heels from his position sorting through his knives on his knees. His gaze found mine. "This is our world, Moonbeam, and our way."

"Batu, you know I see violence and killing differently than you do. If this is being done on my behalf, then can you not show mercy?"

He rose and approached me, automatically taking me in his arms. "You despise violence and killing, yet they are a part of who I am. Do you despise me as well?"

"No," I said firmly. "You are a good man, Batu."

"This is a good cause. A just cause. If I show him mercy, do you know how many others might step up to try to harm you? Because they, too, see that I will not follow through with my duty if they do?"

I touched his stubble roughened cheek, enamored by him even during such a topic. My heart was hammering, as much out of fear I'd disappoint him as fear for a man who didn't deserve my mercy at all.

But that didn't mean he should be tortured and then murdered.

"I understand your logic," I said slowly. "Do you go into this with no compassion for your uncle? No desire to see him live?"

Batu touched my face with tenderness, studying me. "This gives me no pleasure, and I know it will pain Ghoajin as well. But I must perform this duty. She will understand." He hesitated. "Will you understand, Moonbeam? Or will this come between us?"

I didn't know how to answer.

"It will," he said, reading my features.

I withdrew from his embrace and hugged myself. I could mute any of my twenty first century judgments of this era – except for excessive violence and death. That switch just wouldn't go out. I moved away to keep his scent from teasing me back into his arms, trying to negotiate with my conscience.

I didn't want this to cost me Batu. I didn't want anything to cost me Batu.

"You wish me to bend my will," he said quietly. "Are you willing to bend yours?"

"What do you mean?" I asked, meeting his gaze again. I was four feet from him and felt like it was a million miles. I ached to be close to him.

He was hard to read, except that he was intent and his tone measured. "You once swore never to marry again after Taylor. I would like you to be my wife."

The words floored me. The idea hadn't crossed my mind at any point during our tryst. Coming from any other man, it might sound like blackmail. But I knew what he was doing: compromising in his unique way.

What left me breathless: marrying Batu didn't elicit the reaction I expected. As before, there was no tiny voice urging me to refuse, no resistance whatsoever in my thoughts. It made little sense to me that I was not only considering his proposition after swearing I'd never let down my guard again, but *thrilled* by it.

To spare the man who hurt me, all I had to do was marry Batu. I chewed on it for a moment before realizing it wasn't just his uncle's looming death that bothered me. It was the potential death of every man who crossed our paths from here on out.

Because I was here for good. I understood this better now, even if there were some nights when a whisper of hope of seeing my home again flickered to life. If I were to stay with Batu forever, then this … issue had to be resolved now. I prepared what I wanted to say. My insides churned with fear he'd reject my request or view me as not worth the sacrifice.

"You know how … why I swore the oath never to marry again," I started. "I am willing to bend my will, Batu. But in return, I need your will to be bent on an issue related to your uncle's fate but not directly. I want to ask you not to kill unless necessary. I do not ask you to forsake your duty as a warrior or to dishonor yourself, but to kill only when absolutely warranted, when disarming or disabling is not enough, when mercy means one of us is at risk."

He listened, head tilted to the side. "You would dictate who I kill?"

I shook my head. "I would ask you to make that decision but to weigh the risk or danger to us rather than kill indiscriminately. I, in turn, will trust your judgment to determine who that is and never doubt you. I know how honorable you are." My mouth went dry. Nervousness set in, the kind of anxiety I knew stemmed from my experience with Taylor. There was no red flag in my mind at the prospect of marrying Batu, but the scars of Taylor remained.

He was thinking it over, gaze glued to mine. I had asked only what I felt I needed for us to make it without me flipping out eventually over him murdering people.

"Yes, Moonbeam. I will bend my will as you ask," he said softly.

"Then I will be your wife." *Holy shit.* I was starting to panic. It had nothing to do with Batu and everything to do with the emotions I hadn't dealt with yet originating from my trip to the Old West. The sense of detachment crept upon me, and I wobbled.

He closed the distance between us and rested his hands on my hips. I leaned into him, steadied by his heated strength. "Hear me, see me, touch me, taste me," he whispered and kissed me.

I focused on him, on how his arousal was thick and hard at my belly and the flavor of his mouth stoked a fire that never really went out and burned solely for him. A lifetime with Batu …

It wasn't enough. I didn't think any amount of time ever could be. I wrapped my arms around his neck and broke off the kiss, burying my face against his chest to breathe his scent. He held me tightly, his warmth engulfing me.

"You are frightened?" he asked, lips moving against my car.

"A little. I cared about Taylor. It hurt losing him. But Batu, if I lost you …" I couldn't even register the idea.

"You will not."

You don't know that. I had no idea if I was free and clear of Carter and Taylor's people. I hoped that, if they hadn't found me by now, they wouldn't. I had been in this place and time for over three months. But if they did … the issue was what might happen to Batu, if he'd meet the same fate as Taylor.

"I must deal with my uncle. Wait for me here," Batu said and eased away.

I almost asked what he intended to do – but stopped. I had promised to trust his judgment, and I meant to do so, no matter what that meant.

I watched him leave. When he was gone, the tears began. I didn't even know why they appeared or who I cried for, except that I was more scared than I had been in the tent when Batu was ill.

Trying to calm myself, I sat down by the warm fire and did my best to pull some logical reasoning out of my thoughts. I still had the occasional nightmare when I relived the tragic deaths of the people I had met in the Old West. Of them all, Taylor's was the one that plagued me, because I had an indirect hand in it.

Batu wasn't a time traveler or a target to Carter or his enemies. Carter had discussed me moving forward in time a hundred years, not seventy, which meant I never would've met Batu. So it didn't seem likely Batu was on Carter's radar to uncreate the way he had Taylor. Batu was a normal person, one I happened to care about more than I recalled caring about anyone else.

It hit me that I was crying for another reason: because giving my heart to Batu meant I was never leaving here. Even if Carter did find me, I was committing to someone whose world was *here*. I was therefore *choosing* never to go home rather than being trapped.

I gazed around at my surroundings. Sorrow was deep within my breast at the prospect of never going home and yet, I'd gradually come to adapt to this place. I might still wear my clothing inside out or on occasion become the center of laughter for the rest of the community, but I was also a part of Batu's clan, a member in every way but one.

Marrying Batu would finish the process. I'd belong here officially, with my new family.

Along with sorrow, a warm emotion bloomed within me as well, one of joy. I would finally have my own family and definite direction to my life. I kind of liked the sound of it, of undoubtedly knowing my place in the world.

And then there was Batu, the most incredible man I'd ever known.

"I can do this," I whispered, calming. "This is my home now."

I didn't feel the sense of resignation I had when I thought I was stuck in the Old West. I wouldn't have to learn to love Batu as I had

Taylor, because I already knew I'd finished falling for the warrior brute the first night I slept with him. As confused as I sometimes was about what happened in the eighteen forties, I also understood I'd never been in love with Taylor. Attracted to him, I'd harbored nothing but deep respect and gratitude for the man who rescued me and helped me navigate my first time travel trip.

But love was not among the emotions I experienced with Taylor.

I had, however, found it here in the unlikeliest of places with the unlikeliest of men.

Wiping away my tears, I drew a steadying breath and realized that yes, Batu was once again right. Against all odds, counter to any expectations I'd ever held about my life, I was meant to be here. My destiny led me back almost a thousand years in time to a man I never imagined existed.

And it was … fantastic, as the Ninth Doctor would say. Absolutely fantastic.

Before I had a chance to clear my thoughts, Batu returned. I met his gaze as he walked in, afraid to ask after his uncle. His weapons were clean, his body free of blood.

He knelt beside me, and I reached out to him instinctively, taking his face in my hands. "I delivered the punishment times nine but spared his life in exchange for a wedding gift," he told me.

I started to smile, my heart swelling. I wasn't going to dwell on the torture aspect – but on the idea the man was still alive, and I'd helped him stay that way. "What gift?"

"It is for you to name." A smile spread across Batu's face, and he peeled off his tunic in a sign of what was going to come next. "I have few horses for your dowry, but he is one of the wealthiest men in the steppes. Is this not clever, ugly one?"

I laughed loudly, impressed by my conniving – yet mercy granting – soon to be husband. "Very clever!"

"Mercy worked this once," he allowed and wrapped his arms around me. "Come here, my wife." He nuzzled my neck. "Or do you wish mercy as well?"

My breath caught. "Never," I whispered. "I want my warrior husband to pleasure me so well, I float back to the moon."

"As long as you always return to me." There was an odd note in his voice.

I leaned back and met his gaze, not expecting the troubled expression marring his features.

"Why do you say such a thing?" I asked, surprised. "Because I came from somewhere else?"

"Because my heart goes where you do, be it Ghoajin's for a feast or the moon from where you came."

"You don't have to worry about that now, Batu. Even if I could return to the moon, do you think I'd leave you behind?"

"I do not know. Would you?"

"Never." I kissed him gently. "I promise, Batu. Nothing can or will take me away, until it is my turn to go to the Eternal Blue Sky in death. I promise never to become lost again, either."

"I can find you anywhere," he assured me. "I will ensure you are never lost."

I liked the idea of him becoming my home. A lot more than I expected. "Thank you. Now shut up and make love to me."

He smiled in response.

Chapter Sixteen

THE WEDDING CEREMONY, I LEARNED THE NEXT DAY, WAS ALL OF sixty seconds long. It was a formality once the clan elders had given their blessing and the people had been informed. It was completed by a three-day celebration, hosted by Ghoajin, and attended even by the uncle who once tried to kill me. I even saw The Persian storyteller and Batu's cousin.

They were the best three days of my life. I spent the days with the family and the nights in Batu's arms being loved physically until I couldn't move. Batu was happy, too. Not that he ever appeared unhappy, but he smiled twice as much and was always within reach. I knew he was a warrior, one who might eventually be called away to serve his Khan, but for those three days, I could forget anything beyond the moment existed.

I had a home, a man who loved me more than I ever imagined possible, and an extended family that adored me.

I had everything I'd ever dreamed of wanting. My first time travel adventure ended in tragedy. My second in heaven.

Batu left early in the morning to train with the warriors of his clan on the fourth day, and I left our home to attend to Ghoajin, who was continuing to educate me about herbs. It was in early December, and the air was frigid. The blue sky was brilliant but cold and the sun bright despite the fact the temperature didn't climb above freezing. Shivering in my clothing, I adjusted the satchel containing herbs wrapped in linen and a couple of wooden containers I had filled with my practice balms.

"Moonbeam."

I turned and smiled at The Persian, whose quick step drew him to me. He bowed his head.

"Good morning," I said cheerfully.

"May I walk with you?" he asked.

"Sure."

We began walking towards Ghoajin's tent.

"You are quite content here," he observed with a trace of a smile.

"No. I'm *ecstatically* content here," I replied. A whisper of an instinct stirred, as it often did around people. I was guessing the empathic memory chip had never fully shut off but on occasion, subtly told me something about the people around me. I had never feared Batu despite seeing firsthand what he could do, and I had once wondered if the earthy Persian was a time traveler.

The sense about him re-emerged, but I dismissed it outright. If I had it my way, I'd never think about Carter ever again. I loved my new life and had every intention of enjoying every second of it.

"It pleases me to hear this," The Persian said. "Batu is an honorable man, more so than his uncle, who I've shadowed for a year or so. I am surprised you don't wish to return to your home, though."

"To the moon?" I asked with a laugh. "No. I'm happy here." I looked around me and felt the truth of those words to my core.

"Good." He appeared distracted or maybe troubled. "Moonbeam, may I tell you something in the strictest confidence?"

I stopped walking, not understanding what this man could possibly say that needed to remain a secret. "Yes," I said curiously and waited.

He faced me, hesitated, and then drew a breath. "Batu is very happy as well. He wishes for nothing more than to remain by your side forever."

I suppressed a smile. "Why do you say it like it's a bad thing?"

"Moonbeam, I know … I know who you are. What you are. Batu is of a similar mold. By deciding to remain here, permanently, he has angered his employers."

For a moment, I was held in such disbelief, I wasn't able to understand a word he said.

"I know you are both happy, and I know Batu much better than I do you. He deserves peace and love." The Persian's smile was genuine. "But … the people who are after you are not likely to care for the happiness of either of you."

The satchel slid from my hands. I didn't even feel it, barely registered the clinking of wood against wood as it hit the hard ground beside my feet. "What're you saying?" I managed.

"For reasons I cannot begin to understand, Carter has found you. It is not like him to pursue any of his agents so tenaciously. He normally lets them go when they wish it." The Persian shifted his weight between his feet, his features taking on a troubled expression. "I … I am not one of his, but he somehow located me and used me to find you, perhaps from some proverb I recorded about you when we met that survived history. I suspected who you were but had no reason to prove it or to pursue you. Sometimes, we cross paths with other travelers. Our missions and purposes are independent of one another, so we bow heads to one another and move on. Batu is a colleague, one I admire greatly and respect. I simply wish to warn you that the powers who seek you are close to finding you, and there is an inherent danger in that."

His eloquence ensnared me once more, managed to keep my shocked mind from processing the meaning behind his pretty words.

"You're saying …" I couldn't process the warning, not with the more incredible claim beating at my thoughts. "… Batu is a time traveler."

The Persian frowned as he studied me. "You didn't know."

I shook my head, mouth dry.

"I, uh, would've thought you both discussed your uh … outside employment before marriage. My agency assigned him to you on the onset of your travels, first to assess then to protect once we determined the level of technology in your brain. No one has ever mastered what Carter did. The microchips in your head are beyond belief," he explained. "Every agent in our organization knows about this singular success after decades of failure. Carter … interfered, as he is wont to do. I am not privy to the details, but I believe he conscripted Batu somehow – perhaps through force or blackmail – to work for him when you arrived in this era."

"I'm sorry … I'm having some …" *Shit.* I needed to talk and think and right now, my sense of detachment was yanking me into unconsciousness. I sagged and felt myself hit the cold, solid ground. My eyes closed despite my attempt to fight the darkness.

Stuck in-between places, I was vaguely aware of being lifted and carried somewhere, of the worried voices gathered around me, of the attempts to wake me.

But I stayed where I was, overwhelmed and straining not to plummet into darkness of emotion that was far, far deeper than where I had gone when Taylor passed.

I saw the man who saved me at the well on the Old West in my visions. It wasn't the first time I sensed him, but it was the first time I saw him. He had followed Fighting Badger – or perhaps me, since the Native American was stalking me – almost since I had arrived in the Old West.

But the shadowy figure, the one who saved me, had made only two appearances: once at the well and once in the tent of Ghoajin seventy years ago when he forced me to swallow the pills Carter sent with me.

The Persian was claiming that was Batu.

The man I loved, the man I thought I knew, had been lying to me.

Ask him first. He deserved a chance to refute what The Persian was saying or to deny it all. If The Persian hadn't known what he did, I would dismiss his words, because nothing was coming between Batu and me. Hanging onto the thread of hope that The Persian was wrong, his warning was then able to sink in.

Carter was close. I was being hunted. I wasn't freed or left to history; I had been lost, like a set of car keys, and both Carter and his enemies were searching. One of them, or perhaps both, had found me.

But this is my home now.

"Goddess!"

I wrenched awake. Ghoajin was leaning over me and sat back in satisfaction when she saw my eyes open. Suvdin and a couple other women in Ghoajin's entourage were present. I gazed at them briefly and tried to right my thoughts as I sat up.

I'm endangering everyone around me. I hated the feeling. It made me want to weep, reminded me I was meant to remain on the outside looking in wherever I was. Swallowing the emotion, I accepted a goblet of milk and focused on breathing steadily.

"Are you well, Moonbeam?" Suvdin asked, dark eyes searching my features.

"Yes, thank you." I offered a weak smile. "I think I need to lie down at home, though."

"I have sent for Batu," Ghoajin said. "He can escort you home."

Panic swirled within me. I needed some me-time before confronting him to sift through what The Persian had said, to be able to think straight. "I should go now." I hurried to my feet. "Excuse me, please."

Without waiting for them to respond, I fled. Tearing out of Ghoajin's *ger*, I raced through the tents towards minc, no longer caring about the biting chill or the peculiar looks I received.

I didn't stop running or feel safe until I was in the familiar tent that smelled of Batu. Only then did the frantic fear begin to subside and my reeling mind begin to process everything I'd heard.

Sitting by the fire, I wrapped myself in a blanket and stared into it, raw and numb, betrayed and desperate for what The Persian said not to be true. I didn't notice the passage of time or the disappearance of light as night fell. I didn't notice anything, just sat and stared.

And wished I'd never met Carter.

"Moonbeam!" Batu's voice was concerned as he strode into the tent. "We were hunting. I returned as soon as …"

I looked up at him, and he stopped. Wiping my face, I moved stiffly for the first time in hours and wrapped my arms around my knees.

"What is it?" he asked as he removed his outerwear and weapons. "Are you ill?"

"No." I had spent all day thinking about what to say and still couldn't figure out a good opening line. Gazing at my husband, the man I wanted to spend my life with, all I could think about was that I was about to lose him in one way or another. "Do you love me, Batu?"

"Yes, Moonbeam." He sat beside me. "More than the moon or sky or grass."

I believed him. Even The Persian had claimed it to be true. "I need to ask you something."

He waited.

"Are you a traveler? Were you with me in the Old West?"

Batu stiffened. For a moment, I thought he was going to walk away. Instead, he pulled me into his body and hugged me hard. "They found us."

My heart broke. *He lied to me.* "Why didn't you tell me?" I whispered.

"You did not speak of it either."

"Because I didn't think you'd understand." I pulled away to stare at him through tear-filled eyes.

"And you would understand what I was?" he challenged gently.

He made sense, as usual, but this was more than an oversight or an error made in good faith. This was deception from a man I viewed as too honorable to deceive me. "I don't know you, Batu. Is any of this ... *us* real? Am I a mission to you?"

"No, Moonbeam," he whispered. "You are my heart."

"Then tell me why you lied!"

He took my hands, quiet.

"Batu, I love you. I want to spend my life with you here. And then I find out it may not even be possible, not because of me, but because you're a time traveler who could disappear at any moment."

"I resigned," he said with mild humor. "Moonbeam-"

"Tell me everything."

He searched my features for a moment before drawing me into his arms again. I wanted to push him away, to sit at a distance that would allow me to discern how truthful he was without the distraction of his body.

But I also needed him at this moment. I shook out of emotion, and he had always been the one to steady me.

"I am from this time. I was … found when I was young and recruited into the agency. Trained in traveler ways as well as Mongol warrior customs. After ten years, I was returned here with the knowledge I'd be called upon from time to time to assist the agency as directed. My life was generally mine, except that I was ordered to become the guardian of the Goddess of the White Path. I was called upon to assess the threat you posed to history after Carter sent you to the eighteen forties and then to protect you, as my handlers had grown interested in your abilities.

"It was about that time that Carter approached me," he paused.

I listened, my stomach in knots. Clinging to Batu's tunic, I couldn't quite shake the fear that I was going to lose him or maybe already had lost the man I thought he was.

"I will say he was convincing." A troubled note, one containing resentment as well, was in Batu's tone. "I could travel forward and backward in time, and he could only send you backward. He needed you at a certain point in time, so I was ordered to make you take the magic beans he gave you, but the agency told me you needed to awaken earlier. So, I destroyed several of the magic beans as they directed, destroyed my connection to Carter and woke you twenty years before Carter wanted it so, in my era. My agency gave you the task of protecting Flowers and me the mission of protecting you. After that, they said I was free."

His deep voice calmed me, but I wanted to return to yesterday so badly, to erase the knowledge he'd lied to me and continue to live a blissful life with him on the steppes.

"I had planned to live with you here until we were too old to ride horses," he added softly. "I do not know when exactly I began to love you, but I was prepared to take you as my wife before the plague."

His explanation jived with what The Persian had told me.

But … I was still crushed, because I knew better than to let myself get attached and I had not only related to the people of this time but fallen in love and planned on spending my life here. I was a fool to think I could love Batu in peace.

Carter had damned me the moment we met, even before he put the microchips in my head that were so fascinating to Batu and Taylor's people.

"He won't let me go, Batu," I whispered hoarsely. "He won't let us stay together."

Batu's grip around me tightened. "We don't know that."

I do.

"The Persian. He told you," Batu guessed.

"Yes."

"I destroyed the ability for Carter or the agency to track me. When we stopped at the trading post, it was so I could return my tracking device to another time traveler there as part of my resignation. But if The Persian spoke to you, Carter spoke to him. He will know how to contact Carter."

I looked up at him. "You want to talk to Carter?"

"Yes, and tell him to let us go," he replied with resolve. "The agency will, once I assure them you will not harm the timeline of history."

"I don't even know why Carter sent me here. The Persian said his interest is unusual. He sent me on my first journey to … to uncreate … Taylor." The tears began again. "If I'm supposed to uncreate … you …"

"No, Moonbeam," Batu said. "Whatever Carter's intent, it is not this. I knew Taylor. We are the only people who can remember him. He was a good man, a very noble one."

It was nice to know Taylor was remembered by more than me. Whether or not it should have, Batu's admiration for the man who was uncreated took some of the burden of being the only person to recall Taylor from me.

"Carter was as adamant about me as he was you," Batu added. "He will not kill me. He may strand me somewhere in history, like he does his other agents, but he will not hurt either of us."

"I wouldn't be so sure of him. He destroyed Taylor, and I don't even know why."

"Nor do I. But, we have a means to contact him. If he intends to come for you or me, it is better we meet him head on."

The warrior side of him was speaking. I didn't know enough about Carter to know if being proactive was going to work, but I suspected he wasn't going to let me go. I didn't know his deal with Batu.

"I feel like I'm losing everything," I murmured. "I feel like I had the world, and now it's slipping away."

"We have one another, Moonbeam," Batu reassured me. "Carter can't take our love."

I smiled weakly.

"Do you still love me, my goddess?"

"Yes." I lifted my head to meet Batu's gaze. He touched my face gently. "In any time and place, I will always love you, Batu."

"And I you, Moonbeam. I will find The Persian now. We can face Carter together." He released me and rose, striding out without bothering to stop and grab his outdoor layers.

I watched him, unable to shake my fear and doubt about Carter letting us go.

I curled up by the fire for a short time, mentally wired yet spent from the emotional extremes of the past few days. It took me a moment to register the strange buzz coming from my pocket. Shifting, I reached in and instantly recognized the cool combination of plastic and glass.

I pulled the cell phone out and stared at it, dread charging my system once more. I sat up, heart pounding, and swiped the screen awake.

Josie? Please respond. Carter had written the message three times.

My stomach felt like it dropped to my feet. I unlocked the phone and stared at the messages briefly before responding.

Leave me alone, Carter. I'm happy here. I want to stay with Batu. Tapping the send button, I waited.

Carter's answer brought tears to my eyes. *You can't stay, Josie. You have to trust me. You have to leave that era immediately before his people pull you in and dissect your brain or worse. I know about you and Batu. You being there places him in grave danger as well.*

I began sobbing. I had never quite shaken the fear of my presence hurting those around me, and Carter knew exactly what button to push. I texted him a lengthy message, blasting him in a way I wanted to do in person.

You have to trust me. He responded.

"Well I don't!" I said, anger bubbling forth from the depths of my hurting soul. I told him as much.

I understand, Josie. You have no reason to trust me – but you must know that Batu's people will steamroll right over him to get to you. And honestly, if I need to flip that switch, I can do to Batu what I did to Taylor. But I don't want to – believe me. I don't. I want Batu alive as much as I need you alive. I'm banking on you being happy in the long run, but that's not here and now in Mongolia.

"I … hate you." Terror tore through me and left me breathless at the thought of Batu being uncreated before my eyes the way Taylor was.

Please do as I tell you, and I swear to you, Josie, I'll protect Batu against even his own people. He is better off being left in his home time and you moving on. I'll protect him. I swear it. If you stay … Josie, even if I don't uncreate him, he will be slaughtered by his own people. Give him a chance to find happiness and leave this era.

Carter made too much sense. If Batu stayed here, he might one day marry again or at least, he'd be surrounded by his family. Even if I never recovered from the pain building inside me, he would have that chance.

As if knowing I was leaning in his direction, Carter texted once more.

Go to the hill at the north side of the camp. Bring your phone. There's a rock the size of a large tortilla at the very top of the hill and beneath it, the pill you need to take to knock you out for time travel. I've always, ALWAYS protected you, Josie, and I will continue to do so, and Batu. Just do as I say, and he'll eventually end up happy.

"I hate you. I hate you. I hate you." I stood and swiped the tears away. I'd do anything for Batu, and Carter had figured it out. Maybe that was why he waited to find me, to give me time to fall in love with the man he planted in my world. "God! I hate you!"

Batu deserved so much more than this – but he also deserved to live, to have the opportunity I was losing to be happy.

I looked around at the first place that had ever felt like home and wanted to break down and weep. Carter wouldn't be reasoned with by Batu; this much I knew. Carter's plans for me had never been understood, but I didn't want him uncreating or hurting anyone else I cared about.

Putting on my over tunic with shaking hands, I picked up the bag of Moldavite Batu had given me.

This hurts so bad. My chest was tight and aching, and the pain inside me was the kind that would never go away. At times, I still felt it from the death of my parents. "Do it for Batu." I drew a shaky breath and tucked the phone and Moldavite away.

I left my home and listlessly made my way towards the small hill where I'd once had lunch with Ghoajin, Suvdin and the other women. Wherever Carter sent me next, whatever he did to me, I'd never forgive him for this, never stop loving Batu, and never, ever let myself grow attached to anyone else.

Ascending the hill, I found the pill beneath the stone. Sitting back on my heels, I gazed out over the encampment that had grown to ten times its original size from the influx of clans migrating south for the brutal Mongolian winter.

Batu was there somewhere, maybe looking for me, or possibly trying to negotiate with Carter.

I knew what he didn't: there was no negotiating with Carter, and we would never see each other again. If I didn't do this, Carter would kill him. Knowing Batu lived through this meant more to me than signing his death warrant by staying.

I bent over in physical pain from the idea of losing Batu and reminded myself incessantly that this was the only way Carter was going to let him live.

"I hate you, Carter," I whispered again and stared at the pill in my hand. Tears splashed onto my palm. "And I love you, Batu. More than life, more than anything. Stay alive and find happiness. I will always be your Moonbeam."

Not giving myself the chance to back out, I swallowed the pill and washed it down with water.

It acted quickly. Darkness swept through me, and I sagged, tumbling away from my emotions into unconsciousness.

Chapter Seventeen

I DIDN'T FIGHT OR TRY TO UNDERSTAND EXACTLY WHAT WAS happening this time when I emerged from the darkness to feel the sensations of time travel. I didn't care. Whether or not he meant to, Carter had destroyed me with the last trip through time. The Old West softened me up, and the Mongol Empire smashed my heart into a million fragments.

My thoughts were on Batu, on the raw pain of learning who he was and the knowledge I'd never see him again. My only solace – knowing he had a shot at a normal life. Hopefully. At the very least, he was going to live. Carter had sworn as much.

The final boom hit, and the intolerable heat reached its peak. The sense of floating began to subside.

I waited for the cool touch of the outside world of wherever Carter had sent me to begin to dispel the heat. I wasn't anxious at all to open my eyes and see where I was. In fact, I was half tempted to just lay there and see what –

Freezing water swallowed me, jarring my senses. I freaked out. My eyes opened, but all I could see was darkness, and water flooded my mouth and into my nose. Panicking, I kicked my legs and clawed at the liquid around me. My fingertips were numb already and coldness touched my bones.

I broke free of the water and coughed, sucking in deep breaths of air laced with sea spray. It was salt water, and fear shot through me.

If Carter dropped me into an ocean …

"Over there!"

Thank god. I bobbed, at the mercy of tall waves that tugged me under, released me, then smacked the back of my head. Stars were bright in the velvety night sky above, and I struggled as my limbs quickly grew numb. I was shaking and cold.

A lantern attached to the bow of a small boat morphed out of the darkness, headed towards me. "I'm … here!" I shouted. The waves pulled me under, and I barely had the strength to kick back to the surface.

Someone grabbed me by the back of my neck and dragged me roughly over the edge of the rowboat and dropped me into the bottom. I strained to catch my breath and blinked away water to determine what I could about where I was.

"You are far out for a night swim," a male voice said.

The other two men in the rowboat laughed.

The face of the speaker leaned over me. He was a large man with pale skin, long, dark hair and blue eyes that glinted silver in the moon. He wore little more than a fur-lined vest and leather pants despite the cold night and flung a blanket of fur over my shaking body.

I was going to freeze to death. I just knew it.

"Jorgensen, who swims so far out at this time of night?" someone shouted from nearby.

"A brave soul!" The dark-haired man named Jorgensen said in approval. "One of our women, no doubt to impress her man."

Whatever. Even if I could respond, I wouldn't. As it was, I was far too cold to attempt to speak through my chattering teeth. I tasted blood and assumed I'd bitten my tongue but couldn't feel it.

The bow of a massive, wooden ship came into sight above my head, and I struggled to sit, taking in the dress of the blond and brown haired men peering over the edges and the size and make of the ship.

Vikings. It was yet another era I knew nothing about, and I stared at it, cursing Carter for not sending me somewhere civilized and warm, like Greece or Rome or something.

"You are a brave girl," Jorgensen said. "But you should not swim so far if you cannot make it back."

"Tell me, woman, who is your man? Where is he this night?" another called from the ship.

They were staring at me, waiting for my response. I huddled into the fur-lined blanket irritated and cold. "I don't need a man," I proclaimed. "I'm perfectly capable of swimming wherever I want and rescuing myself."

And in that moment, I knew I meant it. I was done being reliant upon anyone for survival, and I would never, ever again risk my heart, my sanity or my health for anyone else.

"You have no man," Jorgensen assessed. "But you are old enough you should have been wedded at least once. Are you a widow?"

Ugh. I didn't think it was any of his business, and I didn't like the reminder that yes, I was a widow – twice over.

"Yes," I replied. "I am."

"You seek to impress Odin this night?" someone else joked.

I didn't want to impress anyone. I wanted to be left alone forever so I could wallow in my misery.

But self-pity wasn't in my personality, and I was already looking around out of curiosity at my new surroundings. The rowboat bumped against the warship while Jorgensen and a blond man on the ship spoke. I wiped my face, desperate to get out of the soaking clothing to warm up but not about to strip around a group of strange men who probably didn't have twenty first century morals about naked women in their midst.

I was going into this experience with a completely different mindset, one as cold as the waters of wherever I was. No attachments, no love, no happiness, no hope for a happy ending.

I hurt too much to take a chance on anyone ever again. A familiar sense hit me, one I hadn't yet experienced traveling back in time.

Scooting over, I leaned over the side of the boat and threw up. I wasn't able to see if it was black like my vomit was when I went forward in time. I had the headache of traveling to the past but had yet to throw up. My stomach was empty, and I dry heaved for a few minutes.

Jorgensen grunted as he sat on the bench nearest me. "Olaf, take us back to the village. Our wayward swimmer needs warmth." His gaze fell to me.

I pushed myself up from the edge of the boat.

"Do you have your own hearth or are you in need of one?" he asked.

"In need of one."

"You are recently widowed then." He was studying me. "I know a man who will want to speak to you."

Oh, god. Here we go. I sighed and turned my gaze to the sky. *Bring it, Carter and the universe.* I had no choice but to find a way to deal with whatever mess I'd been dropped into.

I missed Batu already. Fighting back tears, I did what he had taught me and practiced grounding my senses in the present.

Lanterns glowed in the windows of wooden homes with thatched roofs lining the bay of a small port. The sea air smelled of fish and salt, and the gentle rocking of waves bumping the boat helped ease some of my fear. Carter swore he'd put me somewhere safe. I didn't quite know for certain where I was or how I was going to be safe around Vikings known for pillaging and burning down whole villages, but I had learned a few things about surviving over the past two adventures.

I was going to make it through this, if not with Carter's help, then because if I had learned anything, it was that I was strong enough to do it. Although … I'd trade everything I'd done and everything I was to return to the steppes and spend my life with Batu.

Whenever you are, I love you, Batu. Raw and hurting once more, I willed the words into the universe and hoped they'd find him.

The men rowed to a dock, and I prepared myself mentally for my next challenge as much as I could. No matter what, I had to survive. I had to discover what Carter's end game was.

It was all that mattered now that he had taken everyone else from me.

That and finding a way to beat him at this twisted game.

Exclusive Excerpt from

Black Moon Draw

By Lizzy Ford

Chapter One

The Shadow Knight of Black Moon Draw lifted his boar's head to the sky, worn yet energized by the day at battle. As the battle-witch had promised, he had won shortly after sunset and stood, triumphant, over the body of his slain enemy. The battlefields were littered with the dead and dying, enemies slaughtered by his bloodlust and brute strength, and the bodies of men who served him. He counted the dead then nodded in satisfaction.

It was a good day. Except he needed a new witch. His lay among the corpses, her purple robes fluttering in the late summer breeze.

With six kingdoms conquered and three remaining to oppose him, he did not have time to celebrate his victory with a feast. The end of the era was coming, and with it, the fulfillment of a thousand-year curse that gave him little time to find the last great battle-witch he had sought for ages. The Heart of Black Moon Draw was depending on him. There was no way he was going to fail.

My phone rings, jarring me out of the reading zone where I've been hiding from reality all day. I blink at the words on the screen of my laptop to help me return from the world of Black Moon Draw and then snatch the cell phone on the desk beside my mouse.

"Hello," I answer groggily. Sitting back, I wipe my nose with my palm. The tears stopped a while ago. My nose is still running.

"Hey, baby. Saw your Facebook post," my mother says. "Sorry to hear about Jason."

"Shit happens, Mom," I mumble. "Real life's so much stranger than fiction."

"Is the wedding really off or is this something you're both working through?"

I flinch, lost for a moment. I've spent the past year preparing to dedicate my life to the man I thought was my true love, only for him to tell me he's found someone else, a week before the wedding.

Someone more *grounded*, he claims.

I hope she's ugly. It's a terrible thought, but I can't help it.

"It's off, Mom," I answer. "He says I spend too much time with fictional people when I should be in the real world with real people."

My mother is silent.

I know she's working hard not to utter an *I-told-you-so.* Jason isn't the first person to try to pry me out of the land of the nonexistent and he isn't the first to leave my life over it.

Probably not the last. I'd like to think I *have* to lose myself in books. I've been a librarian for a year now and one of my tasks is to help identify great books to feature at the library. It's a perfect job. All I do when not behind the desk at work is read. If I don't keep reading, how will I know if I've found the next great thing? There's some vindication for a bookworm who reads an awesome book before it's mainstream.

"He was good for you," my mother says. "But what's important is your happiness. Maybe this will encourage you to try to get out more?"

"I don't *want* to get out more. I'm happy being an introverted hermit. I don't care how poor or anti-social I am! If that's not good enough for him . . ." I fight back tears.

"Okay, baby." My mother clears her throat. "Anything I can do for you?"

"No. Thanks, Mom."

"Let me know if you want to go out for a cinnamon roll or something."

"Okay. I'll call you tomorrow." I hang up, tired of being upset. My eyes blur as I stare at the screen of my laptop.

Black Moon Draw is the name of the story that's waiting for me, an unfinished fantasy novel I found on Wattpad, a site where authors write books in real time by uploading a new chapter every so often.

I discovered it this morning, after finishing everything in my Kindle on my to-be-read list and then surfing the net for more books by my favorite author, a mysterious figure who goes by the initials LF. There's no website or bio anywhere for this author and I was thrilled to discover this partially finished story after rolling through her catalog over a period of three days. I assume LF is a woman – most romance writers are.

This book was written for my shitty week.

It features the ultimate, non-redeemable character, the Shadow Knight of Black Moon Draw, whose soul is so black, the sun can't warm its depths. The violent, half-man, half-beast knight rules a kingdom where there is no daylight, only the perpetual fog and grayness of twilight. He spends his lifetime in battles and steamrolls over everyone in his path.

There's no peace, no love, no hope in Black Moon Draw. Only death and destruction and a knight who doesn't know mercy or forgiveness.

"I love this. I wish I could chop off people's heads with one strike," I murmur, rereading the last little bit before the chapter ends. "Freaky but cool."

The book speaks to me, which is why I keep hitting refresh on my browser in the hopes that the author has updated in the time it took me to read. Thinking about the knight makes me shiver. He's sexy in a very caveman way. Definitely not civilized, which fits my brittle mood today.

I glance at the television and sit up straight, exhausted after spending the day alternately crying and reading. I've had my four all-time favorite movies – *Labyrinth, The Princess Bride, The Neverending Story,* and *Pride and Prejudice* – playing on a loop all day. I'm on vacation this week and supposed to be in the final stages of planning a wedding, not stuck in my house.

Now I'm just gonna spend what's left from the wedding fund on books to help me escape my miserable life.

Pushing away from the desk, I go to the bathroom and stare at my bleary appearance. My hair is in a lumpy ponytail, my eyes rimmed with red, and nose red as well. I've spent the day eating ice cream and am almost surprised it doesn't already show on my otherwise trim body. A true bookworm introvert who hates to leave the house, I've done a thirty-minute yoga video religiously every day in my living room for the past three years since leaving my mom's house. With striking blue-green eyes and dark hair, I'm pretty but also plain.

According to Jason. What a bastard. I can count the number of compliments he's given me since we met on one hand. Our relationship is always like a rollercoaster: brief periods of euphoria followed by months of despair.

I wash my face before returning to my desk.

"Take me away, mysterious LF," I tell the laptop.

I go down the checklist I made of essential characters that appear in every one of LF's books. Part of the fun is figuring out who is whom before the author reveals it.

"I've got the Fool, the Betrayer, the Devoted-but-Doomed guy, the Red Herring, the Loyal Second-in-Command, Beautiful Maiden, Love Interest, Villain, a bunch of minions . . ." I pause. My thoughts go to the Shadow Knight. "The Hero. Hmm. Can the biggest, most violent, mysterious, and relentless badass - with no possibility of redemption - be a hero?"

I lean back and sigh.

"No, he can't," I answer my own question. "And a . . . creature like him can never have a love interest. No one in their right mind would want to be with him." Normally I'm able to spot the end game of a novel a couple of chapters in, but this is something different entirely. "How can a book have no hero or love story? What the hell is LF doing?"

The Shadow Knight is unlike any of the characters LF has ever written about. He doesn't fit any of the profiles of the characters LF includes in her books and thinking about him makes me feel . . . edgy. Scared or uneasy because he seems so real. When I read his passages, I can almost hear his deep, gravelly voice and smell the scent of horse leathers.

Which is silly. It's the sign of a great author, not me going crazy. Besides, what reader fears fictional characters?

"So we have a romance with no hero and no love story." I rest my head on my desk, exhausted. "I didn't think that was possible. At least he's sexy."

Unable to see how his mind works like I can the other characters, I've been locked in a silent battle with him since starting the first chapter. I want to hate him for being what he is, but find myself compelled to reread every one of his passages instead.

Fed up, I close the laptop. The *last* thing I want today is a story I have to dissect. I need a distraction, not another stupid man intent on infuriating me.

"You're giving me a headache. You and every other man on this planet," I mutter to the imaginary knight. "What the hell are you waiting for? Why don't you just tell me your story the way every other character does? And why is it taking LF so long to upload a new chapter?"

A fictional man, of course, can't answer.

"At least you're mortally wounded at the battle of Brown Sun Lake, you bastard. I'm hoping she leaves you that way. I can't believe she misspelled *coincidence* twice in the first two chapters, either. Ever heard of spell-check, LF?" I ask no one in particular. "You're stressing me out! You know what will make this easier? Wine."

I've got a couple of nice bottles I had been saving for the wedding rehearsal. I'm halfway to the kitchen when I realize there's something else I've been saving for that occasion.

The gorgeous, purple dress my mother bought me.

Halting, I debate whether or not drinking wine in a fancy dress at home makes me desperate or is a reasonable way to cope.

One of my three cats meows from his spot on the kitty jungle gym in one corner. My shoulders slump.

"You're right. I really am gonna end up a crazy, single, cat lady," I whisper, new tears forming. "Why can't the heroes in books be real?"

My cat blinks at me, but doesn't answer.

"I hate my life. There's no happily-ever-after in the real world." I'd give anything for a do-over, another chance to be someone worthy of a fictional Hero instead of a wallflower with insecurity issues.

Pretty certain I'll die a crazy old maid, I decide to wear my prettiest dress, break out the wine and chocolate and watch *Pride and Prejudice*. Maybe when I wake up in the morning, there will be a new chapter waiting for me.

Chapter Two

The Shadow Knight paced across Blue Star Bridge, the wooden and stone walkway that arched across the river dividing his kingdom, Black Moon Draw, from his eastern neighbors of White Tree Sound.

He stopped in the middle, listening to the sounds of night. Somewhere, an animal splashed into the shallow waters, probably chasing its dinner, while the calls of owls and other night birds rose from the forest at his back. He didn't register the night chill that skated across his muscular form. Built with the power of a bear and the agility of a panther, he was poised and ready to fight. The sword at his back was taller than a full-grown woman and the axe, daggers, whip, and other weapons at his belt were polished and waiting for their next kill.

Ignoring the nervous band of White Tree Sound sentries that stood on one end of the bridge, he swung his massive boar's head around to observe his surroundings. Moonlight trickled through the fog shrouding Black Moon Draw and reflected off the slow moving river below.

"M'lord," a quiet voice said from behind him. "You will cross Blue

Star Bridge this night?"

The bridge was the established border of his lands. He had paid little heed to the kingdom on the other side, with whom he had a truce born out of necessity rather than desire. He had too many other battles to fight to worry about this peace-devoted enemy. He alone could take the forty sentries bunched around the end of the bridge, but the army beyond the forests would require some planning and more men than he had to spare in order to defeat them.

"Not tonight," he said in his low, deep growl. "I need a new battle-witch."

"And you think to find one here?" His most trusted advisor, the man who trained his armies, drew abreast of him. He wore the head of a wolf, the silver eyes and sharp fangs gleaming in the night.

"In my dreams, this is where she appears." There were no sounds other than those he expected to hear, no unusual scents picked up by his sensitive boar's nose.

"Perhaps the Red Knight of White Tree Sound has her." His master-at-arms eyed the restless men belonging to the neighboring kingdom.

"No. She has not come yet."

"From where do you expect this battle-witch to come?"

"From the edge of the world." The Shadow Knight flipped a dagger in his hand, caught it, and sheathed it once more. "Come. She is not here."

"Did these dreams say when she would come?"

"Dreams are like shadows. Even I cannot capture them fully," the Shadow Knight replied. He pulled himself effortlessly onto his massive steed with one arm.

"Except the one about your battle-witch." His second mounted his horse as well.

"'Tis how I know it's different. She will be here." His gaze lingered on the bridge. "'Tis my destiny to reclaim the lands lost by my bloodline before this era ends."

"We have less than a fortnight."

"She will come," he said, resolute.

"I know the value of a good battle-witch. We can post a sentry, if it pleases you."

"Aye. A dead battle-witch does me no good." The Shadow Knight pulled off the Heart of Black Moon Draw – a medallion carved from a rare, black gem and containing the magic of the kingdom – from around his head and tossed it to his master-at-arms. "Instruct our scout to claim her on my behalf."

"Aye, sire."

The Shadow Knight wheeled his horse to face the forest. Squeezing his calves against its belly, he raced into the trees, towards the army preparing for tomorrow's battle.

Chapter Three

OH, GOD. MY HEAD!

I'm afraid to move, knowing once I do, the world's worst hangover will kick my ass. The dull, brain deep throb is already there, waiting to explode when I try to stand. Instead, I listen for the familiar sounds of my apartment in the morning: the neighbor's annoying alarm, the honking of traffic, shuffling of people down the hallway as they leave for work . . .

. . . the gurgle of a stream?

I smell flowers that aren't anything like the vanilla plugins in my bedroom, and something is tickling the sensitive inside of my forearm.

Spiders!

Only such an irrational fear could make me snap up into a sitting position without considering my head.

I groan, gripping it.

I blink, trying to focus, to see my bedroom wall instead of the dead forest where the wall should be. Squeezing my eyes closed, I open them again. My hands drop to my sides and I stare.

The trees are still present, their bare, sagging branches rattling in a cool morning breeze that makes me shiver. Wildflowers litter the grassy area around me, dancing in the wind. Fog clings to the branches of trees and covers the sky.

I slap my cheek lightly to make sure I'm not stuck in a dream. This . . . place certainly seems real. The source of the gurgling is a wide stream whose banks are connected by a graceful, arching stone and wooden bridge. It feels like morning, but is gray out, like the period of graininess between sunset and night.

Where the hell am I? I could have drunk myself to death and maybe the bridge leads to heaven.

Do people in heaven get hangovers?

My head hurts too badly for me to freak out. It's definitely a fitting ending to my week. I'm wearing my pretty purple dress, my feet bare, and dark hair hanging around my shoulders. At least I left the earth dressed decently.

"Oh, my poor mom!" Deep sorrow is building within me at the thought of not saying farewell to my mother and I shift onto my knees. Branches snap from somewhere across the bridge. I concentrate on controlling the headache. My stomach hurts and muscles ache, like I spent the night in some awkward position sprawled across the couch watching my favorite movies.

"Are you the witch?" The male voice makes me jerk.

I face him – and scream. Crouched ten feet from me is a creature with a man's body and a panther's head whose golden eyes are watching me like he's hungry. The unholy combination of man and beast is terrifying.

"Stay away from me!" I shout.

Maybe this isn't heaven. I stagger to my feet, smash to my knees, and then stumble up again.

I fling my arms out to either side to help me balance. The ground isn't moving, but it feels like it is. When my head stops spinning, and I'm fairly confident I won't fall, I look again at the half-man . . . thing. He's dressed in brown leather leggings and a long shirt cinched at his waist by a thick belt. A sword dangles from the belt.

From the neck down, he's a man in every way I can see, from his very human hands and fingers to normal shaped feet in boots.

But his head . . .

"What *are* you?" I ask.

He's watching me closely with his round panther eyes, his jaw open in a noiseless pant. He hasn't moved out of his crouch, as if he's trying to figure me out the way I am him. "You are from the edge of the world?"

"I'm pretty sure I'm not from here." I gaze around in confusion. "This isn't heaven, is it?"

He laughs, a strange, half-growl, half-guffaw.

I take a step back.

"Black Moon Draw has never been mistaken for heaven," he replies.

Black Moon Draw?

"Oy!" someone shouts from the bridge.

I turn, gripping my head again at the sudden movement. A man – a *normal* man – is standing in similar clothing in the middle of the bridge. His tunic is white and bears the symbol of a tree on it.

"Will you be claiming that witch?" he calls to the man with the panther head. He has a Cockney accent I have trouble understanding.

"She's on our land!" The panther-man snarls, standing. "You would be wise to heed my warning. If you cross that bridge, none of the gods will stand between you and my master!"

The other guy is hanging out in the middle of the bridge. It's clear he's not going to cross it and I don't blame him one bit.

"Did you say Black Moon Draw?" I ask the panther-man.

"Aye." He glances at me then returns his golden glare to the man with the tree on his shirt.

"No, really. Black Moon Draw?"

"Aye."

"Terrifying, isn't it?" the man on the bridge calls. "White Tree Sound is at peace and ruled by a man nothing like the beast of Black

Moon Draw."

"My master is not a beast!" Panther-man retorts.

My ears are buzzing and I'm starting to think I either didn't wake up or I woke up in hell.

"Is your master the Shadow Knight?" I ask. "The one with a boar's head who knows no mercy and chops off the heads of pretty much everyone he meets?"

"Aye." Panther-man says with a hint of pride.

"He'll deflower and kill you. Come to us and we will treat you well. Our last battle-witch was made a lady and died of old age," the man on the bridge yells.

At least, I think that's what he says. His accent is heavy enough I'm filling in some of the words.

Black Moon Draw. Shadow Knight. Battle-witch.

I rack my brain. There must be a reasonable explanation for what's going on. Perhaps I didn't wake up from a weird dream? Or did my misery turn into an all-out break with reality?

It's all I can think of. I can't remember most of last night after cracking open a second bottle of wine. This place certainly seems real, from the cool mist settling into the trees to the freak show beside me.

But it *can't* be real. If I were going to be dropped into a book, it'd be *Pride and Prejudice* or, better yet, *Fifty Shades of Grey*, both of which contain civilized worlds with Heroes who only need their Heroines to make their lives complete. From what I read, this nightmarish world is plagued by death and war. Why would I be here of all places?

The two are arguing. I'm having difficulty making out their words and more trouble standing. I sink onto the ground and stare, dazed, confused, horrified. There's a tiny voice in my head telling me that if I thought my life was bad before, it just got a helluva lot worse.

Panther-man clasps my shoulder and kneels before me.

I blink his animal face into focus and recoil.

"I claim you in the name of the Shadow Knight of Black Moon

Draw. Do not cross Blue Star Bridge. They will deflower and kill you." He places something heavy and cold in my hand. "This will grant you safe passage through our kingdom, should you need it. I will not be gone long." He stands and leaves.

It takes me a minute before the sensation of wanting to faint passes. I'm clutching a black jade or obsidian medallion with strange carvings strung on a thick, worn piece of leather. Studying it, I'm trying not to be weirded out by how heavy and real it feels, as if this whole place isn't a flimsy dream that'll dissipate soon.

How can this be real? I'm perfectly sane, or thought I was. Psychosis brought on by mental trauma sounds more likely than I'm stuck in a *book.*

"M'lady." Another voice calls from the bridge.

Looking up, my gaze lingers.

Wow. Dressed in a rich red cloak lined with fur, the brunet man on the bridge has the chiseled features of a model. He's smiling, a perfect, white, even grin, that renders him boyish, charming.

"I'm the Red Knight of White Tree Sound. I rule all of this." He motions to the forest beyond the bridge. "I would like to invite you into my lands and home."

I really hope Prince Charming has a castle. It figures I have to go to a fictional world to find the perfect man.

"I think I'll stay here," I reply. "In case I can go home."

His eyebrows lift. "Home is Black Moon Draw?"

"Oh, god, no. Never. From what I know of that place, it's hell."

His brow is furrowed.

I swallow hard. I'm not going to cry, at least, not until I'm fully convinced this isn't a dream or psychotic break.

"I would encourage you to cross the bridge," he says. "Before the Shadow Knight comes to claim you. We are in need of a battle-witch. You will be safe and protected."

"Battle-witch?" I'm thinking hard through my headache to recall what LF wrote about the mysterious women that the warriors of this world believed could predict and influence the outcome of battles.

"Every knight-ruler in the realm has heard of your coming. The last great battle-witch," he replies. "Come. We have food and clothing to warm you."

It's kind of hard to say no. Jason definitely wasn't a looker and I've never had a man this handsome give me the time of day. While I know nothing of his little kingdom, I do know that I don't want to be here when the violent Shadow Knight shows up.

Getting to my feet, I make my way through the grasses to the stone path leading across the bridge. I pull on the medallion Panther-man gave me, just in case.

Just in case WHAT? I wake up in a different book? Get lost in the forest?

Nothing is making sense right now, except that I'm definitely hungry and could use a blanket or warmer clothing.

"No tricks? I'll be safe?" I ask, pausing at the foot of the bridge.

"You have my word," the Red Knight responds quickly.

Why not? Maybe this man is the elusive Hero I hadn't yet discovered in LF's book. Or maybe he's the Red Herring meant to lead me astray or the Betrayer . . . How the hell do I figure it out?

The panic bubbling within me makes my head pound worse. Whatever I think of the Red Knight, I at least know the Shadow Knight will probably behead me if he finds me.

I walk and join the Red Knight in the middle of the bridge, pausing to gaze up at him. My god – he's utterly beautiful.

"You will need new robes," he observes, gaze lingering on my breasts. "You are in the correct color, but not the correct cloth."

Purple. I'm remembering more details now. The battle-witches of this world wear purple. The color is rare and only the elite seers wear it.

What happens when they realize I'm not a battle-witch?

The thought makes my head pound. I touch it gingerly.

"You are unwell?" the Red Knight asks.

"Drank too much wine last night."

"Ah. A common ailment." He waves over one of the three men waiting in the area between the bridge and forest. "Come." He starts down his side of the bridge.

I glance over my shoulder, noticing for the first time how the mists hanging in the branches of trees on the Black Moon Draw side of the bridge are absent in White Tree Sound. There are birds on this side of the forest, and it smells of pine. The forests are different – one alive and one dead – yet divided only by a stream. It's sunny on this side of the stream, too.

This is too weird. I need time to think or maybe to get rid of my headache first because thinking is too difficult right now.

Trailing the Red Knight off the bridge, I pass the three guards waiting for him and follow him onto a deer trail. We don't walk far and stop on a rustic road hedged by trees. A shoebox looking, wooden wagon with four horses out front and a driver waits in the middle of the road.

Another guy in white opens the door for the Red Knight, who sweeps off his cape before climbing in. I get in as well and sit opposite him. There's a trunk between the two benches and a lantern hanging from the low ceiling in the center whose light doesn't reach the corners of the wagon.

The wooden benches are covered by pillows. It's warmer in here and I rub my upper arms to help warm me.

"'Tis a half day ride to my hold," he tells me. "You are hungry?"

I nod.

He taps the trunk. The top slides off as if by magic and he reaches into its depths to lift a tray of food: jerky, cheese, bread, and whole fruit. A pitcher and two stocky goblets are present as well.

Another tap and the trunk slides closed.

"Eat," the Red Knight urges me. "The moon apple is a specialty of my lands." He holds up a white apple.

"Thanks." I accept it and put it in my lap. I'm not much of one for apples. Bread, though, is my weakness, as evidenced by my thighs, and I grab a piece. "You said you've been waiting for me?"

"Battle-witches are rare. The knight-rulers of our realm are sent visions or dreams when a new one is to come," he explains with another charming smile. "The Shadow Knight has been eyeing my lands for many years. We are at peace, but I'd like to be ready."

What do I say to that? "I don't blame you," I reply awkwardly. I take a huge bite of bread and then a sip of wine. The bread is dry and hearty, the wine a little stronger than I'm used to.

The carriage jolts into movement and I rock back, catching myself on a pillow.

"His was recently killed," he adds. "I know he is looking for a new one."

"What happened to yours?" I ask.

"'Tis the fate for any battle-witch captured by an enemy. Deflowering and death. But mine died of old age since there has been no war in years."

"Deflower? You mean rape?"

"Rape or seduction. Most battle-witches are young like you and fall for a handsome knight who brings them flowers. I barter such services to any kingdom that needs it. It's how my coffers stay filled with gold and I stay on good terms with all."

He's a damn gigolo. Why am I not surprised?

"Why not just kill her?" I demand, not understanding the need to seduce a woman before lopping off her head.

He laughs, like I've asked the stupidest question on the planet. "Because your kind can't die! If I chop off your head, it'll grow back by tomorrow morning. But you can lose your powers, if you are no longer pure, which makes you vulnerable."

I lower the wine. Do I make a joke about it being too late to be pure and risk him beheading me to prove a point, or do I play along and hope

I'm never challenged to prove I'm a battle-witch?

You wake up. That's what you do. I close my eyes and will myself out of this mess.

"They say if an ordinary man even kisses a battle-witch, his man parts will fall off. I have a certain immunity to such a fate," he adds.

Are these wacky rules made up by LF? Because they don't make much sense to me. Have these people ever chopped off the head of an alleged battle-witch to test their theory?

Opening my eyes, I'm not surprised to see I haven't been magically transported back to my home. I start eating again. I'm guessing sleeping with the fine specimen of a man before me is off the table as well, though I'd rather not sleep with a man-whore in the first place.

Unless he *really* knew what he was doing in bed, à la Christian Grey and unlike Jason.

"The guards said you appeared last night," the Red Knight says and leans forward, as if he doesn't want anyone to hear his words. "You were not there and suddenly you were. From whence came you?"

I sip my wine, once again at a loss as to how much I should say. The Red Knight is waiting patiently, his friendly, open features encouraging me. He's not giving me the vibe I'm used to, that I'm about to be judged or made fun of.

"From another world," I reply honestly. "I don't know where or how. I went to sleep there and woke up here."

"Someone sent you here," he guesses.

"Yeah. How'd you know?"

"Let's just say you're not the first who's been sent." He's frowning, his eyes moving to stare at some point in the distance.

Is it possible the people of this world are aware of mine? How crazy would that be?

"My head hurts so bad." I can't even entertain such a deep thought.

He's too distracted. "This world, is it magical?"

A glance around reminds me these people don't know what

electricity is let alone the Internet. "You can say that."

He sits back, pensive.

I eat quietly, uncertain what's bothering him. The cheese is awesome, much better than the bread and wine. I'm not a fan of jerky and quit after choking down one piece.

"What is your name, witch?" he asks finally.

"Naia."

"Naia." A flicker of surprise crosses his features. He shifts forward again. "You must not tell others of this magical world from whence you came or the person who sent you or even your name."

"Why not?"

"A battle-witch, such as you are, is expected to have knowledge of the unknown and magic. But another world?" He shakes his head gravely. "You will be flogged or worse, put to death, for even mentioning it. And . . ." He pauses, as if not sure he should continue, before he does. "I'm going to track down the person who sent you. I don't need others getting in my way."

Ummm . . . yeah, right. No book character can find its author, because they aren't real.

Listening and growing more confused, I'm surprised by the severity of his expression and the sudden way he's looking at me as if he wants to feed me to Panther-man after all.

It hits me then that this man, the Red Knight, is a warrior, one trained to lead men into battle and kill, even if his kingdom is at peace. It's not like he's a Starbucks barista or coworker at the library. He's armed with a sword and knife and friendly – but dangerous. If he wants to track LF down, I doubt it's to thank her for creating his world.

"If you find that person, tell her to send me home," I reply finally.

"I shall," he said. "In the meantime, listen to me carefully. When asked, battle-witches always say they are from the edge of the world. You and I know differently. No one else can know."

"I'm sorry." It seems like the right thing to say. "I didn't know. I won't say anything to anyone." I want to ask him if he knows he's just a fictional character. By the look on his face, it's not a good time to point that out.

"And if you are asked by anyone, you are to tell them you were found on my side of the river. Do you understand?" His gaze is piercing, his face stony.

"I think so."

"You must *know* so. I will ensure you never return home if you admit the truth to anyone."

Things just got real a little too fast for me. I nod and then find my voice. "I understand." My heart is slamming into my chest, adrenaline racing through me as my instincts warn me of danger. It's hard to keep in mind that none of this is real when he looks like he's ready to stab me with a knife.

The intensity around him fades and the smile returns. "I have never found a new battle-witch. I am eager to learn how well you predict battles."

"Yeah." My head is feeling better from the food. My appetite has fled. "Me, too." It seems like the only safe answer and I start to retreat into my shell, the way I do around anyone else in the real world. I know the world of this book is dangerous. I'm starting to think it's dangerous to *me*. "Um, do you know how I'm supposed to predict battles?" I venture.

"My last battle-witch would look at her hand. When there was aught to share, she shared."

I glance down instinctively at my hands. To my surprise, there's something on my right palm, written sloppily in a maroon Sharpie.

"Can you see it?" I ask, holding out my palm to him.

"I cannot. What does it say?"

Maybe I am a battle-witch. How weird would that be? Squinting, I study the writing. It appears to be moving, scrolling like the ticker at the bottom of a news station. Beneath it is a digital clock marking days, hours, minutes, and seconds.

"There's some sort of countdown," I say, watching the seconds tick down. "What happens in about ten days?"

"The end of this thousand-year era," he replies.

"Is that good or bad?"

"It should be neither." He's rubbing his jaw, gaze growing distant. The tension is back in his frame, a sign I take as bad.

"Should be," I repeat.

"If it 'twere any other era, aye."

If television and movies have taught me anything, it's that countdowns are never good.

"What else is there?" he asks.

"It says there are others seeking me who will attack you before the fork." I reread it, puzzled. "Does that make sense?"

Across from me, the Red Knight has gone rigid, one hand on the hilt of his sword. "Are you certain?"

"Yeah. Why? What's wrong?"

He reaches back and slaps the wall of the carriage twice. "The fork is less than a candlemark from where we found you."

I have no idea what a candlemark is – a measure of time? distance? – but judging by his reaction, it's close, and that's bad.

The wagon stops quickly enough that I barely catch the cheese that comes hurling at me.

"You mean they're coming now?" I ask in alarm.

"Stay here." He shoves the door open to the wagon and leaps out, slamming it closed behind him.

Black Moon Draw

is available in ebook from your favorite ebook store and paperback from Amazon and special order from your local bookstore!

About The Author

Lizzy Ford is the award winning, internationally acclaimed author of over thirty five books written for young adult, new adult and adult romance readers, to include the internationally bestselling Rhyn Trilogy, Witchling Series and the War of Gods series. Lizzy has focused on keeping her readers happy by producing brilliant, gritty romances that remind people why true love is a trial worth enduring.

Lizzy's books can be found in every major ereader library, to include: Amazon, Barnes and Noble, iBooks, Kobo, Sony and Smashwords. She lives in southern Arizona with her husband, three dogs and a cat.

Connect with Lizzy:

WEBSITE:
www.LizzyFord.com

FACEBOOK:
www.Facebook.com/LizzyFordBooks

or find her on TWITTER!
@LizzyFord2010

Also by Lizzy Ford ...

OMEGA SERIES
Omega
Theta
Alpha

OMEGA BEGINNINGS SERIES
Alessandra
Mismatch
Phoibe
Lantos
Theodocia
Niko
Cleon
Herakles

HISTORY INTERRUPTED
West
East
North
South

NON-SERIES
Black Moon Draw
Highlander Enchanted

SONS OF WAR (STANDALONES)
Semper Mine
Soldier Mine
SEAL Mine

UNNATURAL SERIES
Unnatural
Unmade

STARWALKERS SERIALS (with Julia Crane)
Severed
Trapped

Exiled
Revealed
Escaped

Heart of Fire

Charred Heart
Charred Tears
Charred Hope

Rhyn Trilogy

Katie's Hellion
Katie's Hope
Rhyn's Redemption

Rhyn Eternal

Gabriel's Hope
Deidre's Death
Darkyn's Mate
The Underworld

War of Gods

Damian's Oracle
Damian's Assassin
Damian's Immortal
The Grey God

Damian Eternal

Xander's Chance
The Black God

Anshan Saga

Kiera's Moon
Kiera's Home (novelette)
Kiera's Sun

Santa's Ninja Elves (short stories)

Natasha
Hunter

Non-series titles

Star Kissed
A Demon's Desire
The Warlord's Secret
Maddy's Oasis
Rebel Heart

By Lizzy Ford and Published by Evatopia Press

WITCHLING
Dark Summer
Autumn Storm
Winter Fire
Spring Rain

INCUBATTI
Zoey Rogue
Zoey Avenger

BROKEN BEAUTY NOVELLAS
Broken Beauty
Broken World

VOODOO NIGHTS
Cursed
Chosen

... and many more coming soon!

With so many books, it's hard to know where to start! Here's a quick list of suggestions!

FAN FAVORITES (paranormal): "Katie's Hellion," “Dark Summer,” “Damian’s Oracle”

ABOUT A READER WHO GETS SUCKED INTO A BOOK: "Black Moon Draw"

CONTEMPORARY ROMANCE: "Semper Mine"

SPICY URBAN FANTASY/PARANORMALS: "Zoey Rogue","Charred Heart"

SWEET (FADE TO BLACK SEX SCENES) PARANORMAL ROMANCE: "Damian's Oracle," "Katie's Hellion," "Xander's Chance"

NOVELLAS: (paranormal) "A Demon's Desire," (contemporary romance) "Maddy's Oasis"

TEEN PARANORMALS: "Dark Summer," "Cursed"

TEEN LITERARY FICTION: "Broken Beauty"

LIZZY'S FIRST BOOK EVER: "Damian's Oracle"

TIME TRAVEL: "West"

SCI-FI ROMANCE: (dystopian) "Rebel Heart," (alien) "Kiera's Moon," (futuristic) "Star Kissed"

FIRST BOOKS IN EACH SERIES

"Damian's Oracle" (War of Gods)
"Katie's Hellion" (Rhyn Trilogy)
"Gabriel's Hope" (Rhyn Eternal)
"Charred Heart" (Heart of Fire)
"Dark Summer" (Witchlings)
"Zoey Rogue" (Incubatti)
"Hear No" (Hidden Evil)
"West" (History Interrupted - standalones)

"Semper Mine" (Sons of War - standalones)
"Severed" (Starwalkers)
"Cursed" (Voodoo Nights)
"Broken Beauty" (Broken Beauty Novellas)
"Xander's Chance" (Damian Eternal)
"Elle's Journey" (The Foretold Trilogy)
“Kiera’s Moon” (Anshan Saga)

44369902R00171

Made in the USA
Charleston, SC
26 July 2015